Texas Widow

Mary Lou Hagen

Dec 1, 2007

To Irene Schiemenz, I hope you enjoy the story of Johanna and Hofer.

Best wishes

Mary Lou Hagen

PublishAmerica

Baltimore

First printing

ISBN: 1-59129-499-1
PUBLISHED BY PUBLISHAMERICA BOOK PUBLISHERS
www.publishamerica.com
Baltimore

Printed in the United States of America

DEDICATION

To my good friend Norma Lauderdale Barker-Schultz,
without whom this book could not have been written
and the memory of Charlene DeViney Palkowski—
may the beautiful butterfly fly free forever.

ACKNOWLEDGMENTS

There were many people involved in the writing process of TEXAS WIDOW. First and foremost, I want to thank Norma L. Barker-Schultz for giving me the idea for weaving a fictional novel around her maternal grandmother's life story.

Once I began to put words on paper, I soon realized I needed help in preparing the manuscript. I found such a person in Charlene DeViney Palkowski. She was physically handicapped, operated a secretarial service from her home and had computer experience. She became my sounding board, my critic and my friend. We worked together for almost two years. Shortly after the last page came out of the printer, Charlene died of a massive heart attack. It was her wish to be cremated and to "escape from this obese body and become a beautiful butterfly."

In addition, I want to thank the staff at the San Antonio Public Library, especially the McCreless Branch, the Castroville Public Library, Castroville, Texas, and the many historical institutions that provided me with information and encouragement.

To my good friends, Rosemary Croom and Charlene Nelson, my thanks and gratitude for the many hours they spent reading, critiquing and editing the manuscript. Their input was invaluable.

I used a number of references while researching TEXAS WIDOW.

The following is a partial list of books that provided me with authentic information:

Bracken, Dorothy Kendall and Maurine Whorton Redway. *Early Texas Homes.* Southern Methodist University Press, 1956.

Cox, Paul W. and Patty Leslie. *Texas Trees.* Corona Publishing Co., 1988.

Fehrenbach, T. F. *Lone Star.* American Legacy Press, 1968.

Lich, Glen E. *The German Texans.* University of Texas Press, 1996.

Mills, Betty J. *Calico Chronicle.* Texas Tech Press, 1985.

Nonte, George C., Jr. *Revolver Guide.* Stoeger, 1980.

Tarnowska, Marie. *Fashion Dolls.* Hobby House Press, Inc., 1986.

Webb, Walter Prescott. *The Texas Rangers.* University of Texas Press, 1965.

Texas has been blessed with a wealth of historians who have spent years researching the state's colorful history. Consequently, there are many wonderful books and sources of information available to those who want to delve into the past.

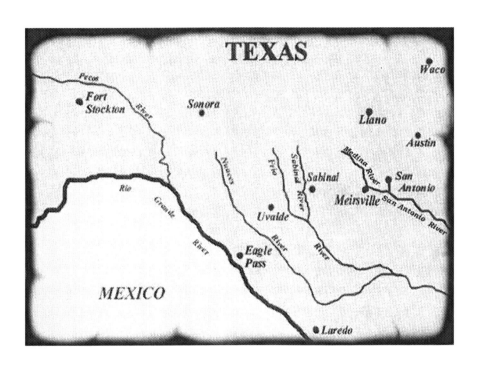

PROLOGUE

Texas 1863

The purple shadows of early twilight spread their delicate fingers over the small green meadow. The last rays of the dying sun transformed the water of the shallow pond into a bottomless black abyss. The call of the dove settling in for the night broke the silence, then quiet descended once more.

The girl sat on a huge rock keeping a silent vigil. The sharp ring of metal against stone brought her to her feet. She rose and turned in the direction of the approaching horse and rider. The rider leaped from his mount, hurried to the girl and caught her by the shoulders.

"Johanna! I was afraid you wouldn't come."

She smiled faintly, a deep sadness in her eyes. "Hello, Will." She stood rigid in his embrace. As he bent to kiss her, she turned away.

"What's wrong, Johanna? Tell me! What is it?"

"I'm going to marry Josef Bauer."

"No, you can't! He's an old man. What about us?" His hands tightened on her arms. "Don't do this. I'll go to your father. I'll make him listen."

Johanna reached for his hands and clasped them tight. "No. That would only make things worse. You know how he feels about you. You're not German, but worse than that, at least in his eyes, you're Catholic. There is no way he would give his consent."

"You're nineteen. You don't need his consent."

Johanna's eyes grew wide with shock. "I could never marry without Poppa's blessing."

"You would marry an old man because that's what your father wants you to do?" He pulled away from her, eyes wild and fists clenched.

Tears stung Johanna's eyelids. "I'm sorry, Will. I do care for you, but you don't understand." She fought back the tears and swallowed the sob in stuck in her throat.

"I understand, all right. Your old man has convinced you I'm not good enough for you. Well, maybe I'm not, but that won't matter when old Josef crawls into bed with you. You just think about that!"

Thankful Will couldn't see, Johanna knew her face was flaming. She hadn't allowed herself to think about the physical aspect of marriage to Josef. He was sixty-six years old, so maybe... She pushed the indecent thoughts from her mind.

Without another word, Will turned his back and strode to his horse. Mounting, he reined the animal around, dug in his spurs and lashed it into a run. He disappeared in the gathering darkness.

CHAPTER ONE

Texas 1873

"Be still, Fritz," the boy said, holding tight to the dog's collar. The large black and tan animal continued to bark and strain to get loose.

Johanna watched a horse and rider coming down the lane. She did not recognize them. The rider slowed the big black stallion to a walk and stopped a short distance away. The boy patted the dog, whose bark turned to a soft whine. It sat down on its haunches.

"Good morning, ma'am. Could I trouble you for some water?" The rider pushed his black Stetson back from his forehead, and Johanna glimpsed a lock of coal black hair. A faint smile revealed a flash of even white teeth. She found herself looking up into a pair of deep blue eyes, startling in his dark face. He was a handsome man; Johanna judged him to be in his mid-thirties. An uneasy feeling settled over her. In her close-knit German community, she was not accustomed to being around strange men.

"Certainly. The well is over there," she pointed to the side of the house. "The horse trough is in the barnyard."

The stranger swung his leg over the saddle, his movements fluid and graceful. Over six feet, he was broad in the shoulders, narrow of waist and lean in the hips. His clean-shaven face contrasted sharply with his dusty clothing. He was clad in snug-fitting black trousers and a black shirt. Although of good quality, the clothing showed signs of wear. The black leather vest and boots, with their silver spurs, looked to be handmade. The bright blue bandanna around his neck was made of silk. Her eyes widened when she saw the pistol riding on his right thigh, the holster tied down with leather thongs. Johanna's heart fluttered. Would the man try to harm them?

"Name's Logan Delaney, ma'am. How far is it to Meirsville?"

"It's about six miles." A tiny shiver ran down Johanna's spine. She twisted her bonnet strings around her fingers. Everything about the man told her he was dangerous.

He removed his hat and a breeze ruffled his thick hair. It had a slight wave and curled where it grew low on the nape of his neck. The stranger's eyes focused on her, and Johanna knew he saw a plain, overworked farm wife in a faded rose calico dress.

Holding the reins in his hand, Logan strode forward, taking in the woman's appearance. She was tall and slender with golden hair, and her tanned complexion was smooth and clear. She was not a classic beauty, but she was mighty pleasing to the eye. In her pink dress she looked as sweet as cotton candy, but he sensed she had more substance than spun sugar. He shifted his gaze. His taste ran to women who offered pleasure that lasted only for the moment.

"I'm Johanna Bauer. This is my daughter, Heidi, and my son, Karl."

"Hello, young lady." He smiled and made a slight bow. The child was a miniature copy of her mother.

"Hello," she whispered, clinging to Johanna's hand.

"Howdy, young man." Logan acknowledged the boy and offered his hand. Karl, with a look of amazement, shook hands.

Gustav came from the barn and hastened to Johanna's side.

"This is my friend, Gustav Schultz. Gustav, Mr. Delaney is on his way to Meirsville."

Logan held out his hand. "Mr. Schultz." The old man's grip was firm and steady. Logan noticed Johanna introduced him as her friend and wondered about her husband.

He led his horse to the water trough. While the stallion drank its fill, Logan surveyed his surroundings. The large rock barn had an attached corncrib on one side and a shed for wagons and implements on the other. A wire corncrib, a pigpen and a shed took up one corner of the large barnyard. In the opposite corner, a chicken house and pen held a flock of dark red chickens busy scratching in the feed strewn about. The privy, outside the barnyard fence, was almost concealed by a clump of juniper bushes.

Logan saw pride of ownership in the neat farm and, for a moment, let his mind think of home. Maybe it was time he went to see his father.

Letting the reins trail on the ground, Logan untied his canteen. He walked to the well and drew a bucket of water. After quenching his thirst, he filled the canteen and retied it. He swung into the saddle and tipped his hat.

"We appreciate the water, ma'am." Logan patted the horse with an affectionate hand. His eyes lingered on the woman, then he turned the big stallion and rode out of the yard.

"Mama," Karl whispered, "I bet that man is a gunman."

"He may be, but he was polite and caused us no harm." Johanna's manor betrayed none of her concern.

"*Ja,*" Gustav said, "but I would not want to be his enemy."

The shiver that ran down Johanna's spine had nothing to do with being cold. The dark stranger with the compelling blue eyes made her uncomfortable. Was it because he was different from the men in her life? She didn't know but it didn't matter. He was gone now. Mentally shaking herself for her foolish thoughts, she forced his image from her mind.

* * *

"He is nine years old, Johanna. It is way past the time." The old man's voice was gentle but firm.

"I know, Gustav," she said, "but you know how the sight of blood upsets him. He had dreams for months after Josef died."

"*Ja, liebchen,* but he has not had the dreams for many months now. Karl is a strong boy and will grow up to be a fine man like his poppa. Do not worry." Gustav patted her hand and followed Karl out of the house.

Johanna watched as they entered the chicken pen. Gustav handed Karl the hatchet. Her throat tightened, and she clasped her hands tightly together. Although too far away to see his features, she knew Karl was struggling to hold back the tears. Her mind's eye brought the scene into focus: the frightened chicken, its feet bound, its body quivering and Karl's hand trembling as he stretched the bird's neck over the chopping block. She saw him raise his arm and bring the hatchet down. The headless bird flopped grotesquely and bright red blood spurted high in the air. Karl jumped back, letting the hatchet fall to the ground.

Gustav wiped the blade with a rag from his pocket and buried the hatchet deep in the chopping block. He gestured to the chicken and Karl retrieved the lifeless bird.

Johanna swallowed the lump in her throat, her hands clenched into fists at her sides. She felt so helpless. Sometimes the responsibility of raising the children alone overwhelmed her.

"Mama." Heidi broke into her thoughts. "Is it time to pick the feathers?" She was learning to pluck and clean fowl just as Johanna had done when she was a child.

"Yes, are you ready?" Johanna's voice betrayed none of her inner tumult.

Heidi nodded and skipped out the door. Johanna followed, glancing at the big kettle in the side yard. Streaks of white vapor rose in the air. The water was hot enough to scald the chicken and loosen the feathers, which would be dried and saved to stuff pillows and feather beds.

Johanna looked up to see Karl, his arm extended, carrying the dead fowl. The coppery smell of fresh blood hung in the air, reminding her of Josef's fatal accident two years ago.

* * *

"Mama, Mama, come quick! Poppa's been hurt." Karl stumbled into the house.

Johanna, baking the weekly supply of bread, turned to see her son standing in front of her, his dark eyes enormous in his pale face. His hands stained with blood, he reached out to her. The bread pan clattered to the stone floor.

"Hurry, Mama, he's hurt real bad." Tears coursed down the boy's cheeks.

Johanna fought to control the panic that threatened to surface. She must remain calm. Josef needed her. Leaving the pan where it fell, she grabbed Karl's arm and started toward the door. She stopped abruptly. Heidi was napping in the bedroom.

"Karl, stay with Heidi. She'll be frightened if she wakes up and no one is here." Looking at his bloody hands, she tried to swallow the lump lodged in her throat. "Wash your hands. Quick now! You don't want Heidi to see them like that."

Without waiting to see if Karl obeyed, she flew out the door. Heart pounding, she ran through the pasture behind the house and through the fallow cornfield. The wagon stood at the edge of the trees with the horses grazing nearby. Gustav came out of the woods and started toward her.

"You cannot help him." He shook his head as if to deny what had happened. Blood smeared his clothing, his hands and arms up to the rolled sleeves of his shirt, a bright red.

Johanna struggled to pull air into her tortured lungs. Chest heaving, she took a step forward. "Gustav, what...what happened?"

"*Er ist tot*, Johanna," the old man's voice wavered. He swallowed hard and blinked back the tears. "We had the dead oak cut through, and it fell before Josef could get out of the way. I tried to help him, but...so much blood. He was moaning and Karl was crying and..." Gustav's voice broke.

Later, she could never recall how she and Gustav had gotten Josef's broken body into the wagon and back to the house. The preparations and the funeral remained a merciful blur.

* * *

Johanna pushed the painful memories aside and took the chicken from Karl's outstretched hand. Although his face was pale, Johanna saw the pride of accomplishment shining in his eyes. Josef would be proud of his children. Rumors had circulated that Will DeVore had made vague references to her virtue because of Josef's age. Josef had never mentioned the ugly gossip, and their life together had been pleasant. Johanna forced the thoughts to the far recesses of her mind.

"The table looks very pretty, Heidi. Thank you for the flowers." Johanna smiled at her daughter. The brilliant bluebonnets and scarlet Indian paintbrush, the blue and white checked tablecloth and blue willow dishes together added a splash of color to the dim interior of the small rock house.

Heidi kept a watchful eye on the dumpling pot to make sure it did not boil over. Her voice held a note of pride when she answered. "I know how much you like bluebonnets." Then she asked, "Did I use the right napkins?"

"Yes, dear, they're fine."

The back door opened and Karl and Gustav entered carrying pails of milk to be strained and put in the springhouse to cool. Karl, a slender, dark-haired youngster, often displayed the same tenacity that Josef had possessed. Johanna was grateful this trait had manifested itself in her son, because she knew it would be needed in the years to come.

Stout of body and limb, Gustav's once-dark hair was now iron gray and his face deeply lined from a lifetime spent out-of-doors. Since Josef's death, a large part of the farm work fell to Gustav, and this gave Johanna cause for concern. Nick and Sam, her brothers, helped out whenever their own work schedule permitted.

"Supper is almost ready. By the time you get the milk put away, it will be on the table." Johanna reached for a bowl in the cupboard.

After hoeing weeds from the corn all day, Gustav and Karl needed a filling as well as tasty meal. Fresh vegetables from the garden, and Johanna's home-canned relishes accompanied the chicken and dumplings. She had used the last of the dried apples to bake a pie, and the spicy odor of cinnamon lingered in the air.

Seated at the table with heads bowed, Johanna said grace. "Come Lord Jesus and be our guest. Let the food thou has't given us be blessed. Amen."

Josef had held to many of the old world customs. He and Gustav had discussed farm matters during mealtime, but Johanna and the children had been expected to remain quiet unless spoken to. Now, she and Gustav made the decisions together. Johanna also encouraged the children to talk about their daily activities.

"We should finish the corn tomorrow," Gustav said in his heavily accented English.

"Will you need supplies to repair the barn?" Johanna asked as she passed the bowl of chicken and dumplings.

"*Ja,* we are almost out of nails and maybe a board or two where old Gertie kicked through her stall."

Johanna sighed. The endless repairs to buildings and farm implements and money for the children's schooling demanded constant sacrifices. Self-denial came easily to her, but the desire for a better life for Karl and Heidi was the driving force behind her efforts. Josef had left her the farm free of debt. Glad she was not beholden to her family, Johanna was learning to be independent.

"We can get the staples and whatever you need when Heidi and I go in to town tomorrow. I'll make a list after supper."

Disappointment flashed across Karl's face, and she knew he wanted to go with them.

"Gustav, why don't we all go in to town? You could use a day's rest."

"*Nein,* you and the *kinder* go. I will stay here and finish the corn. But I do need tobacco." He glanced at Karl, a twinkle in his eye.

"All right. I know you don't like to go into town on a weekday. I'll bring your tobacco." She rose to get the pie from the pie safe in the corner.

Johanna pretended not to notice the way Karl's face lit up. There were few pleasures in their young lives or her own either for that matter. Though she did not dwell on it, she looked forward to the occasional function she could attend without an escort. She refused to think about marrying again. Many of the young men had gone away to fight for the Confederacy and had never returned. She suspected the few unmarried men in the community were more interested in her farm than they were in her. Widowers looking for a mother for their children would only add more responsibility and hard work to her life. Besides, she was twenty-nine now, too old for such foolish thoughts.

Unbidden, the handsome stranger's face flashed before her, his deep blue eyes raking her from head to toe. Johanna blinked and the image was gone. She pushed back her chair. "Let's clear the table, Heidi."

Heidi carried the leftover bowls of food to the cabinet.

"You need to feed Fritz." Johanna handed Karl a bowl of scraps.

Gustav settled in his rocking chair, filled his pipe and puffed contentedly.

As she poured hot water in the dishpan, Johanna again gave thanks for the sturdy home Josef had left them. The farmhouse's thick walls kept it warm in winter and cool in summer. A center beam ran the length of the galvanized pitched roof. Large brick chimneys had been built at each end of the rectangular building. The lean-to on one side was also constructed of rock. Small casement windows flanked the double doors leading into the house.

Johanna picked up the glassware and began washing it, reflecting on the spring-cleaning that lay ahead. The interior walls and woodwork, a combination of mesquite, cypress and oak woods, needed to be polished. One large room served as kitchen, dining room and sitting room and ran the length of the house. Two small bedrooms opened off the main room. Bedding would have to be taken outside and aired.

The large fireplace with a built-in Dutch oven dominated the kitchen, and the massive chimney required a thorough check and sweeping. Johanna smiled as she wiped the top of the big iron cook stove. Josef had suffered the good-natured teasing of his friends, because he had wanted his young bride to have every convenience he could afford. Although her love for Josef had been much like that of a daughter for her father, he had shown her more consideration than her father ever had. She kept those memories buried and seldom let them surface.

Johanna removed the tablecloth from the large oval table and shook the crumbs into the fireplace. Made of native oak by German cabinetmakers that immigrated to America, the furnishings were simple pieces except for the cherrywood cupboard with its leaded glass doors. It held the precious china dishes that had traveled with her parents from their native land. Poppa had passed them on to her since she was

18

the eldest daughter. Her eyes grew dreamy thinking of the time when Heidi would display them in her home. Perhaps they would become family heirlooms.

Joining Gustav in the sitting room, Johanna took up her mending. Karl played with his toy soldiers while Heidi rocked her doll in the little chair beside her mother. Soon the children's heads began to nod.

"Children, it's time for bed. We want to get an early start in the morning."

With the prospect of a trip to town, Karl and Heidi made their preparations without further urging. Johanna heard their prayers and kissed them goodnight. She returned to the sitting room to find Gustav knocking ashes from his pipe into the fireplace.

"I am going to bed, too, *liebchen.* I will see you in the morning." After Josef's marriage to Johanna, Gustav had moved into the lean-to.

"Good night, Gustav." Johanna closed the door and slid the bar into place. Heaving a sigh, she blew out the lamp on the kitchen table. Her mending lay on the seat of the rocker. Tired and weary, she could not finish it. Picking up the remaining lamp, she walked into the bedroom. Before Josef's death, the children shared a bedroom. Now, Heidi slept in Johanna's room. She was curled up asleep in her small bed in the corner.

Johanna poured water into the china bowl, quickly sponged off and donned her nightdress. Taking the pins from the bun at the nape of her neck, she let the heavy tresses fall to her waist. It felt good to relieve the ache caused by the tightly-bound hair. The hundred brush strokes seemed to take forever. Was it worth the effort? A soft smile curved her lips as a secret part of her remembered that Will had said her hair was the color of honey.

After plaiting her hair into a single braid, Johanna blew out the lamp and crawled into the brass bed that had been Josef's wedding gift. She pulled the covers up to her chin. Stretching out, she sighed as her tired body relaxed. She tried not to think of the long years ahead and the responsibility of raising two fatherless children.

Johanna rose at dawn and cooked a hearty breakfast. She tidied up the house and prepared food for Gustav's dinner. No self-respecting German housewife left dirty dishes and unmade beds.

"Would you like to wear your pink dress today?" Johanna asked Heidi as she opened the clothes press.

"What are you going to wear, Mama?"

"I think I'll wear the pink gingham, too. I wore it to church last Sunday. Then I can put it in the wash." Johanna removed the dress from its hanger.

"Then I will wear my pink dress," Heidi said.

Johanna often sewed Heidi's dresses from matching material since it made the seven-year-old feel grown up. Fastening her buttons and helping her with her hair, Johanna completed Heidi's toilette. She admonished the little girl not to get dirty and allowed her to go outside.

Johanna adjusted the high round collar and long full sleeves of her dress. She liked the delicate color although she knew it emphasized her tanned complexion. One petticoat sufficed. Few farm women, especially older ones like herself, bothered with corsets. She wound her hair into its customary bun. Taking her shawl and bonnet from their hooks, she hurried outside.

Johanna stepped into the yard and appraised Josef's legacy to his children. The farmhouse was built on a slight rise, and the rock smoke and springhouses were situated nearby. Water trickled from the spring to form a shallow creek. Pungent marigolds and multicolored zinnias edged the vegetable garden and served as a deterrent to the insects that preyed on the produce. She inspected her carefully nurtured roses and breathed in their delicate scent. Several large pecan, live oaks and mesquite trees provided welcome shade from the fierce Texas sun. Johanna's lips compressed into a straight line. *No sacrifice is too great to keep the farm for Karl and Heidi.*

"Come, we need to get started. I want to stop and see Mrs. Wolfe. She's ailing, and I know she would appreciate a loaf of fresh bread." Johanna tied her bonnet strings and pulled them tight. "Gustav, there's food for your dinner. We should be home by late afternoon."

Karl boosted Heidi onto the wagon seat and jumped up beside her. Gustav gave Johanna a hand up. She adjusted her skirts and picked up the lines.

"Wait, don't forget the rifle." Gustav handed her the gun, and she placed it under the wagon seat.

Although danger from Indian attacks was non-existent, renegades occasionally roamed the countryside. Snakes and wild animals could spook the horses.

"Getty up," Johanna called to the horses and snapped the lines. The wagon moved out of the yard.

In spite of her resolve to put the stranger from her mind, Logan Delaney's handsome visage surfaced again. Would she see him in Meirsville?

CHAPTER TWO

Logan rode into Meirsville from the west at midday, passing by a big stone church and cemetery. A stone and frame schoolhouse and a small stone dwelling nestled among the trees. He surveyed the neat little town with a practiced eye. The wide street made up the business district, and several side streets formed the residential area.

A large sprawling building on his right, Schmidt's Mercantile, dominated the end of the street. He noticed a doctor's office and a gun shop and remembered his rifle needed adjustment. Farther on, the sheriff's office and the bank were constructed of stone. A wooden sign identified Martin Koenig as the sheriff. Considering their proximity and solid construction, Logan concluded bank robbers would think twice about holding up the bank. The town looked deserted except for a few women going about their daily shopping.

Logan dismounted in front of the saloon across the street from the sheriff's office. Between the bank and the Medina River, which formed the east boundary of the town, the vacant land held a scattering of makeshift tables and benches. A bridge spanned the river, and San Antonio lay several miles to the east.

A livery stable and corral occupied the area next to the river. Several vacant lots separated it from the saloon. The barbershop, marked by a red and white striped pole, shared a large structure, *The Gasthaus*, with a small shop painted pale blue with snowy white trim. An elegant sign above the door read Amanda's Fashion Shoppe. A vision of a golden-haired woman flashed through Logan's mind. *Johanna Bauer! Whoa there. You don't have time to fool around with a woman. You've got a job to do.*

Most of the buildings had false fronts with rooflines projecting over the boardwalk to provide protection from the elements. Logan cataloged the town's layout in a matter of minutes. Years of experience had taught him that such knowledge was vital to self-preservation. Trouble always came when you least expected it.

Logan looped the reins over the hitch rail and crossed the street. The door to the sheriff's office stood open, and he stepped inside. It took a minute for his eyes to adjust before he saw the man seated behind the desk. The lawman stood up. He was of medium height, slender and wiry, and his face was lined and tanned to a deep brown. His brown hair, lightly touched with gray, contrasted with a luxurious mustache the color of fresh-ground coffee. The star pinned to his brown cloth vest glinted dully in the half-light. A pistol in a worn holster rode low on his right hip. *Tough as a piece of rawhide.*

"Howdy, stranger. Somethin' I can help you with?"

"I have business with the sheriff."

"You're lookin' at him."

Logan reached into the top of his left boot to a secret pocket and brought out a folded piece of deerskin. He handed it to the sheriff. "I'm Logan Delaney. I work out of the Waco office under Captain Montgomery. We got word that Joe Greene had been seen in San Antone. I'm here to check it out."

The lawman unfolded the leather square to reveal the silver star of the Texas Rangers.

"Martin Koenig." He offered his hand. "Have a seat." He resumed his position behind the desk.

Logan pulled up a chair and straddled it.

"I ain't seen any strangers around here lately, but I'll keep my eyes open and ask around."

"I'll be staying here overnight. I could use a square meal and some sleep. It would probably be better if we don't seem too friendly. I'll keep in touch."

Koenig nodded, pushed back his chair and stood up.

"Good luck," he said, handing Logan his badge.

"Thanks." Logan returned the badge to its hiding place.

Stepping off the boardwalk into the bright sunshine, he saw a wagon enter town and stop in front of the mercantile. A woman handled the lines and two children sat beside her. She climbed down from the wagon seat and held out her arms to a little girl. The boy jumped off from the other side. Logan couldn't make out her features, but she was wearing a pink dress.

Koenig had followed Logan to the door.

"Sheriff, who is that woman going into the mercantile?"

Koenig looked up the street to see Johanna and the children enter the store. "It looks like Johanna Bauer. Why?"

"I stopped at a farmhouse this morning to water my horse, and I talked to her. She had two youngsters, and there was an old man there," Logan explained.

"That would be Gustav Schultz. Fine woman, Johanna, even though there's them that would say different."

"Why is that?" Logan asked.

"Well, about ten years ago Conrad Neicum, Johanna's daddy, made her marry Josef Bauer. He was old enough to be her father, even older. Them two kids come along right away, so I guess he wasn't too old for that." Koenig let a slight grin surface.

"Anyway, he was killed a couple 'a years ago when a tree fell on 'im. Johanna has been tryin' to keep that farm goin' ever since. Gustav and Josef Bauer come over from the old country together. Johanna would really be up against it if it wasn't for Gustav. 'Course, there's them that's always ready to wag their tongues, but I've knowed Johanna since she was a girl, and she's a good, decent woman."

Logan tried to ignore his growing interest in the attractive widow. It was true his father was anxious for him to marry and provide him with grandchildren, but Logan did not intend to tie himself down with a ready-made family.

"Yeah, there's always people ready to talk." He nodded to the sheriff and made his way across the street. He wanted a room, a bath and a hot meal, but first he needed to take care of his horse. Rangers provided their own mounts and gear, as well as weapons.

Logan's stallion, *Él Campeon,* came from the blooded stock raised on the Delaney ranch, the Spanish Spur. His lineage went back to the original stud Logan's father had bought in Louisiana many years ago. Sean Delaney not only acquired a stallion on that trip but a bride as well. He met the lovely seventeen-year-old Kathleen Logan, who captured his heart. They were married six weeks later. The harsh Texas wilderness and the complications of childbirth proved too much for the delicate southern beauty, and she died when Logan was born. Devastated, Sean never remarried.

Logan mounted up for the short ride to the livery stable. No self-respecting cowboy ever walked when he could ride. Logan had been a cowboy long before he became a cavalryman in the Confederate Army and a Texas Ranger.

A big live oak tree stood in front of the livery stable and, on the opposite side of the building, cottonwoods grew along the riverbank. Logan dismounted and led *Él Campeon* into the building. The pungent odors of hay and oats, straw and manure permeated the dusky interior. Dust motes danced in the sunlight that streamed through the cracks. A big man in a leather blacksmith's apron was coming out of the office just inside the door.

"What can I do fur ya?" he asked in a deep voice that carried a hint of Scottish brogue. Wide of shoulder, his arms in their rolled up shirtsleeves, bulged with muscles. He had fiery red hair and a thick red beard.

"Can you take care of my horse for a day or two?" Logan asked.

"Aye. Two bits a day not includin' oats. Fine lookin' animal," he answered as he appraised the stallion.

Él Campeon was a big animal with long legs, a deep chest and a small white blaze on his forehead. Although dusty from the trail, his coat reflected care and attention.

"Name's Frank McCray." He offered his hand. Like the man himself, his grip was powerful.

"Logan Delaney. Just passin' through on my way to San Antone." Logan reached into his pocket and pulled out a silver dollar. "This should cover it."

"We'll take good care of 'im. Roberto," he yelled. A young boy appeared at the back of the building and ran forward.

"*Sí, Señor* McCray,"

"This is Mr. Delaney. Take his horse to stall five. He gets a ration of oats, too," McCray instructed.

"*Sí, señor.* He is a fine looking *caballo*. I will take good care of him." The boy looked to be about nine or ten years old. His black hair was long and shaggy, and his light olive skin made his black eyes appear huge in his small face.

"Yeah, *Él Campeon* and I have been together since he was a foal. I'm mighty partial to him," Logan responded.

"Ah, The Champion. It is easy to see he is a winner. He is well-named, *señor.*"

Logan slapped the horse lightly on the rump, took his saddlebags from behind his saddle and pulled the rifle from its scabbard.

Roberto took the reins and led the horse away.

"Much obliged."

Carrying his saddlebags over his left shoulder and his rifle in his right hand, Logan headed toward the saloon. He needed a drink to cut the dust from his throat.

The sign painted on the saloon window read Bier & Schnaps, Emil Stein, Prop. The Germans had this town nailed down. Logan pushed open the swinging doors and stepped inside.

The building, narrow but with considerable depth, was devoid of the usual odors of stale smoke, liquor and unwashed bodies. A partition at the back with two doors divided the long room. To Logan's left, a mahogany bar took up the rest of the wall, and a huge mirror behind it reflected the highly polished surface. Rows of sparkling pitchers, glasses and mugs, together with bottles of liquor, occupied the shelves. Shiny brass spittoons sat at regular intervals in front of the bar, and the brass foot rail glowed in the half-light. The floor was spotless and lightly covered with a layer of sawdust. Sturdy oak tables and chairs were scattered intermittently around the room.

Logan grinned. *No rough stuff or soiled doves here. Those prim and proper German housewives probably saw to that!*

The establishment was empty and quiet except for the muted conversation of the two men sitting at a table in the corner. It was spring and a weekday. Farmers and ranchers were busy tending their crops and rounding up their cattle.

In fact, Logan reminisced, the cattle drives were probably getting underway about now. His memory went back to the drives he had made when he first came home from the war. Texas ranchers had lots of land and cattle but little money. Thanks to Charlie Goodnight and John Chisholm, who discovered the Eastern markets, two or three trips up the trail to the railheads in Kansas put a rancher's failing spread in the black again. Logan had made three drives himself, but as soon as the Spur was back on its feet, his restless nature led him to join the Rangers.

Logan strode to the bar and laid down his rifle.

"Whiskey."

The barkeep, stocky and well-muscled, with gray hair and mustache, filled a glass with clear amber liquid and placed it in front of him. His snowy white apron and striped shirt, the sleeves held in place by black holders, were stiff with starch.

"That'll be two bits," he said.

Logan placed a coin on the bar. "Nice place you got here." He downed the contents to find it smooth and mellow.

"*Ja,* it was my *vater's* before me, and I hope to pass it on to my son. He's ten years old now, but Anna, my wife, don't want the boy near the place. She does let him help me in the storeroom, when he's not goin' to school." Like most saloonkeepers, Emil liked to visit with his customers.

"Women are funny that way. How far is it to San Antone?"

"Easy day's ride."

"Thanks. Could I get a bite to eat here later?"

"*Ja,* but only cold food. Don't have any cookin' facilities here. I bring meat, cheese and bread from home. The hotel dining room serves up a fine hot meal."

Logan finished his drink, picked up his rifle, nodded to Stein and left the saloon.

The barbershop, located between the saloon and hotel, advertised baths. He was going to treat himself to a good scrubbing with plenty of hot water. Camping out on the trail, using cold water to shave and wash up was anything but satisfying. There was a change of clothing in his saddlebags.

Bright red geraniums bloomed in the flower boxes lining the hotel windowsills, and contrasted sharply with the dull buff color of the building. A row of chairs was lined up on one side of the door and to the right was an outside entrance to the dining room.

Logan went to the desk and asked for a room. The woman behind the desk was nearing middle age but still attractive.

"Yes, we can accommodate you, sir. Rooms are $1.50 per night." She spoke in a cultured voice with an eastern accent.

Logan signed the register and she glanced at his signature. "How long will you be with us, Mr. Delaney?"

"A day or two, ma'am."

"I am Mrs. Reynolds. My husband and I operate this establishment. If there is anything you need, just let us know." She handed him a key marked 203. "Up the stairs, second door on the left."

"Thank you, ma'am."

The woman watched as Logan climbed the stairs.

The room, while not luxurious, reflected careful attention. The bed was covered with a bright patchwork quilt, and a small table beside it held a lamp. A chest, washstand with china pitcher and bowl, a rocking chair and a straight chair completed the furnishings. The room's only window overlooked the roof of the building next door. Logan recognized the pale blue color of the ladies shop. He grinned. *Some female sure has grand ideas.*

He pulled out his change of clothes and headed for the barbershop. He could drop his rifle at the gunsmith's later. Pure luck had put the new model Winchester '73 in his hands, and he meant to keep it in prime condition.

Logan locked the door and made his way down the stairs. The tantalizing aroma of beef and hot bread wafted into the lobby. Before Logan reached the door, it opened and a young woman entered carrying a large hatbox.

"Jane," she called, "I have your hat finished."

Mrs. Reynolds came out of the dining room. "Amanda! I wasn't expecting you this early."

Not wanting to encounter the woman, Logan stepped back out of sight.

Amanda's glossy auburn hair was confined in a net-covered chignon low on her neck. Her perfectly formed features emphasized an air of elegance. She was wearing a white pleated waist with a lace-edged collar and cuffs. Her dark green skirt had the new-fangled contraption called a bustle. She looked as if she belonged in a fancy parlor serving tea. No doubt she was married. A woman that beautiful wouldn't be single

When the women had disappeared through a doorway behind the desk, Logan continued on to the barbershop. After a good soak in a big wooden tub, he dressed in dark gray trousers and a gray cambric shirt. He donned his black leather vest and, buckling his gunbelt, tied the leather thongs around his thigh. A red silk bandana, knotted loosely around his neck, completed his attire.

He needed a good meal under his belt and headed for the hotel dining room. Carrying his soiled clothing in a bag the barber had provided, Logan came out of the bathhouse. A small Mexican boy, who had not been in the shop when Logan arrived, approached him.

"Shine your boots, *Señor,*" *he* asked.

Logan looked down at his dusty boots. They could use a good cleaning and some polish. "*Sí, muchacho. Cuando?*"

"You speak the language, *Señor,*" the boy exclaimed. "*Cinco centavos.*"

"*Un poco,*" Logan replied. He handed the boy a ten-cent piece and seated himself in the chair.

The coin quickly disappeared. "*Gracias, senor.*"

Consuela, his father's housekeeper, who was the closest he came to having a mother, had taught him her native tongue when he was a boy.

By the time Logan returned to his room and picked up his rifle, the dining room was nearly empty. Jane Reynolds was standing at the entrance.

"Would you like to leave your weapon behind the desk, Mr. Delaney?" she asked, walking toward him.

"Yes, ma'am, that would probably be best. Don't want to scare your customers." Logan's white teeth flashed in a grin.

Jane indicated a shelf beneath the desktop, and Logan placed the rifle on it. She guided him to a table by the windows. A young woman in a blue and white checked gingham dress covered by a white apron approached carrying a glass of water.

"Good afternoon, sir. Our special today is *sauerbraten*," she said.

Logan couldn't recall ever having eaten the dish and was not sure he knew what it was. *What the hell!* He had eaten worse during the war. He ordered coffee and apple pie for dessert. The food was tasty if a bit unusual. Logan finished his meal and laid a silver dollar on the table.

Logan found that a distinguished looking gentleman in a black broadcloth suit had taken Mrs. Reynolds place at the desk.

"May I help you?" His voice had the same cultured accent as the woman's.

"I left my rifle here while I was in the dining room."

"Ah, yes. Mr. Delaney, isn't it? I'm Jonathan Reynolds." He handed Logan the gun. "It's a Winchester '73, isn't it? I've heard about them, but this is the first one I've seen. Looks like a fine weapon."

"Yes, it is. Needs a slight adjustment, though. I noticed a gunsmith's shop when I rode into town."

"Max Hemmerlein knows his business. I'm sure he can take care of it."

Logan nodded and made his way across the street. The gunsmith was of average height with light brown hair and a mustache that looked as if it had been groomed with a garden rake. Logan handed him the rifle and explained that the trigger malfunctioned at times.

"Might take awhile. Fact is, I've only seen two or three like this. Can you come back in the mornin'?"

"Yeah. Name's Delaney." As he left the shop, Logan glanced down the street and saw a wagon coming from behind the mercantile. The woman driving the team wore a pink dress. *Johanna Bauer!* He increased his pace.

Logan caught up with Johanna as she pulled the wagon into the street. He saw the recognition in her eyes, stopped beside the wagon and tipped his hat.

"Mrs. Bauer, Heidi, Karl."

The little girl hid her face behind her mother's back. Karl gave him a cautious nod.

"Hello, Mr. Delaney, I see you had no difficulty finding Meirsville."

"No ma'am. It's a right nice little town "

"Yes, it is. Of course, I've lived here all my life, so I really don't have any place to compare it with." Her hands tightened on the lines.

Searching for a way to prolong the encounter, Logan focused his attention on the big horses hitched to the wagon. "That's a mighty fine looking team. I don't recall ever seeing horses quite like them."

"No, there aren't very many in this part of the country. They're Percherons. Their ancestors were brought over from the old country. Most of the German families in this area have them."

Logan stepped forward and examined the animals more closely. He judged the gelding to be about seventeen hands, the mare slightly smaller. Mottled gray in color with short heads, they had massive arched necks and the distinctive fetlocks common to their breed.

"How's their temperament?" Logan asked, wondering at Johanna's ability to control the large beasts.

"Oh, they're very gentle. That's what makes them such wonderful animals. They have lots of stamina but are easy to work with." Her smile reflected her affection for the horses.

The children remained quiet although Heidi squirmed around on the wagon seat. Logan could feel Karl's eyes watching him.

"I hope you have a pleasant stay in Meirsville," Johanna said. "Good day." She urged the horses forward.

"It was nice to see you again, Mrs. Bauer," Logan said. Either Johanna did not hear him or chose not to respond. He watched, his gaze pensive, as the wagon moved out of town.

CHAPTER THREE

The beauty of her surroundings was lost on Johanna. Mesquite and huisache trees displayed their new feathery green leaves. Delicate pink primroses, multicolor phlox, vivid bluebonnets and fiery Indian paintbrush provided brilliant displays of color. Karl seemed to sense his mother's mood and kept Heidi's attention focused elsewhere.

After years of silence, Johanna had received a letter from her sister, Margareth. Five years younger than Johanna, she had been determined not to be forced into marriage with an old man. She had run away with a stranger passing through town, bringing shame and disgrace to the family. Her name was never mentioned. It was if she were dead.

Although surprised at the unexpected correspondence, her encounter with Logan Delaney still lingered in her mind. What was there about the handsome stranger that she kept thinking of him? An aura of danger seemed to hover around him. She forced her thoughts to the tasks ahead.

By the time they reached the farm, Gustav had started the milking. She guided the wagon into the shed, unhitched the horses and turned them loose in the barnyard. "Children, hurry and change your clothes. Karl, you need to help Gustav, and Heidi, you can help me with supper."

Jumping down from the wagon, Karl took the bag of sugar from Johanna while Heidi carried Gustav's tobacco. Johanna picked up the basket holding the remainder of her purchases and followed the children into the house.

She quickly prepared a meal of fried potatoes, ham, and *schmierkase* rounded out with relishes, canned peaches and sugar cookies. After finishing the dishes, Johanna reluctantly took up her mending. The chore seemed unending. Tired after their long day, Heidi and Karl began to bicker.

"That's enough," Johanna scolded. "Off to bed now." She followed, tucked them in and heard their prayers. Returning to the sitting area, she fingered the letter in her apron pocket. She had no idea what to do about it. All her old guilt feelings resurfaced. Perhaps she could atone now for telling Poppa about Margareth's meetings with the stranger. Pacing the sitting area where Gustav sat enjoying his pipe, she drew a deep breath. "Gustav, there was a letter from Margareth today."

"Margareth!"

"Yes. She's in Colorado. Let me read it to you."

> *Dear Sister,*
>
> *I take pen in hand to write to you, hoping you will find it in your heart to help me. I have nowhere else to turn. I know Poppa has never forgiven me.*
>
> *My husband was killed a few days ago, and I find myself with little money and no means of support. There is no work here for decent women, and I am a decent woman although I was married to a gambler. I would like to come and stay with you for a while until I can decide what to do. Maybe I can find work in San Antonio.*
>
> *Please write as soon as you can. I have money for stage fare.*
>
> *Your loving sister,*
> *Margareth*

"Oh, Gustav, I can't refuse, although I know Josef would not approve. And what about Poppa and Sam? You know what they will say." Johanna clutched the letter in her hand, her voice filled with anguish.

"Your poppa will be angry, but Josef is gone. Is it right to go to church, to claim to be a Christian, then turn your back on your sister in her time of need?" Gustav patted her arm as she sat down beside him.

"You're right, of course. But what about Margareth? How will people treat her? They haven't forgotten." Tears gathered behind Johanna's eyelids and choked her voice.

"*Nien*, but I'm sure she expects that."

"I wonder if I should tell Poppa right away?" Johanna asked, more of herself than Gustav.

Gustav shook his head. "He will find out soon enough."

"Yes, and so will everybody else."

They said their goodnights and Johanna prepared for bed. Although tired from an eventful day, she could not sleep. Her mind went back to her childhood with Margareth. They shared the same coloring and family resemblance, but Margareth had been the pretty one. Always fussing with her hair, she loved ruffles and frills. *I wonder how she looks after all these years?*

With their mother's illness, Johanna's responsibilities as the oldest daughter increased. Even had she been inclined to vanity, she had no time. After her mother's death she married Josef and became a mother herself, leaving even less time for her appearance. Since she did not intend to marry again, she told herself it was not important. Unbidden, a man's face flashed before her. Logan Delaney! She had no time for the likes of him. With a determined will she forced his image from her mind.

Letting her thoughts go full circle, Johanna made her decision. She would write Margareth and tell her to come and stay as long as she liked. The eastbound stage stopped in Meirsville on Saturdays, and Johanna had two days to compose her reply. As for her family, she would face them later. Johanna worried about telling the children their aunt was coming. The scandal occurred before they were born, and Johanna did not want to dredge up the ugly details.

After supper on Friday, Johanna made her announcement. "Children, listen. You remember Mama has a sister, your Aunt Margareth, who went away a long time ago?" Wide-eyed, they stared at her. "Her husband died and she wants come home for a visit."

"Mama, was that who the letter was from?" Karl quickly tied the two events together. "Yes. She's in Colorado so it will be awhile before she gets here. I want you to be especially nice to Aunt Margareth and make her feel welcome."

"Oh, Mama!" Heidi exclaimed. "You said she was real pretty, and that I look like her."

"You do, *liebchen*. The three of us, your Uncle Nick, Aunt Margareth, and I, have the same color hair and eyes. But we haven't seen your Aunt Margareth for many years, and she may have changed a lot. I want you to promise not tell anyone she is coming. Not your grandfather, your cousins, not anyone. I will tell them later." Johanna rose and began clearing the table.

"We promise," they chorused.

"She will be happy to meet her *niche* and *neffe*." Gustav smiled. "She got into much mischief when she was your age."

After the children were asleep, Johanna sat down at the kitchen table to answer Margareth's letter.

> *Dear Sister,*
>
> *I was very happy to get your letter but sorry to hear of your loss. I know how difficult it can be. Joseph was killed in an accident two years ago.*
>
> *Of course you may come and stay as long as you like. I haven't told Poppa or our brothers but plan to do so before you arrive. I don't know how they will accept the news, but I pray you can put your differences aside. It won't be easy, but I will help in any way I can.*
>
> *You have a niece and nephew who are anxious to meet you. Karl is nine years old and Heidi is seven.*
>
> *Let me know when you will arrive. It will be wonderful to see you again.*
>
> *Your loving sister,*
> *Johanna*

Gustav offered to take the letter to Meirsville, and Johanna gave Karl permission to go with him. She needed to make soap before churning butter and making *schmierkase*. Heidi stayed home to help her mother. The big iron kettle used for dozens of chores sat in the side yard not far from the well. Johanna lit the fire Karl laid when he filled the kettle. While the water heated, she carried ashes from the fireplaces and grease she had saved to make soap. Sometimes she added dried flowers to the mixture to give it a pleasing fragrance, but last year's supply had been depleted.

Johanna dumped the ashes into the boiling water and mixed the ingredients thoroughly. She added the grease and stirred again. It would need to cool overnight before she could cut it into squares. The gelatin-like substance in the bottom of the kettle would be saved for tasks requiring a strong cleaner.

A dedicated servant of the Lord, Pastor Mueller tended to preach long sermons. Johanna didn't mind, because it gave her a chance to rest a bit longer. Today, his sermon seemed short. Too soon they sang the closing hymn, "God Be With You 'Til Meet Again."

Her emotions in a turmoil, Johanna dreaded telling her family about Margareth. After speaking with the pastor and his wife, she walked toward the wagons.

"Hello, Johanna. And Heidi, how pretty you look," Jane Reynolds greeted them. Jane was stylishly dressed in a pale green silk gown with overskirt and bustle in beige taffeta, and a matching hat completed her ensemble.

"Hello, Mrs. Reynolds." Heidi smiled, lowering her gaze.

The Reynoldses were childless, and Jane had taken an interest in Heidi. Johanna imagined how Jane would dress Heidi in expensive clothing and teach her all the social graces. Well, she was Heidi's mother, and she would teach her daughter all the things a good farm wife needed to know.

Jonathan and Gustav exchanged greetings, then Jonathan spoke to Karl. "You're growing like a weed, son." He smiled at the boy.

"Yes sir," Karl replied. He stood stiffly beside his mother.

"Hello, Johanna. Isn't it a lovely day?" Amanda and her mother joined them.

"Yes, it is." Johanna secretly admired Amanda's deep blue silk gown with its ivory lace trim. Her auburn hair under her flower-trimmed hat glowed with fiery highlights in the bright sunshine.

Mrs. Blair, Amanda's widowed mother, wore her customary black garments. A petite lady, she had a soft voice and gentle manner. The Blairs had come from Boston shortly before Josef died. Mr. Blair took a position at the bank, but the doctor's recommendation that he move to a drier climate came too late. He died the following year. A few months later, Amanda opened her dress shop. Although George Taylor called on her, they were not formally engaged.

Being from the East, the Blairs, the Reynoldses and Taylor had formed close friendships. Outside their church affiliation, Johanna had little contact with them.

Johanna followed the children toward the conveyances and saw her family waiting. Margareth's letter ran through her mind, and she had a sinking feeling in the pit of her stomach. She dreaded the confrontation to come.

"Johanna," Jane called, "can you help with the Fourth of July picnic this year? You know how everybody loves your chocolate cake."

Turning, Johanna replied, "I'll do I what can, Jane." She didn't know what problems would arise when Margareth returned.

"*Grossvater, Grossvater*!" Heidi and Karl ran to Conrad, who stood talking with Gustav. A stout man with gray hair and a full beard, Conrad ruled his family with a strict hand.

Johanna often felt had her mother lived, she would not have been forced to marry Josef. But Karl and Heidi made it all worthwhile.

Johanna's brothers and their wives waited at the wagons. Unbidden, the idea came to her. She would not tell them until she had more privacy, and she would tell them in her own home.

"Poppa, why don't you all come for dinner next Sunday. We haven't been together for a long time."

"We will come," Conrad accepted for all them.

Johanna's older brother, Sam, resembled their father. Sam's wife, Mary, a plain, somber woman, wore her brown hair pulled back in a tight knot. She was in her fifth month of a difficult pregnancy.

Nick was a handsome young man, three years younger than Johanna. His wife, Anne-Marie, small and delicate with blond hair and blue eyes, saw the good in everybody and everything. Married nearly a year, they lived with the Neicums and were anxious for a home of their

38

own.

The men removed their sack coats and rolled up their shirtsleeves while the women donned their bonnets for the trip home.

"I hope you feel better and will be able to come to dinner next Sunday," Johanna told Mary. Mary nodded and called her children, a boy and two girls, playing an impromptu game of tag with Karl and Heidi.

Anne-Marie hugged Johanna. "See you next Sunday." Nick swung his pretty wife onto the wagon seat. The children climbed into the back with their grandfather while Sam helped Mary into the buggy.

The week before the family dinner seemed to fly. There were the usual chores, and Johanna sewed new clothing for Karl and Heidi. She spent Saturday preparing the food for Sunday dinner. Deciding on a ham from the smokehouse, she added fresh vegetables from the garden and jam torte for dessert. Her father's favorite, the recipe had been handed down from her grandmother.

All during church, Johanna's thoughts raced and tumbled through her mind. How she dreaded the coming events. She did not want to cut herself off from her family, neither could she turn Margareth away. With a start, Johanna realized the congregation was singing the closing hymn.

Sam and Mary and their children joined them. Johanna knew Sam would not be inclined to accept her decision concerning Margareth.

"Catch me," cried five-year old Emily as she tagged Heidi on the arm. "Me, too," three-year-old Laura squealed, trying to keep up with the older girls. Pretty little girls, Emily and Laura wore dresses passed from oldest to youngest. This resulted in faded garments without frills, but both girls were sweet and even-tempered.

Karl and his cousin Michael disappeared in the crowd of boys waiting in line at the privy. A year younger than Karl, Michael was short and stocky, quick to anger and slow to forgive. Karl had locked horns with him on more than one occasion. To Karl's continuing mortification, Michael always emerged the victor.

*

Johanna elected to serve the meal outdoors. A picnic atmosphere prevailed, and everybody relaxed after the heavy meal. The children played some distance away as Johanna gathered her courage and spoke.

"I have waited until we could all be together before telling you the news." Her stomach roiled, and she feared she was going to rid herself of what little she had eaten. With all eyes focused on her, she took a deep breath and gripped the edge of the table. "I received a letter from Margareth last week."

Shock registered on their faces, but no one spoke. Conrad sat up straighter. The color left his face as his dark eyes flashed.

"She is in Colorado," Johanna continued. "Her husband died, and she wants to come home."

"*Nein*! She is not welcome in my house," Conrad thundered, rising from his chair.

"Wait, please, Poppa," Johanna pleaded, on the verge of tears. "Hear me out. She has no place to go, and I have already answered, telling her she can come and stay with me."

"Josef will turn over in his grave," Conrad roared.

Sam and Mary exchanged glances.

"Pa, it's done." Nick tried to calm his father. "Besides, it all happened a long time ago."

"People have not forgotten!" Conrad pounded the table with his fist.

"No," Mary spoke up. "It will start all over again. What about your children, Johanna?"

Before Johanna could reply, Nick broke in. "I don't think Karl and Heidi will be harmed by a visit from Margareth. When will she get here?"

"I don't know," Johanna said. She clenched her hands together, and she could feel the nails digging into her palms.

"I think we should try and make her feel welcome," Anne-Marie declared, watching Conrad from the corner of her eye. "We don't know anything about what kind life she has had."

Conrad's face colored. "It was her choice," he said, his voice cold. "Come, we must leave."

Gustav had said nothing during the exchange. Now, he dared challenge his old friend. "Don't feel unkindly toward Johanna, Conrad. What else could she do?"

Conrad shook his head. Without answering, he turned and walked away. Mary called her children, and they scampered toward the wagon.

"I think you did the right thing, Johanna," Anne-Marie said. "Nick told me about Margareth. I love Poppa Neicum, but you know how stubborn and unforgiving he can be." She smiled to take the sting from her words.

"Yes, but I was hoping..." Johanna's voice trailed off.

"It will be all right," Anne-Marie said, hugging Johanna.

"I pray that it will," Johanna replied.

Conrad did not speak to Johanna again. After saying goodbye to his grandchildren, he climbed into the wagon, and the rest of the Neicums followed.

Deep anguish filled Johanna's heart as she struggled to hold the tears at bay. Her worst fears had been realized. Poppa still refused to forgive Margareth and had chastised her for taking her sister in.

* * *

In a shack nestled among the rocky hills ten miles away, five men sat around a rough pine table. The yellow glow from a smoky lantern defined their rough features. They were engrossed in a game of cards and coins and bills were scattered in front of them. The center of the table held a large pile of money. Suddenly, one of the men jumped up, an angry scowl on his face. "Damn it, Joe," he cursed, "you're cheatin'!"

The man at the head of the table stood and shoved back his chair. He flushed dark red, and his eyes narrowed as he looked at the man who challenged him. "Cooper, you son of a bitch, you asked for it!" Before anyone could react, Joe drew his gun and fired.

A bright red stain blossomed on Cooper's shirtfront. Eyes wide with shock, he stared at Joe, a look of surprise frozen on his face. He tried to speak, and a bloody froth appeared on his lips. For a long moment he remained upright, then pitched face down on the table.

Coins and bills spilled off. One of the men caught the lantern before it hit the floor. Silence fell over the room. Joe gave each man a long searching look. In spite of his unkept appearance, he was a handsome man. Tall and slender with dark brown hair, his brown eyes confirmed the streak of cruelty he had just revealed. Receiving no response from his unspoken challenge, he holstered his pistol.

"Pick up the pot!" he ordered. "We'll it split up. Then git that carcass outta here!"

CHAPTER FOUR

Air thick with smoke, the smell of liquor, sweat and strong perfume filled The Hanging Tree Saloon in San Antonio. It was crowded with cowhands, businessmen, gamblers and saloon girls. The piano player pounded out a tune that barely could be heard above the loud voices and bawdy laughter.

Logan sat at a table in the corner with his back to the wall. Earlier in the day, he had contacted City Marshal Tom Davis. Davis had not heard anything about Greene being in the area. A dark-haired woman in a short red satin dress and black net stockings came down the stairs. She paused on the bottom step and surveyed the room before walking in Logan's direction. She stopped several times to talk with the customers, and lewd laughter accompanied the conversations.

"Hello, stranger. I'm Sally. Care to buy a lady a drink?"

Logan stood and pulled out a chair. "It would be my pleasure, ma'am." He motioned to a woman serving drinks at the next table. After giving her his order, he turned to Sally. She was pretty under the heavy face paint, but there was something in her dark eyes that told him she had long ago given up hope for a better life.

"Haven't seen you in here before." Her red lips curved in a practiced smile.

"No, ma'am. Just passin' through. Thought I might run into a fella I know," Logan lowered his voice. "Name's Joe Greene. 'Course he may not be usin' that name." Logan winked, as if sharing a secret. "Good lookin' cuss. Tall, dark hair, 'bout my age."

"I don't know anybody by that name, but the description could fit a hundred men." Sally's eyes narrowed. "What did you say your name was?"

Logan often posed as a half-breed bounty hunter. "I didn't, but it's Hunter."

The woman nodded as the bargirl delivered the order. With a seductive smile, Sally edged closer and laid her hand on his thigh. The vision of a golden-haired woman flashed before his eyes. *Damn!* He didn't even know Johanna Bauer. Why did he keep remembering her? Logan forced his thoughts back to the task at hand. He slid his arm around Sally's bare shoulders as she finished her drink in three quick swallows.

"Can I buy you another drink?" he asked, running his fingers down her arm.

"Sure."

The piano player, who had stopped playing for a few minutes, began again. The tempo increased, and the women coaxed their unwilling partners onto the floor.

Logan changed his tactics. "Would you like to dance?"

She nodded and Logan rose from his chair. They moved onto the dance floor. Her strong perfume stung his nostrils as she pressed her body against him. In spite of himself, he felt his body responding. *Lord!* Thankfully the music stopped, but Logan kept his arm around her waist as they walked back to their table.

Marshal Davis threaded his way through the crowd and approached them. "Evenin', Sally."

"Hello, Marshal." A genuine smile softened her painted features.

"Haven't seen you around before, stranger." The marshal's eyes narrowed thoughtfully.

"Just passin' through, Marshal. Name's Hunter." Logan had told Davis he didn't want it spread around that he was a Ranger.

"Looks like you're enjoying yourself. Just keep it under control." He winked at Sally and pushed his way through the crowd.

Logan almost sighed with relief. He had no desire to sample Sally's charms. If he could make her think he was worried about the law, he could avoid taking her upstairs. He watched the marshal walk away. "He a good lawman?"

"Tom? Oh, he tries real hard, but it's a tough job." She eyed Logan from under lowered lids.

"Yeah, I reckon it is." Logan kept his eyes on the departing lawman. "Well, I've had a long ride. I think I'll call it a night. Thanks for the company, Sally." He pushed back from the table.

Disappointment flickered in her eyes, but she recovered quickly. "Oh, sure. Hope you find your friend."

"Thanks."

Logan checked out of the Brackett Hotel the next morning. He had made the rounds of the saloons without success. Instinct told him Greene was not in San Antonio, and he had learned long ago to trust his hunches. He wanted to report to headquarters, take leave time and be on his way to the Spanish Spur.

Located on Camarron Street, The Bracket Hotel backed up against San Pedro Creek. The Bat Cave building at the corner of Camarron and Houston Streets housed the Bexar County offices and jail. The city offices occupied space in an adjacent building facing Houston Street. Davis would want to keep an eye out for Joe Greene, and Logan made a trip to his office. The marshal was out, but Logan left a message with the deputy that he was leaving town.

Logan mounted up, rode down Houston Street and crossed the San Antonio River. Several bathhouses were located along its banks. He entered Alamo Plaza, and the sight of the mission where the bloody battle with Santa Ana had been fought caused his throat to tighten. His father had been with Sam Houston at San Jacinto, and Logan's pride ran deep. He continued on, passing a brewery, two gristmills, a foundry and various businesses. Reaching the Main Plaza, he entered Military Plaza and discovered he had made a complete circle. The town was larger than he remembered.

The rough country above Austin gave way to rolling hills with tall grass and fewer trees. Cattle dotted the landscape, and Logan saw an occasional rider in the distance. He found a sheltered spot near a small creek and made camp. Water flowed smoothly over the rocky bed, and cottonwood trees grew profusely along the banks. Logan unsaddled the stallion and staked him out to graze.

He poured his second cup of coffee and pulled out the makin's. There were times when tobacco filled a void, but not tonight. *Maybe Pa's right, maybe it's time I settled down.* He stared into the dying campfire, and the red-gold flames formed a vision of a golden-haired woman in a pink dress. *Christ*! This had never happened to him before. *I should have taken Sally upstairs!* He flicked the last of his smoke into the fire and climbed in his bedroll.

Lightning flashed and thundered rolled. *Él Campeon* snorted and pranced around, drawing the picket rope tight. Logan came awake with a start, his hand going to the gun beside his head. His eyes strained, trying to see through the darkness. It was nearly dawn, and it would be a good idea to move on before the rain came. Logan broke camp and was on his way when the storm hit. His slicker provided some protection from the downpour, but there was no shelter in sight.

As abruptly as it started, the storm was over. The sun peaked through the clouds, shedding pale gold streaks of light over the sodden landscape. Following the creek in a northerly direction, Logan saw the water had risen and turned muddy. More rain had fallen upstream, and the little brook was now a raging torrent. He dismounted and stood looking down at the churning brown water.

"Help! Help!" The cry was barely audible.

Looking across the ever-widening creek, Logan spotted a man clinging to a log that was bobbing crazily downstream. His reaction was instinctive. "Hang on! I'm going to throw you a rope." In a matter of seconds, he had a loop in the air and spinning out over the boiling current.

The man managed to snag the rope and pull it over his shoulders. Quickly dallying the lariat around the saddle horn, Logan called out encouragement. "Hold on! We're going to pull you out."

The man hesitated then let go of the log. Arms flaying, he struggled with the current while Logan urged *Él Campeon* backward. The powerful stallion pitted his strength against the raging water and pulled the man to safety. Dripping wet, his clothing plastered to his slender body, Logan saw the man he had rescued was little more than a boy.

His long hair clung to his head, and a sparse beard covered his features. "Thanks mister. I'm...I'm sure much obliged to ya," he managed to stammer.

"I'm glad I happened along," Logan returned. He untied his bedroll and took out a blanket. "It might be a good idea to get out of those wet clothes."

"I'll dry out quick enough. Thanks agin." His body shivering, he wrapped the blanket around him.

Logan shrugged. "Name's Hunter. Headed for Waco. There some where I can take you?"

"Bud...Bud Anderson." Silent for moment, he nodded his head. "We're not fur from the Patterson place. I kin git a horse there to git back to Llano."

Evidently the kid didn't intend to tell him how he happened to be in the middle of a flash flood. If a man volunteered information, it was because he wanted to. If he didn't, you didn't ask. Logan strode to *Él Campeon* and climbed into the saddle. Holding out his hand, he pulled the boy up behind him.

Stopping to rescue Anderson added a half-day to Logan's trip. He rode into Waco in the late afternoon. Ranger headquarters consisted of several frame buildings, a large barn and corrals. A barracks-like structure housed the Rangers, and a smaller building served as the captain's office and living quarters. As Logan dismounted, a man left the office and walked toward him.

"Delaney! Haven't seen you in a coon's age."

"Howdy, Bartell. It has been a long time."

They shook hands. Bartell was a stocky man with black hair, a thick mustache and deeply tanned skin. He and Logan had ridden together on several occasions.

"Captain in?" Logan asked.

"Yeah," Bartell answered. "Looks like you've had a long ride."

"Too long." Logan slapped the dust from his clothing. "Captain heard Joe Greene might be in San Antone. I was in Uvalde, and he sent word for me to check it out. No trace of him, though."

"That's how it goes, sometimes. Been around Mineral Wells myself. Trackin' a bunch of renegade Comanche. Trail just plumb petered out. Sure is a mystery where them red devils disappear to," Bartell exclaimed.

"They know more tricks than a medicine show magician," Logan agreed. "Guess I'd better check with the captain."

The man behind the battered desk stood up. Tall and powerfully built, Wes Montgomery was in his early forties. His light hair and pale blue eyes contrasted with his ruddy complexion.

Logan touched his hat brim in an informal salute.

"Delaney." Montgomery offered his hand.

Logan settled in a chair facing the desk. "I'm afraid I don't have anything good to report, Captain. I contacted Sheriff Koenig in Meirsville. Same thing with Marshal Davis in San Antone. Nobody's seen Greene, or if they have, they're not telling. It's hard to pick up leads when we don't have any more to go on." Logan was tired and discouraged, feelings he rarely experienced.

"I'm working on that. We're trying to put his likeness on some new posters," Montgomery told him, fiddling with the stub of a pencil.

"Sure would help," Logan admitted. "When will they be ready?"

"I'm not sure. Couple weeks, maybe."

"Since I have some leave coming, I'd like to go home for a spell."

"I don't see any problem with that. By the time you get back, the posters should be ready. If anything turns up before then, I know where to find you." Montgomery grinned.

"Thanks. I'll be pulling out tomorrow."

Logan topped a slight rise and reined *Él Campeon* to a halt. It had been a long three-day ride from Waco. He pushed his hat back, wrapped his hands around the saddle horn and leaned forward. The Spanish Spur lay sprawled in the late afternoon sun. An original land grant from the King of Spain to a nobleman killed by Indians, it had been awarded to Sean Delaney for his service to the Republic of Texas. Covering one hundred thousand acres, three thousand head of longhorn cattle roamed its vast lands.

A wide grin split Logan's features, and he urged *Él Campeon* into a run. "We're home, boy!" He slapped his hat brim against the horse's rump. As he rode up to the house, the heavy wooden doors opened and a woman stepped outside. She stopped, shielding her eyes from the sun.

Logan dismounted and opened the iron gate in the adobe wall surrounding the house. The old hacienda, freshly whitewashed, had a red tile roof. The windows and doors were set into arched openings covered with iron grillwork. A rock path led to the front entrance. Logan's mother had brought live oak trees to the Spanish Spur and, with careful nurturing, several had survived. Cultivated cacti and agave grew in the rocky soil, and pots of blooming plants decorated the stone courtyard in front of the house.

"Logan, Logan, you are home, you are home!" The woman ran down the path waving her arms.

"Consuela! You get prettier every day," Logan teased, enveloping her in a tight hug.

"That is not true, and you know it." She spoke in heavily accented English. Consuela was nearing fifty, but her black hair showed mere traces of gray, and her face was youthful and unlined. "Don Sean will be very happy to see you. It is good you have come home, Logan. He needs you." Her tone and manner grew serious.

"Where is Pa?" He put his arm around her ample waist and walked with her to the door.

"He rode out with Pat and the men to check the waterholes on the south range. He will be back in time for supper."

"That'll give me time to scrub this dirt off."

"I will have Pedro bring hot water to your room. It is ready for you, as always." She smiled at him, her dark eyes filled with happiness.

"*Gracias.* Before he brings the water, I'd like him to put *Él Campeon* in the corral. He needs rubbing down and a good ration of oats. He's been on the trail for quite a spell."

Going to the corner of the house, Consuela called out, "Pedro! Pedro, come quickly."

A Mexican boy, about ten years old, came from behind the house.

Seeing Logan, he ran to him shouting, "*Señor* Logan, you have returned!"

"Pedro." Logan grinned and rumpled the boy's shaggy hair. He motioned to the stallion tied outside the adobe wall. "Take good care of him. He's earned a long rest."

Logan followed Consuela into the house. The roof projected out over the *hacienda*, and the double doors opened into a large *sala*. A second pair of double doors at the opposite side of the room led to an inner courtyard. A large dining room opened off one end of the *sala*, and beyond it were the kitchen, a storeroom and Consuela's bedroom. The library and bedrooms were off a wide hallway in the other wing.

"Are you hungry?" Consuela asked. "I will fix you something to eat."

"No, I'll wait till supper." Taking in his surroundings, Logan realized how much he had missed his home. The heavy dark wood furniture gleamed from frequent polishing. Black iron sconces with tall white candles, and Spanish crests of the nobleman's family decorated the walls. Deep red velvet draperies hung at the windows. The afternoon sun played hide and seek on the dark tile floor.

Logan's gaze lingered above the fireplace where the portrait of a young woman reigned supreme. Painted when Kathleen was sixteen, the portrait had captured her image in all its youthful loveliness. She was very beautiful, with long black hair and deep blue eyes, and it was plain that Logan had inherited the masculine counterpart of her beauty. It was the only likeness of the mother Logan had never seen.

Logan made his way to his bedroom, which was next to the library. Spacious and furnished with the same dark heavy pieces, a dark red leather chair and ottoman, it invited relaxation. The bed and window coverings were heavy woven cotton in shades of deep blue and dark red. A wool rug with a blue and red pattern covered the tile floor.

After shaving off four days worth of whiskers, Logan relaxed in the big copper tub. He scrubbed off the accumulation of trail dust and washed his thick black hair. Donning brown denim pants and a blue chambray shirt, Logan exchanged his dusty black boots for highly polished brown ones. A red cotton print bandana replaced his customary silk one. What a relief to leave off his gunbelt and pistol. It felt good to relax and let down his guard. A careless Ranger soon became a dead Ranger.

Logan found Consuela in the kitchen preparing the evening meal. Long ago it had been a separate building, but the walkway had been enclosed making it part of the *hacienda*. Strings of red and green peppers and garlic hung from the ceiling providing a colorful contrast to the stark white walls. The kitchen was Consuelo's exclusive domain, and touches of her Mexican heritage were visible.

"Sure smells good, Consuelo."

The spicy aroma of chili peppers and *frijoles* permeated the room. Turning from the huge black range, Consuelo smiled. "Tomorrow I will fix the *aroz con polo* and *flan* for you."

"You haven't forgotten my favorites," Logan teased.

She shook her head and smiled. "No, *muchacho*."

"Think I'll help myself to Pa's whiskey before supper," Logan told her. The library served as the ranch office and showed signs of hard use. The windows were curtained with heavy brown fabric. Kathleen had filled the floor to ceiling bookcases with a fine collection, and a large rolltop desk sat nearby. The huge fireplace, built of native stone extended along one wall. A large table in the center of the room held a silver tray, several bottles of liquor and sparkling glassware. The large brown leather-covered sofa and two matching chairs provided comfortable seating.

Logan poured himself a generous amount of whiskey and drained half of it in one swallow. Ah, his Pa never skimped on good liquor. Glass in hand, he walked down the hallway and through the first arch into the courtyard. All the rooms, protected by the wide overhang, opened into the inner courtyard. Here again, Consuelo had created an attractive desert garden.

Logan surveyed his heritage. The ranch buildings, about two hundred yards from the *hacienda*, sat on slightly lower ground.

A small creek lined with scraggly cottonwoods, wound its way south. Logan could see *Él Campeon* in one of the corrals getting reacquainted. *Damn, it's good to be home.*

Hoofbeats thundered in the distance. Logan returned to the *sala*, looked out the front window and saw a cloud of dust on the horizon. He finished his drink and set the empty glass on the table. Striding quickly through the *sala* into the courtyard, he opened the iron gate and took the path down to the corral. Riders were rounding the house, and Sean Delaney was in the lead with Pat Riley at his side.

As Logan reached the corral, Sean spurred his horse and raced toward him. He came out of the saddle and grabbed Logan in a bear hug. "Son, you're sure a sight for sore eyes." The hint of an Irish lilt colored his voice.

Logan's grandfather, Flynn Delaney, had come to Texas from Ireland in 1814 with a group of Catholic priests to bring Christianity to the Indians. The missionaries settled near Corpus Christi, and Flynn fell in love with a young nun. They had run away and were married by a traveling preacher.

Sean, shorter than his son, shared the same broad shoulders and lithe body. He carried his fifty-seven years well. His dark brown hair was streaked with gray, but his blue eyes were clear and direct.

"Pa, it's good to be home."

The horsemen reached the corral, and Logan recognized Frank Butler who had been with the Spur for several years. The other man was a stranger. Riley, a big grin on his face, dismounted. "'Bout time you come home, boy!"

The two men shook hands, slapping one another on the back. "Did Tim go on the drive?" Logan asked.

"Yeah, left last week. Your Pa and I are too old for that anymore."

The cowhands were standing behind Pat. Sean introduced the new man as Ed Jones. "Pat, check out the rest of the water holes tomorrow," Sean instructed. He put an arm around Logan's shoulders. "And plan on coming up to the house for supper tomorrow night. I know Consuelo will cook up a feast."

Pat nodded and followed the men to the corral. Logan and his father entered the *hacienda* through the kitchen.

"I need to clean up before supper, but let's have a drink first. It's not every day my son comes home."

Consuelo was putting the finishing touches on the meal. "Don Sean! I thought I heard riders. Supper is ready when you wish to eat."

"Give me a few minutes," Sean requested. "Pat will be having supper with us tomorrow night," he added as they left the room.

Father and son relaxed over their whiskey. "Well, Logan, have you come home to stay?"

"No, Pa, I'm on leave. I'm due back at headquarters in a couple of weeks." Logan saw disappointment flash in Sean's eyes, and then it was gone.

"I'm trailing an outlaw named Joe Greene. Maybe when I catch up with him..." He left the sentence unfinished. He wouldn't make promises he couldn't keep.

"Consuelo's waiting with supper," Sean said, coming to his feet. "I'll wash up and we'll eat."

The dining room table was set with a linen cloth and napkins and colorful Mexican pottery. Seeing there were only two place settings, Logan called to Consuelo, "Aren't you eating with us?"

She came from the kitchen carrying a large tureen. "Not tonight, *muchacho*. You and your father have much to discuss. There will be time later."

Logan smiled and kissed her on the cheek. She was very dear to him. Father and son discussed ranch business during the meal. Afterward, they went into the courtyard where Sean took out his pipe and filled it.

"Tell me about this Joe Greene, son."

Logan related what knew about the outlaw and his fruitless search in San Antonio. Unbidden thoughts of Johanna crept into his mind.

"What's really bothering you, Logan?"

"It's not Greene, Pa," Logan admitted as he pulled the tobacco sack from his shirt pocket. "It's this woman I met." He built a smoke and told Sean about Johanna Bauer.

"She's a widow, you say?" Sean's tone was casual.

"Yeah. Has a boy nine or ten, and the prettiest little girl you ever saw."

Sean chuckled. "Son, I'd say you're between a rock and a hard place.

CHAPTER FIVE

Heavy rain lashed the countryside, and Johanna's mood was as gray as the weather. There had been no communication with Poppa although Nick had told her not to worry, everything would work out. Anne-Marie eagerly awaited Margareth's arrival, but Mary had not hesitated to express her displeasure. The news shocked those who remembered Margareth and aroused the curiosity of those that didn't.

Karl and Heidi were gathering eggs and Gustav was feeding the livestock.

"Karl, I've been thinking. Where is Aunt Margareth going to sleep?"

"With Mama, I suppose. Why?"

"Well, you know Mama and I don't have much room. Remember I used to sleep in your room before Poppa died? I think I should move back there. That way Mama and Aunt Margareth won't be so crowded."

Karl stared at his sister. She surprised him sometimes with her grownup ideas. "I guess it would be all right. We don't want Aunt Margareth to think she's putting us out. She might if you stay in Mama's room."

During supper, Heidi turned to her mother. "Mama, Karl and me have been talking about Aunt Margareth. Where she going is sleep?"

"Karl and I," Johanna corrected automatically. Her heart skipped a beat. Had the children heard the ugly gossip?

"Karl and I," Heidi parroted. "We think I should move back into Karl's room. That way you and Aunt Margareth would have more room."

Saved from an embarrassing explanation about Margareth's past, Johanna gave a sigh of relief and focused on Heidi's remarks. "Children, are you sure you want to do this?"

"Yes, Mama," they chorused. Karl was more interested in the cake she was serving for supper than talking about Aunt Margareth.

"I think it's very nice you are concerned about your aunt." Johanna poured herself another cup of tea.

Gustav added, "She will be pleased to have such a thoughtful *niche* and *neffe*."

"There is much to do before Margareth arrives," Johanna said. "We will need to take Heidi's bed down and set it up in Karl's room. That would be a good time to wash the bed clothes and do some spring cleaning."

"I will help, *liechben*," Gustav volunteered. "There is not much work in the fields until time for haying."

The rain stopped during the night, and the day dawned bright and clear. Johanna breathed in the fresh air. *If only human beings had the ability to cleanse their minds as thoroughly as the storm has cleansed the earth.*

While the water heated in the big kettle, Johanna and Heidi gathered the soiled clothing. It took most of the morning, but Johanna was proud of the spotless laundry hanging on the lines. With dinnertime fast approaching, she hurried to prepare the meal. She cut thick slices of ham and placed them in a skillet to fry. Hot potato salad and green beans would be topped off with cake left over from yesterday.

As Johanna set the food on the table, Karl and Gustav came into the house. The tantalizing aroma of fried ham and the pungent smell of vinegar mingled in the air.

"Smells real good, Mama," Karl complimented his mother as he eyed the repast.

Johanna smiled. The boy had a healthy appetite. "Get washed up," she told him.

During the meal, they discussed moving Heidi into Karl's room. "Do you want to do it this afternoon or wait until tomorrow?" Gustav asked as he cut into a thick slice of ham.

"We might as well get started after dinner," Johanna replied.

Karl and Gustav took Heidi's bed apart and set it up in Karl's room. Johanna and Heidi moved the little girl's small trunk to the foot of the bed. Heidi arranged her dolls, and Johanna hung the child's dresses on the extra hooks on the wall. The room was too small for a clothes press. Bright patchwork quilts covered the beds, and curtains made from sewing scraps hung at the windows.

The next morning Johanna was busy rearranging her bedroom to accommodate Margareth and did not hear Heidi run into the house until she called out. "Mama, Mama, Pastor is coming down the lane!"

I'll bet it has something to do with Margareth. "I'll be right out." Johanna glanced in the mirror. She had a smudge of dirt on one cheek, and her hair was escaping from its pins. She quickly wet a cloth, ran it over her face and repinned the loose tendrils. Grabbing a clean apron from the drawer, she tied it over her faded calico dress.

The minister alighted from the buggy as Johanna stepped through the doorway. "Good morning, Pastor."

"Good morning, Johanna. And Heidi, how are you today?"

"I'm fine," Heidi answered softly.

"Please come in," Johanna gestured toward the house. "I was just about to have a cup of tea. Karl and Gustav are cutting hay this morning. Nick will be here tomorrow to help with it." Johanna knew she was chattering, but she couldn't seem to stop.

"A cup of tea would be most welcome," the pastor returned, removing his hat. He pulled a handkerchief from his pocket, wiped his brow and followed Johanna into the house.

Heidi went to the cupboard and began gathering cups and saucers. She set them on the table and added the sugar bowl and cream pitcher. "Mama, there was *kuchen* left from breakfast," she reminded her mother.

Johanna nodded. "If you will it set it out, I'll get the cream from the spring house." Johanna excused herself. She returned with a small pail and poured the heavy cream in the pitcher.

"This is very thoughtful of you, Johanna," the pastor told her, gratefully sipping his tea. "When you were in church Sunday, I didn't know I'd be coming out this way. Mrs. Wolfe sent word she wanted to see me. I'm afraid she has given up." He shook his head.

"I'm sorry to hear that, Pastor. Is there anything I can do?"

"Pray for her. But I know you're already doing that," he acknowledged, smiling.

The conversation continued in the same vein for several minutes, but Johanna knew the minister had something else on his mind. Past middle age and stout of build, he had thinning gray hair and a short, well-trimmed beard. His eyes behind their metal-framed spectacles twinkled most of the time but could, when the occasion demanded, cause the mildest sinner to squirm in his seat.

"I hear Margareth is coming for a visit."

Johanna heaved a sigh of relief. It was finally out in the open. "Yes, but we don't know when she will arrive." Turning to her daughter, she said, "It's very warm today, Heidi. Fritz might need fresh water. He's tied and can't get to the creek."

Hedi jumped up from her chair. "I'll tend him, Mama."

"Thank you, dear."

When Heidi was out of hearing distance, the pastor spoke. "I know this is difficult for you, but you have nothing to feel badly about. What happened with Margareth was a long time ago."

"I don't know how much you have heard, but Margareth's husband died, and she has no place to go. Poppa is furious and won't even talk about it. Nick thinks it's time to put the past behind, but Sam is too much like Poppa to agree."

Johanna refilled the pastor's cup. "I know Josef would not approve of me taking her in, but I can't turn her away." Joanna's voice was strained.

"No, and you shouldn't. 'Let he who is without sin cast the first stone.' We both know there are those who are only too willing to forget that, but you can't let them keep you from doing what you believe is right. We all have a Christian duty to help those in need. I may just remind the congregation they need to be merciful if they expect mercy in return."

"What am I going to do about Poppa? I know he won't come here and Margareth can't go home." Johanna looked down at her lap to hide the moisture in her eyes. "I have prayed and prayed about it. There doesn't seem to be anything else I can do."

"Perhaps we could pray together now," the pastor said.

Johanna bowed her head while Pastor Mueller offered a short prayer that God would guide and direct Johanna and her family during this trying time.

Nick came the next day, and to Johanna's delight brought Anne-Marie with him. After the men left for the fields, Johanna showed her the children's room.

"That was very thoughtful of them," Anne-Marie told her. "But then, Heidi and Karl are thoughtful children."

"Most of the time," Johanna smiled. Then, her voice serious, she asked, "What about Poppa? Has he said anything at all about Margareth?" Her legs went weak, and she sat down on Karl's bed.

"Not in front of me, but Nick said he is still angry. I feel like telling him how wrong is, but you know I can't do that," Anne-Marie replied, sitting on the edge of Heidi's bed.

"No. It would only make matters worse." Johanna told Anne-Marie about the pastor's visit.

"Maybe Pastor could talk to Poppa Bauer."

Johanna shook her head. "I don't think it would do any good."

The men did justice to the meal Johanna and Anne-Marie prepared. Savory sausage, sauerkraut, potatoes and fresh green beans were topped off with blackberry cobbler.

"How is Mary?" Johanna asked as she passed the pitcher of fresh cream. Johanna tried to be discreet since pregnancy was never discussed in front of children.

"I think she's going to be all right. She just has to be careful," Anne-Marie replied. "It's going to mean rearranging the bedrooms, though. We're pretty crowded. I wish Nick and I had a place of our own," she smiled wistfully, glancing at her husband.

"Be patient, sweetheart. It's just going take a little longer than we planned. But we'll make it," Nick promised, his smile tender.

"Oh, I'm not complaining. I'm just anxious," Anne-Marie hastened to add.

"By the way, Johanna." Nick turned to his sister. "I ran into Will DeVore in town last week. His father is real sick, and Will had to leave the cattle drive and come home. He asked about you."

"Will DeVore! Why, I've only seen him once since Josef died."

"I wouldn't be surprised if he comes calling one of these days," Nick teased as he reached for the cream pitcher.

"Well, I would. I'm not interested in him or any other man for that matter." In spite of her denial, Johanna's face colored a delicate pink.

Wide-eyed, Karl and Heidi listened to the exchange between their mother and their uncle.

"Mama don't need a husband," Karl stated emphatically. "Me and Heidi and Gustav can take care of her."

Anne-Marie and Nick exchanged glances while Gustav seemed not to hear and continued eating. Johanna quickly changed the subject and asked about the haying.

"We should finish this afternoon," Gustav told her.

The afternoon passed quickly, and all too soon Anne-Marie and Nick were their way home.

Taking the quilts from off the line, Johanna looked up to see a rider coming toward her. For an instant her mind replayed the scene of another rider stopping for water. Logan Delaney! He popped into her mind at the slightest provocation. She gave herself a mental shaking. *You will never see him again and, you'd best forget all about him.*

The rider reached the house and reined his horse to a halt. Johanna felt a stab of disappointment. The horse was a big bay gelding with three white stockings. The man swept off his brown Stetson, and she recognized Will DeVore. Leaving the basket of clothes, she walked toward him.

"Howdy, Johanna," he greeted her as if ten years ago had been yesterday.

"Hello, Will."

He was a big man with strong features, and his pale gray eyes looked colorless in his tanned face. He was dressed in range clothing and wore a pistol on his right hip. "May I step down?" he asked, maintaining the courtesy of the range country. "I'd like to talk to you."

"Of course."

Will dismounted and tied the horse to a fence post.

Heidi came out of the house carrying her doll. Seeing the stranger, she stopped abruptly.

"It's all right, Heidi. This is Mr. DeVore. We were friends when we were young," Johanna explained.

"I hope we still are. Howdy, little miss," He smiled and touched his hat brim.

"Hello." Hiedi took a step forward.

"Can I offer you something to drink, Will? Coffee, tea?"

"Water will do just fine."

From the corner of her eye, Johanna saw Heidi slip back into the house. *It's just as well. I'm sure Will doesn't want an audience.* After he quenched his thirst and watered his horse, Johanna led the way to the benches beneath the trees.

Will stood looking down at her. "Johanna, I won't beat around the bush. I saw Nick in town, and he told me you haven't remarried. I've come to ask if I can call on you. I let your pa scare me away once, but I won't be put off so easy this time."

Johanna hesitated. She had never considered this might happen. "I don't know, Will. I've never thought about being courted. I'm not sure I want to be. I have two children, you know." She pleated her apron fabric.

"That don't matter. I don't mean to push you, but neither one of us is gettin' any younger. You think about it, and I'll be back next week for your answer."

"All right. But I'm not making any promises." She stood and smoothed the wrinkles from her apron.

"That's good enough for now." He grinned, donned his hat and strode to his horse.

*

At the supper table, Heidi told Karl and Gustav about their visitor.

"What did he want?" Karl asked, his voice sharp.

"Don't take that tone with me, young man!"

"I'm sorry, Mama," the boy apologized, his face flaming.

"Mr. DeVore was just passing by and wanted to water his horse." Johanna strived to keep her voice casual. "We knew each other when we were growing up."

Gustav added. "His *vater* owns the Circle D. They have much land and many cattle."

"You mean he's rich?" Heidi asked, her voice filled with awe.

"*Ya*, I think so," Gustav replied.

Karl scowled and a dark flush crept up his neck. "We don't care about that, do we, Mama?"

Johanna, at a loss for an answer, shook her head and changed the subject.

On Sunday Johanna saw the family at church. Conrad barely acknowledged her presence and made no effort to speak with her. Mary and Sam were not with them. Anne-Marie said Mary was ailing again. "Is there anything I can do? I could follow you home and..."

"*Nein*, we will manage," Conrad cut her off.

Her spine stiffened and she tried to disguise the hurt at her father's curt dismissal. "If you're sure..." She turned to Anne-Marie. "Give Mary my love and tell her I hope she feels better soon."

Johanna had no opportunity to talk with Nick about Will's visit. She didn't know what she was going tell Will when he came back. She was honest enough to admit she once might have given Will more consideration, but a tall dark stranger with deep blue eyes kept creeping into her dreams.

Johanna became more apprehensive every day. She would be relieved when Margareth arrived, although it could only complicate matters. At least she would have someone to share her troubled thoughts. The children and Gustav must never discover how worried and frightened she felt.

Saturday came and it was time to make the trip to Meirsville. They needed supplies and Johanna wanted to purchase materials for summer clothing. The butter and egg money might not be enough, but she could withdraw funds from the bank. With careful management, she had been able hold onto the money Josef had left her and add a bit to it.

The countryside had lost some of its lush beauty. The pastures were turning brown from too much sun and too little rain. The bluebonnets and Indian paintbrush had given way to Indian blankets and black-eyed Susans.

Gustav halted the wagon in front of the mercantile, and Johanna and the children climbed down.

"I will take care of Bruno and Katrina, *liebchen*."

"I have quite a few things to do, but I want to sell the eggs first. Will you meet us down at the river for dinner?" Johanna had packed a picnic basket.

"*Yah*." Gustav slapped the lines, and the wagon moved off.

"Mama, may I go to Henry's?" Karl asked. "I haven't seen him since school was out."

"Yes, but be back by dinner time," she cautioned.

Karl ran off to find Henry while Johanna and Heidi carried the baskets of eggs into the mercantile.

"Good morning, Johanna." Mrs. Schmidt was a short plump woman with gray hair worn in braids wrapped around her head.

"Good morning, Mrs. Schmidt." Johanna set the baskets on the counter. "Here are the eggs and my order. We'll come back after dinner. I want to pick out some yard goods."

"We just got a new shipment in. Some real pretty colors, too," Mrs. Schmidt responded. "Your order will be ready when you come back."

Johanna nodded and called Heidi, who was looking at the merchandise in the glass display case. They continued on to the bank. Several chairs and a large table with an ornate lamp in the center occupied the area inside the door. The tellers' cages took the inside wall, and a wooden railing separated the back of the building where the vault was located. George Taylor's private office took the other corner room beyond the railing.

Johanna completed her business and turned to leave as Taylor emerged from his office.

"Hello, Mrs. Bauer, Heidi. It's nice see you. Is everything satisfactory?"

"Yes, everything is fine," she assured him.

"I'm glad to hear that. If there's anything you need, let us know," he said with a smile.

"Thank you. Good day." Johanna spotted Gustav coming out of the livery stable and motioned him over to the public area. She took the picnic basket from the wagon and began to set out the food. Karl came running up, out of breath.

"I thought I was going to be late," he gasped.

Gustav grinned and patted the boy on the back. "You are never late when it's time to eat."

Packing away the remains of their lunch, Johanna reminded Gustav she and the children would be at the mercantile. "Bring the wagon around in about hour."

"I will go to Stein's for a little visit."

As Johanna and the children walked toward the mercantile, Amanda crossed the street, picking her way through the horse droppings. She wore a navy blue skirt and white pleated waist. A large envelope was tucked under her arm.

"Johanna, how nice to see you. Heidi, Karl, are you having a good time in town today?" Amanda's beautiful face reflected genuine interest.

"Hello, Amanda." Johanna was conscious of her plain calico frock.

"Hello, Miss Blair," Karl responded.

"We had a picnic down by the river," Heidi chimed in.

"That's always a lot fun," Amanda replied. "I'm sorry I can't stay and chat, but I must get to the bank before it closes. See you in church tomorrow." She hurried away.

While Karl wandered around the mercantile, Johanna and Heidi inspected the yard goods. Calico in blue, gray, brown and green, and gingham in red, blue, yellow and green checks made vivid splashes of color among the somber items in the store's inventory. Pristine white dimity, lawn and pique caught Johanna's eye. *Oh, how would it feel to be able to buy whatever you wanted?*

"What color would you like, Heidi? You may choose one and Mama will make you a new dress." Johanna's practical mind took over.

"They are all pretty." Hedi looked at each piece and ran her fingers over the smooth cloth. She liked the green check. "I don't have anything green."

Johanna chose gray calico for herself, muslin for undergarments and material to make Karl and Gustav new shirts. As a special treat, she bought green hair ribbons for Heidi and red braid trim for the gray calico.

Mrs. Schmidt cut the materials and packaged them. She totaled Johanna's purchases and deducted the egg money. As Johanna counted out the balance due, Mrs. Schmidt exclaimed, "I almost forgot. You have some mail. I'll get it for you."

Johanna stared at the letter in her hand. She recognized Margareth's handwriting. Looking up, she saw Mrs. Schmidt watching her. "Thank you." Johanna put the letter in her reticule. She would not give the gossip mill any new fuel.

Gustav had pulled the wagon to the front of the store and was helping Mr. Schmidt load the supplies. Johanna and the children climbed onto the seat. When they reached the edge of town, Johanna pulled the letter out and began to read.

> *Dear Sister,*
>
> *It is with a grateful heart that I accept your offer to spend some time with you. I did not want to cause my family any more pain, and if there had been another way, I would have taken it. I will be leaving Cripple Creek in two days and should arrive in Meirsville around May 15th.*
>
> *Your loving sister,*
> *Margareth*

CHAPTER SIX

"Oh, Mama, it's so pretty!" Heidi exclaimed.

Preparations for Margareth's visit were completed, and Johanna began sewing Heidi's new dress. She pinned and cut the material, making ample allowance for the hem. The dress had short puffed sleeves and a full skirt enhanced with a wide ruffle.

The shirts for Karl and Gustav were sewn in record time, and Johanna started on the gray calico. Always a treat, the new dress with its red trim had a festive look.

While Gustav and Karl helped a neighbor who had broken his leg, Johanna was busy with the ironing. Perspiration dotted her forehead and beaded her upper lip. She heard the sound of hoofbeats and looked out the window to see Will DeVore reining his horse to a halt. Panic threatened to envelop her and she chastised herself. She was an independent woman, free to make her own choices.

There was no time to do anything about her appearance. Wiping her face and tucking the loose strands of hair into place, she went to the door.

"Howdy, Johanna." Will doffed his hat.

"Hello, Will." She stepped outside.

Will came directly to the point. "Have you made up your mind?"

"Let's talk in the yard. I've been ironing and it's much cooler out here. Heidi is resting. She had a stomachache and I put her to bed. Too many cookies, I'm afraid."

They walked to the benches under the trees, and Johanna sat down. Will sat across from her, placing his hat on his knees. Conscious of the dampness under her arms and her wrinkled clothing, Johanna looked down at her lap.

"I don't know what to say, Will." She clasped her hands together.

"You could say 'yes.'" His face lost its somber expression and he grinned. Suddenly, Johanna saw Will as had he looked ten years ago when he was young and in love.

"It isn't that simple. Things have changed," Johanna smiled, a hint of sadness in her voice.

"Some things, but not my feelin's for you. That's why I never married. Never found another woman I wanted."

A bright pink flush stained Johanna's cheeks.

Will continued, "I knew you wouldn't talk to me that first year after Josef died. And then I was away on the cattle drives. You know, since my mother and brother died of the fever, I'm all Pa has left. He's anxious for me to get married, and he's always liked you, Johanna "

"I'm sorry to hear about your father, Will. Are you sure you're still interested in me, or do you just want to make your father happy?" Johanna looked him in the eye.

"You don't believe that! How about the times we met at the water hole?" Will flashed a knowing grin.

Once more Johanna's face flooded with color. She remembered their last meeting, when she had told him she was going marry Josef.

"I'm sure you've heard that Margareth is coming home?"

Will looked surprised at the abrupt change of subject. "Yeah, but I didn't know if it was true."

"Yes, she will be staying with us." There was no need to explain that Conrad had never forgiven Margareth. "Perhaps we can talk again after she gets settled. She's supposed to arrive the fifteenth."

Will's gaze grew speculative. "Then you're not turnin' me down?"

Before Johanna could reply, Heidi called out, "Mama, Mama, where are you?"

Johanna gave a silent sigh of relief. "I'm in the front yard." She rose and turned toward the house.

Will came to his feet.

Heidi came out of the house and stood on the step.

"Is your stomachache better?"

"Yes, ma'am." Heidi walked to her mother's side.

"You remember Mr. DeVore, don't you?" Johanna put her arm around the child's shoulders.

"Yes. Hello, sir."

"Howdy, young lady. I hear you ate too many cookies." Heidi blushed and looked down her feet.

"Well, Johanna, I'd better be goin'." Will clamped his Steston on his head.

"We will remember your father in our prayers."

"I appreciate that and I know it will mean a lot to Pa." Touching his hat brim, he walked to his horse, mounted and rode off.

Johanna saw Karl and Gustav approaching in the wagon. She thought she saw Will nod, but he continued on without stopping.

Nick and Sam stopped by the next day on their way to help the injured neighbor. Heidi was in the yard playing with Fritz, and Karl and Gustav were in the fields.

"I'm glad you stopped by. I've been wanting to talk with you. Margareth will be here around the fifteenth. What can we do about Poppa?"

"I don't think we can do anything," Sam replied, scowling.

"No, if he decides to forgive her, he will do it on his own. Don't fret, Johanna. Everything will work out all right." Nick gave his sister a hug. "By the way, did Will DeVore come around?" He grinned, his eyes twinkling.

"Yes, he did. He's been here twice." Johanna focused her gaze over his shoulder

"Well?" Nick asked.

"Well, nothing. Maybe after Margareth comes..." Johanna's voice trailed off.

"You could do worse," Sam said. "Will has always had an eye for you. Besides, he'll inherit the Circle D someday. He could provide for you and the kids. It's going to be a long, hard road to raise them by yourself."

"Whoa, Sam! Aren't you jumping the gun?" Nick's voice lost its teasing note.

"Stop it! Both of you! I'm not interested in marrying again." Johanna felt her temper rising but managed to keep her voice even.

Nick grinned and winked at her. "We'd best be on our way."

* * *

The long awaited day arrived, and the family rose at dawn. Chores finished and breakfast over, Johanna helped Heidi dress.

"Mama, may I wear my new green dress? I want to look nice for Aunt Margareth."

"Yes, this is a special day." Johanna tied the green ribbons around Heidi's pigtails before beginning her own toilette.

She had finished the gray calico dress. Johanna did not usually spend time or money to embellish her clothing, but she wanted the dress to be special. The bodice opened to the waist, and she had gauged the skirt before attaching it to the bodice. Catherine's sewing basket had yielded pretty red glass buttons that matched the red trim on the high collar and the cuffs of the long full sleeves.

Karl and Gustav, freshly scrubbed and wearing their new shirts, were anxious to get started. "Mama, I need to take care of Fritz," Karl said.

"All right, but don't play with him. We have to leave soon," Johanna replied as she gathered her reticule and bonnet.

With Gustav handling the lines, they made their way to Meirsville. Johanna's thoughts focused on Margareth. What would she look like? Had the years treated her kindly? How would people react to her return?

The westbound stage arrived in Meirsville from San Antonio early every Monday morning. There would not be many people on the street at that hour, and they should be able to avoid the busybodies. The stage stopped in front of the hotel for unloading and picking up passengers and mail. Johanna asked Gustav to pull the wagon in front of the barber shop two doors from the hotel. They remained in the wagon awaiting Margareth's arrival.

A cloud dust appeared on the horizon. As the stage came into view,

Johanna climbed down from the wagon seat. Karl swung Heidi to the ground, and Gustav secured the horses.

Pulling hard on the lines, the driver brought the cumbersome vehicle to a halt. He jumped down, opened the door and assisted a woman from the coach. She wore a black serge traveling suit.

"Johanna?" The woman's voice was low and hesitant.

Both women moved forward.

"Margareth? Is it really you?" Johanna's voice was choked with emotion.

The women embraced, then drew back and looked at one another. Neither seemed able to speak. Margareth's eyes were wet with tears. Johanna took in Margareth's appearance from head to toe, seeing not a girl of fourteen, but a striking woman of twenty-four. She was several inches shorter than Johanna, and the hair visible under the feather-trimmed black hat was the color of spun gold. Although dusty and wrinkled, her dress, cut in the latest fashion, had a full skirt with a bustle and Basque-type jacket. The garment displayed her bosom and narrow waist to perfection. White silk ruffles spilled from the opening at her throat and from beneath the long sleeves of her jacket.

"Ma'am, I've put your trunks on the porch," the driver interrupted the reunion. He set a bulging portmanteau beside Margareth. Dropping the mailbag next to the hotel door, he climbed into his seat. With a crack of the whip and a few well-chosen words, the stage rolled out in a cloud of dust.

"Oh, I didn't even thank him," Margareth lamented as she wiped her eyes with a dainty lace-trimmed handkerchief.

"I'm sure he understood. Oh, Margareth, it's so good to see you! I guess I was still expecting my little sister." Johanna smiled, her eyes misty.

"It's been a long time since anyone called me Margareth," she answered. "Jack shortened it to 'Maggie' when we first met, and I've been Maggie ever since."

"That will take some getting used to, but we'll try." Johanna turned to Heidi and Karl standing by her side. "Come children, meet your Aunt Margareth."

The children stared at the fashionably dressed woman.

"Marg...Maggie, this is Heidi." Johanna urged the little girl forward.

"Hello, Heidi. You look like your mother."

"Hello, Aunt Maggie," Heidi responded with a bashful smile.

Margareth hesitated, then stooped and hugged the little girl. Karl stood quietly observing the exchange between his sister and his aunt but made no effort to join them.

"Karl." Johanna eyed the boy sternly. He came forward, his eyes downcast.

"You favor your father, Karl," Maggie told him.

"Yes, ma'am."

Gustav had been waiting quietly in the background. Now he joined them. "Margareth, you remember me? I'm Gusatv Schultz."

"Gustav? Oh, yes, you lived with Josef and Catherine." Maggie offered her hand.

"I guess I was like Johanna and expected a young girl." He took her soft hand in its black leather glove in his callused one.

"It's been a long time." Maggie lowered her voice. "Johanna, how is Poppa? Sam and Nick?"

Noticing that people were beginning to appear on the street, Johanna answered, "Let's get your things in the wagon. We can talk on the way home."

Gustav and Karl loaded the trunks while Maggie retrieved her portmanteau and put it behind the wagon seat. When they were a short distance out of town, Johanna turned to Maggie.

"You asked about Poppa and the boys." She shook her head, "Well, I'm afraid nothing has changed as far as Poppa is concerned." She touched Maggie's hand in a gesture of comfort.

"Sam and Nick are pleased you decided to come home," she continued. "Sam's wife Mary is expecting again, their fourth. She's not doing very well. Nick married Anne-Marie Witte a little over a year ago. I don't think you know her. She's quite a bit younger than we are. You'll like Anne-Marie. She's a very sweet girl, and Nick is so in love with her."

Johanna smiled and chattered on. "They are trying to save for a place of their own, but you know how long that takes." She glanced at Maggie in time to see a strange expression flit across her face, but it was gone in an instant.

"Things don't seem to have changed a great deal," Maggie said, gazing around the countryside.

"No, not very much," Johanna answered. "There are few new families in the area, and the war did change a lot of lives."

The remainder of the trip passed quickly with Johanna answering Maggie's questions about family and friends. Johanna refrained from asking Maggie about herself. Whatever Maggie wanted to tell her would come in its own good time.

When they reached the farm, Gustav pulled the wagon close to the house. He and Karl carried the heavy trunks into Johanna's bedroom.

"Put them in the corner where Heidi's bed was," Johanna said. "Would you like a cup of tea and something to eat?"

"That would be heavenly. I had to get up early to get the stage to Meirsville, and I'm not used to that. I feel like I could sleep for a week." Maggie stifled a yawn.

"You can sleep as long you like," Johanna told her. "Dinner will be a little late," she said to Karl and Gustav as they left to take care of the horses and wagon.

"Heidi, you need to change your dress. You don't want to get it dirty. You won't be able to wear it to church on Sunday. I need to do the same." She exchanged the gray calico dress for a faded blue one. Tying an apron around her waist, she and Maggie went back to the kitchen.

Johanna put the kettle on and brought out the tea things. She had baked strudel the day before.

"I haven't tasted real strudel in years," Maggie exclaimed.

Heidi came into the room struggling with her buttons.

"Here, let me help you," Maggie offered.

Heidi smiled and turned her back. Maggie's fingers trembled as she fastened the little girl's dress.

"Thank you," Heidi spoke softly.

"You're welcome." Maggie returned her smile.

Johanna indicated that Maggie should be seated at the table and poured steaming cups of tea.

"Heidi, would you like a glass of milk?"

Heidi nodded and Johanna filled a tumbler. She passed the plate of strudel.

"This is wonderful," Maggie said as she savored a bite of the rich pastry.

"Thank you," Johanna said with a pleased smile.

"Mama, don't you think I should untie Fritz? Karl has probably been too busy," Heidi said.

"Yes, dear. That's very thoughtful of you."

Heidi finished the last swallow of milk and scampered off.

"Would you like more tea, strudel?" Johanna asked.

"No, thank you. It was delicious." Maggie patted another yawn.

"You need rest, and I need to get dinner started." Johanna rose and began to gather the tea things.

"I feel like such a bother," Maggie apologized. "At least let me help you get dinner."

"You're no bother. I'm just glad you decided to come home," Johanna said, putting her arm around Maggie's shoulders and hugging her close. Maggie smiled, her eyes tearing again.

"Let's get you into bed." Johanna picked up the kettle of hot water and led the way to the bedroom. She poured hot water into the washbowl. "There's cold water in the pitcher and fresh towels." She indicated the stack of snowy linens folded on the washstand. Turning down the bed covers, she kissed Maggie on the cheek. "Try to get some rest."

When Johanna called Maggie for dinner, she found her sister sound asleep. She decided Maggie needed rest more than food and did not awaken her.

"I need to weed the garden," Johanna said as they enjoyed the quick meal she had prepared.

"Gustav and I are going to check the cornfield," Karl said. "We might have roasting ears."

"*Ya,*" Gustav added as he drained his coffee cup. "They should be ready. I will bring some to the house."

"Good. I will fix them for supper." Johanna was planning a special meal for Maggie. *Weiner-schnitzel* and potato pancakes had been her favorites when she was a girl. Sweet and sour cabbage and blackberry cobbler would complete the menu.

The sun was beginning its descent westward when Johanna finished the garden. Most of the preparation for supper had been completed, but she would have to hurry. Gustav and Karl needed hot water and no doubt Maggie was awake. When she entered the house, she found Maggie was indeed awake. She had changed her traveling suit for a light blue muslin dress and rearranged her hair. She looked fresh and pretty.

"Johanna, why didn't you wake me?"

"You needed the rest. Are you hungry?" Johanna asked, conscious of her grimy hands and messy clothing.

"No, not really."

"How about a cup of tea?"

"I'd like that," Maggie said.

"Let me freshen up first," Johanna hurried to the bedroom.

"If you like, I can help you unpack," Johanna said after they finished the evening meal.

Accommodating Maggie's possessions would require some adjustment. When Maggie opened the trunks, Johanna could not believe her eyes. She had never seen such beautiful clothes. Of course Amanda and Jane were always fashionably attired, but being stylish and well-dressed was necessary to their businesses.

"Jack always insisted on buying me nice things," Maggie said as she fought to hold back the tears. "I know it's hard for you to understand, but we did have a good marriage. We didn't have the kind of life decent people approve of, but we were happy.

"When I ran away," Maggie continued, "I lied to Jack about my age. I told him I was eighteen. I know he didn't believe me, and I'll never understand why he took me with him." Maggie smiled and shook her head. "But he said if I was going stay with him, we had to get married. He was twenty-four. I thought Poppa might try to find us, and he would get in trouble with the authorities.

"I didn't know for a long time that he came from a wealthy family in New Orleans. He was involved in a duel, and they disinherited him. We had good times and bad times, but he never mistreated me." She sniffled and wiped her eyes.

"Oh, Maggie." Johanna's voice was filled with compassion as she embraced her sister.

"I know I have to go on, but right now I don't know what do." Maggie's voice wavered.

"Give it time, Maggie. We're glad to have you with us. Let's just enjoy it."

Maggie began to unpack the trunks. There were gowns in all fabrics, colors and styles. Petticoats with fine lace trim and crinolettes with steel bustle supports, ribbon trimmed chemises and drawers, and heavily-boned corsets spilled from the trunk in profusion. Johanna's eyes went wide like a child's at Christmas.

Digging deeper, Maggie brought forth stockings of fine lisle, worsted cotton and even some in colors and black net. There were high-top shoes and soft leather boots as well as patent leather and satin slippers. Johanna could not have imagined such finery in her wildest dreams.

Maggie hefted her portmanteau onto the bed and began removing an assortment of fancy jars and bottles. "Tools of the trade." Maggie laughed, then seeing Johanna's face color, hastened to add, "Oh no, not what you're thinking! I learned a great deal about taking care of my complexion, from Jack, mostly. He said Creole women are very protective of their skin. They have French ancestry, and you know the French are supposed to know all the beauty secrets."

Johanna unconsciously touched her own tanned face.

"You're welcome to use any of the things I brought with me," Maggie offered.

"Oh, no. I couldn't do that," Johanna protested.

* * *

The village of Llano, situated on the banks of the Llano River, boasted a hotel, several stores and saloons, but no house of worship. The Indian threat that had plagued the early settlers was under control, but the place attracted men who did not want to call attention to themselves. Those who rode on the dark side of the law could lose themselves in the smoky recesses and back stairs of the saloons and whorehouses.

As it neared the noon hour, the sun was a bright yellow ball when a man rushed into the sheriff's office. From his white shirt with black garters holding up the sleeves, a flowered waistcoat, and the white apron tied around his middle, it was obvious the man was a saloonkeeper.

"Sheriff, you'd better git over to my place quick. Tess has been killed."

Powers came out from behind his desk and reached for his hat. A short stocky man, he had dark hair and eyes and a full mustache.

"Killed! When? How?"

"Don't know. Looks like she was strangled. When she didn't come down fer breakfast, Audrey went to see 'bout 'er and found 'er stone cold dead."

Crossing the wide street, they narrowly missed being run down by a loaded freight wagon.

"Better slow that damn thing down," the sheriff yelled at the be-whiskered driver who spat tobacco juice over the side of the wagon, narrowly missing a well-dressed matron trying to cross the street. She glared and shook her fist at the unrepentant teamster, who guffawed loudly and drove on at breakneck speed.

The saloon's inhabitants were subdued in contrast to their usual raucous behavior. Unpleasant odors from the previous night's activities hung in the stale air. Two soiled doves, Audrey and Polly, huddled at a table in the corner over the remnants of their morning meal. They were clad in faded wrappers, their hair uncombed, and their tear-stained faces bare of paint.

"Got any idea who might a done it, Hank?" Powers asked, glancing at the two women.

"No, Sheriff. Them girls was pretty busy last night."

CHAPTER SEVEN

Fiery red streaks stretched across the western sky, and purple shadows gathered among the trees as Logan rode into Ranger Headquarters. He had enjoyed his visit home, but the usual eagerness to resume his duties had vied with a strange reluctance to leave the Spur.

Logan stabled *Él Campeon* and headed for the barracks. There were two men in the building, Bartell and a new recruit he introduced as Lou Helderman.

"Seems like we're keepin' the same schedule," Bartell remarked. "Where you headin?"

Logan pitched his bedroll on an empty bunk. "Don't have an assignment yet. I've been on leave. You still chasin' Comanches?"

"No, there was a big rukus over to Fort Griffith, and the cap'n sent me and Helderman to check it out. Some cowpokes shot up the place and wounded the sheriff."

Logan shook his head. "Never seems to get any better, does it?"

"Delaney, I'm glad you're back." The captain opened a desk drawer, took out a stack of papers and handed one to Logan. The likeness of Joe Greene stared back at him. Dark hair hung to his shoulders, and his eyes were dark under heavy eyebrows. He had a small mustache. The description gave his height as six feet and his approximate weight one hundred and sixty pounds. The reward had been increased to one thousand dollars. It seemed Mr. Greene had added cattle rustling to his accomplishments.

Montgomery placed the remaining posters on his desk. "The sheriff in Llano just sent word that a saloon girl was found dead in her room a couple of days ago. From the description of the man she was with the night before, it could have been Greene. You need to check it out."

Logan smiled grimly and tapped the poster with his finger. "From all we've heard about him, he has a fondness for the ladies."

"Hate to chase you out so soon after that long ride from the Spur," Montgomery said.

"That's all right, Captain. We both know what happens when the trail gets cold. Besides, I didn't do anything but eat and sleep while I was at the ranch." He grinned and patted his flat abdomen.

"How is Sean? Still want you back home for good?"

"Yeah, but you know Pa. He won't pressure me. Pat's worse than Pa is. Tim took the drive this year, and Pat feels like I should be on the Spur."

"Any problems with the Comanches?"

"No. Pa made a bargain with them a long time ago. They take a beef or two when they're hungry, and they don't bother the ranch. 'Course, that doesn't mean he leaves the horses unguarded." Logan grinned. It was a known fact that the Indians valued fine horseflesh above all else.

"Smart man, your Pa." Montgomery separated the posters and handed Logan a small number. "Take these with you. Might run onto a lawman who hasn't seen one."

Logan felt the sweat trickle down his back. Summer had definitely arrived. The landscape was showing the effects of the hot Texas sun. Greasewood, sagebrush and cacti survived the dry, rocky soil, but the prairie grasses had succumbed to the longhorn cattle roaming the thinly populated area.

He had been riding since daylight. Spotting trees in the distance, he left the main trail. A small stream wound its way southward. Its banks were lined with cottonwoods, and the clear water flowed over a rocky bed. Later in the summer the creek would dry up but provided welcome relief now. Horse and rider quenched their thirst, and Logan refilled his canteen. Untying his bandanna, he dipped it in the cool water, run it over his face and neck and sighed with pleasure.

Sitting with his back against a large hackberry tree, Logan reflected on the trouble in Llano. If the killer had been Joe Greene, he would be long gone by now. There might be a clue or two if some idiot had not destroyed them. With the Rangers on his trail, where would Greene go? San Antone? No. Greene wouldn't be fool enough to hang around a town crawling with lawmen.

Pitching his half-smoked cigarette in the water, Logan caught up the reins and swung his leg over the saddle. His eyes focused on a patch of wildflowers near the creek bank. One bright pink blossom stood out against its withered companions. A vision of Johanna flashed before him. He hadn't been able to erase her memory no matter how hard he tried. Her image was burned in his brain. *Damn. If you don't get her out of your mind, it's going to get you killed.*

Logan rode into Llano in the middle of the afternoon. The sheriff's office and jail were located just off the main street. Logan went directly to the lawman's office. He had been in Llano many times and was acquainted with the sheriff. Powers did a fair job of keeping the peace, but Logan knew it would be up to the Rangers to apprehend the killer. Seated behind his desk, Powers stood when Logan entered the office.

"Delaney, I sure am glad to see you," he said, offering his hand.

"Howdy, Powers. Heard you got a little problem. Want to fill me in?" Logan pulled up a chair.

"This stranger showed up the day before the girl was killed." Powers resumed his seat. "He stayed at the Longhorn, played some poker and got friendly with Tess. She's the one that was killed," he added by way of explanation.

"Audrey's room is right next to Tess', and the night before she heard some loud voices but didn't pay much attention. When Tess didn't show fer breakfast, Audrey went to see about her and found 'er dead. Doc Moore says she was strangled. From the way Hank—he owns the saloon—described the man, it could a been Joe Greene. Fits the wordin' on the poster." Powers slumped down in his chair as if the lengthy recitation had exhausted him.

Logan's eyes narrowed and his features tightened. He'd bet his best pair of boots they could add murder to Joe Greene's growing list of crimes.

"I'd like to see the room. Hope the barkeep has kept it locked," Logan said, rising from the chair.

"Yeah, but Hank threw a fit till I convinced him the Rangers wouldn't like it if he didn't." Powers reached for his hat hanging on a peg by the door.

They crossed the street to the saloon, and Powers introduced Logan to Hank. He confirmed Powers' story.

"We're gonna take a look at Tess' room," Powers informed the saloonkeeper.

"All right, but when you gonna release it? I gotta a girl comin' in on the stage tomorrow." He wiped the bar with a dirty rag.

"As soon as I finish my investigation, it's all yours," Logan told him.

At the top of the stairs, a hallway ran the length the of building. A door at the end led to an outside stairway. There were two rooms on each side of the hall. Powers took a key from his pocket and unlocked the door of the second room on the right. The door swung open and Logan wrinkled his nose. The stench of death, sex, sweat and cheap perfume mingled to create a putrid odor. Logan stepped to the single window and raised it high.

"She was layin' in the bed on her back." Powers indicated the iron bed with its rumpled covers. "She didn't have no clothes on," Powers continued, an embarrassed look on his homely face. "That chair was turned over, jist like you see it."

A dressing table in the corner held an array of bottles and jars, some open and their contents spilled. Tess had not been a neat person. Hooks on the wall held brightly-colored dresses, and a small chest was filled with undergarments. A typical saloon girl's room.

"Didn't find nothin'," the sheriff said.

Logan continued looking around. "It's easy to overlook small things." He squatted and looked under the bed. A bright ray of sunlight shining on something metal caught his eye. Reaching for the object, he discovered it was a broken rowel from a silver spur, much like the ones he wore himself. It had been polished recently, and that fit. Joe

Greene was known as a fastidious dresser.

"What did you find?" Powers asked, his voice several notes higher. Logan held out his hand.

"Well, I'll be damned." The sheriff's face turned bright red.

"It happens to the best of us." Logan grinned. "I don't suppose anybody saw him leave the room?"

"Not that I know of. Them other girls had their own customers, and Hank don't ride herd too close. They know what he expects and, if he don't git it, out they go."

"Greene—if it was Greene—probably sneaked down the back stairs. What about his horse?" Logan stared at the broken piece of spur.

"Grover, that's the mucker over to the livery, said the man paid in advance, and the horse was gone the next mornin'. Grover said it was a brown and white piebald, real flashy."

"That fits. I don't see any reason to talk with the mucker. I think I have everything I'm going get."

Logan's instincts told him Greene had lit out for the border. Riding south, he distributed posters to lawmen who did not have them. He mulled over the necessity for stopping in Meirsville to alert Sheriff Koenig. *Admit it, Delaney. It's not Koenig that's on your mind.*

Koenig had received the new posters but was unaware of the incident in Llano. He agreed that Greene had probably high-tailed it to Mexico. There was no reason to linger in Meirsville, and Logan took the trail leading to Uvalde. There were other border crossings, but the place was known as a refuge for cattle rustlers, bank robbers and others outside the law.

Logan told himself that the fact that he was near Johanna's farm had nothing to do with his decision. At the same time he reined *Él Campeon* to the right and walked him toward the farmhouse. What would he say to her? He couldn't think of a good reason to be there.

She was standing at the well with her back to him. Her golden hair gleamed in the sunlight filtering through the trees. Leaning forward to lift the bucket, the raised hemline of her dress revealed a pair of trim ankles.

Logan swallowed hard, then called out, "Mrs. Bauer." She whirled around, water splashing out of the bucket. Logan's face mirrored his astonishment. Although the resemblance was uncanny, the woman was not Johanna.

Logan touched his hat brim. "I'm sorry, ma'am. I didn't mean to startle you. I'm Logan Delaney, and I just stopped to pay my respects to Mrs. Bauer."

"I'm Johanna's sister, Maggie DuPree. I'll tell her you're here." Her eyes searched his face. "Would you like to wait over there?" She pointed to the benches beneath the trees.

"I need to water my horse, ma'am. It's mighty hot today."

Maggie nodded and hurried toward the house, calling out, "Johanna, you have a visitor."

Logan stood as Johanna approached and he saw the transformation. The tight bun was gone, and her golden hair was fashioned into chignon at the nape of her neck. Wispy tendrils framed her forehead and curled around her ears. Even her tanned complexion looked different. Her green calico dress hinted at generous breasts and a narrow waist. Logan could hold his own with the opposite sex, but this time he was at a loss for words.

"Mr. Delaney, it's nice to see you again," Johanna said. She smiled and turned to Maggie. "You've met sister, Mrs. DuPree."

"Yes." Logan managed to recover his voice. "You two sure look a lot alike."

Johanna smiled. "So we've been told. Please have a seat, Mr. Delaney." Johanna moved toward the benches under the trees.

Logan seated himself and balanced his Stetson on his knees. "Where is that pretty little girl, Mrs. Bauer?" he asked, trying to slow his racing thoughts.

"She went with Karl and Gustav to visit a neighbor. May I offer you some refreshment?" Johanna smoothed her apron.

"No, thank you, ma'am. I took advantage of your water for myself and my horse."

"Are you from around here, Mr. Delaney?" Maggie asked. Then she quickly apologized. "I'm sorry, that's really none of my business, but I've been gone a long time and don't remember anyone named Delaney."

"I'm from over west Texas way. Just passing through on my way to Uvalde."

"That's a dangerous place," Johanna exclaimed.

Maggie smiled. "I imagine Mr. Delaney can take care himself."

Logan grinned but made no comment. The silence grew awkward.

Johanna watched Logan from the corner of her eye. He made her uneasy, but she couldn't tell why. It wasn't his behavior. She certainly couldn't fault that. It wasn't his appearance except maybe for the deadly revolver on his hip. He was clad in tight-fitting dark gray trousers stuffed into polished black boots and a light gray shirt with the sleeves cuffed back. A black leather vest covered his broad torso, and a blue silk bandanna the exact color of his eyes was knotted around his neck.

The sound of an approaching wagon intruded into her thoughts. It drew closer, and Johanna saw Karl was driving with Heidi sitting beside him. There was no sign of Gustav. Momentarily forgetting the tall gunman, Johanna gathered her skirts and ran to meet them.

"Where is Gustav? Is something wrong?"

"Mama, Uncle Gustav is hurt real bad." Heidi struggled to hold back the tears.

"He was helping Mr. Scheidler move a hog house when he hurt his back," Karl explained as he brought the horses to a halt.

Johanna hurried to the back of the wagon where Gustav lay propped up with pillows and covered with a quilt. His face was gray and drawn with pain.

"Oh, Gustav, how bad is it?" Johanna reached for his hand.

"Now, *liechen,*" Gustav soothed, "I will be all right."

"Karl, pull the wagon up to the house." Johanna took command. "Heidi, you see to Gustav's bed."

Karl saw Logan for the first time. His eyes narrowed and a slight frown appeared on his face.

"Let's get Gustav to his room and try to make him comfortable. Maybe we should send for Dr. Fischer," Johanna said, anxiety filling her voice and expression.

"*Nein, nein, liebchen,*" Gustav objected, trying sit up.

"Here, let me help you." Logan climbed into the wagon bed and helped the old man to his feet. Then with extreme care, Logan lifted him up and onto the ground.

"This is very kind of you, Mr. Delaney. Between us I think we can get him to his room." Johanna pointed in the direction of the lean-to.

"I'll see to the horses, Mama," Karl called out as he led the team away.

Logan supported Gustav on one side while Johanna and Maggie helped on the other. Heidi held the door open and they took Gustav inside. The small room was scrupulously clean. It contained a bed and washstand. There was a large trunk at the foot of the bed and a rocking chair near the window.

"Gustav, you need to get into bed," Johanna urged. "I have some laudanum in the cupboard. It will ease the pain."

"If you want to get the medicine, ma'am, I'll glad to help Mr. Schultz into bed," Logan said.

"Thank you. I'll be back shortly." She retreated to the doorway where Maggie and Heidi were waiting.

"Johanna, why don't I start supper while you see to Gustav?" Maggie asked

"That's a good idea." Johanna turned to Logan. "We'd be pleased to have you take supper with us, Mr. Delaney."

"That's not necessary, ma'am."

"Do you need to leave immediately?"

"No, ma'am, but..."

"Good, it's settled then." Johanna smiled and left the room. Heidi and Maggie followed.

"*Danke.*"

"No thanks necessary. Just tell me what you need."

"The night shirt is in the trunk."

Between them they managed to get Gustav settled. Johanna returned with the laudanum, and he took it without resisting.

"*Danke, liebchen.* I am sorry I cannot help Karl with the milking."

"Gustav, I know how to milk a cow," Johanna admonished gently.

"I know you do." He managed a weak smile.

"Would you like Heidi to sit with you for awhile?" Johanna asked as she smoothed the covers.

"If she wishes."

"You know it would please her. Try to rest now."

"Mrs. Bauer." Logan had been standing at the door while Johanna made Gustav comfortable. "I'm not much for milking cows, but I can pitch hay and feed the stock."

"We appreciate your offer, Mr. Delaney, but we simply cannot impose on you further."

"I recognize a lady in distress when I see one. Now, you wouldn't want to deprive me of the chance to behave like a gentlemen, would you?" Logan flashed a grin, exposing even white teeth.

"Go along, *liebchen*, let Mr. Delaney help you." Gustav's speech was slurred, a sign the laudanum was taking effect.

"All right. I know Maggie's limitations in the kitchen. And I need to prepare some soup for Gustav. He will need to eat when he awakens." Johanna left the door ajar.

Johanna reached the corner of the house in time to see Karl disappear into the barn with the milk buckets. Logan bent to untie the thongs that held his in holster place. Johanna felt a sudden chill. During the excitement, she had forgotten the danger that seemed to surround him. She took a deep breath and tried to swallow the lump that rose in her throat.

* * *

Soft rays of moonlight played hide and seek with the dark waters of the Rio Grande. The flames from a small campfire outlined the silhouettes of the five men gathered around it. A coyote howled in the distance, answered in a heartbeat by one of its kind.

"Joe," a rough voice interrupted the silence, "do you think the Rangers are on our trail?"

The meager light from the campfire revealed a dark countenance covered with several days' growth of beard. It was difficult to determine the man's age, even his size, because he blended into the darkness. He was known only as Bennett and had ridden with Greene for several years.

"Hell, yes! You know they are. I'm goin' into Laredo tomorra night. I'll keep my eyes and ears open." Greene threw his cigarette butt into the fire.

"That's pretty risky, Joe," another man spoke up. "You better stick to them *señoritas* at the cantina."

Greene's eyes narrowed and a scowl marred his handsome features. "Shut up, Hawkins! You know better'n to try and give me orders. Besides, that bitch had it comin'. She tried to rob me. If you're afraid to ride with us, you can git out now." Greene's hand rested on the butt of his revolver.

"Now, Joe, don't git all riled up. You know I didn't mean nothin'," Hawkins answered in a choked voice.

A feral grin split Greene's features, and the anger left his face as quickly as it had come.

"How long we gonna hole up down here?" The man who asked appeared older than the others. His hair and beard were shot through with gray. He went by the name of Ollie Sims, although a man's name could change whenever the need arose.

"As long as we have to, I reckon," Greene replied, scowling. "There's a herd across the river to the west aways. I plan to wait till things cool off a bit, then round up them beeves and shove 'em across the border for some quick money. You know ol' Don Miguel don't ask questions, and he's always got plenty of cash on hand."

"That's a good idee, Joe. I could sure use some *dinero*. My poke's 'bout gone," a young fellow with stringy blond hair whined.

"Bud, yore poke ain't even broke in yet."

The men guffawed loudly.

"Damn you, Bennett, jist 'cause I'm younger 'n the rest of ya, don't mean I ain't done my share a pokin'," the slender young man bragged.

"Yeah, them little school girls in Llano." Hawkins joined in the fun. "We're talkin' 'bout real women. Like them *señoritas* at the *cantina*. Now, them gals know how to please a man."

CHAPTER EIGHT

"Heidi, supper is ready," Johanna called from the doorway.

The milking chores finished, Johanna had gone to check on Gustav and found the little girl rocking quietly as she watched the old man sleep. Satisfied all was well, Heidi tiptoed from the room. Logan and Karl washed up at the back of the house.

When they came inside, Logan's black hair glistened from the dunking he had given it. Johanna noticed the shadow of a beard on his tanned cheeks. He was not wearing his gunbelt, and somehow he looked undressed without it. That thought caused Johanna's pulse to quicken. *Goodness!* What was she thinking about? She had never seen Josef completely naked in eight years of marriage. Nor had she ever undressed before him.

The years following Heidi's birth had been platonic, and Johanna had felt only relief. That aspect of marriage had not been enjoyable, but it was a wife's duty. Johanna forced her mind away from such unseemly thoughts.

She indicated where they should sit, and Logan took Gustav's place at the table. Maggie kept the conversation going with amusing tales of times spent in the mining camps.

"Mr. Delaney, have you ever seen a shotgun wrapped around a tree trunk?" Maggie asked with a mischievous smile.

"Can't say that I have, ma'am," Logan replied. He set his coffee cup back in the saucer and prepared to hear Maggie spin her yarn.

"It happened at one of the mining camps where my husband and I were living. There was a woman there who did laundry for the miners. She was married to one of them, but Old Hard Rock Pete wouldn't stay on his claim and work it. He'd come into town with a little sack of gold and stay in the saloons until it was gone. His wife—everyone called her Big Ruby—ranted and raved and threatened every time to shoot him if he didn't give her some of the gold before going off to gamble.

"Well, he tried her patience one time too many. He came home, and Ruby was all cocked and primed. She demanded a share of the gold before she would give him his clean clothes. Hard Rock refused. They argued and yelled and name-called until everybody in town heard them. People came out of their houses to watch. The women took up for Ruby and the men egged Pete on. Seeing that the men were beginning to laugh at him, Pete threatened to lock her in the privy, and she stormed into the house.

"He thought the fight was over and went inside. She chased him out with a shotgun, yelling with every breath she was going kill him. He just laughed at her and headed for the saloons. She was hot on his heels, took a bead on him and pulled the trigger. For some reason, the gun didn't fire. By this time Ruby was in such a rage she swung the gun at a tree, and those double barrels wrapped themselves around the trunk like a woman's hair around a curling iron."

By the time Maggie finished her story, Logan was laughing and Johanna barely contained herself. Heidi and Karl listened, wide-eyed. Johanna suspected Maggie had omitted a few unsavory details, but she was grateful for her sister's sense of humor.

After a meal of succulent baked ham, sweet potatoes, green beans and rice custard, Logan complimented his hostess. "That was a mighty fine meal, ma'am. It's not often I have the opportunity to enjoy food like that."

"Thank you," Johanna said.

Karl, who had been quiet during the meal, broke in. "Where do you live, Mr. Delaney?"

"Karl!" Johanna rebuked him.

"That's all right, Mrs. Bauer." Logan pondered the question for a minute. "I guess you could say wherever I hang my hat, but I was raised in west Texas."

Karl scowled but remained silent.

"Karl, will you look in on Gustav? If he's awake, I'll take him some soup." Johanna tried to ease the tension between Logan and Karl.

"May I go too, Mama?" Heidi asked.

"Yes, but don't pester him. He needs rest."

After the children left the house, Logan spoke to Johanna. "Mrs. Bauer, I've been thinking about Mr. Schultz. He won't be able to get around for a few days, and you're going to need help. I'll be glad to stay and give you a hand." He drank the last of his coffee while he waited for her answer.

Johanna stared at him, flabbergasted. It was true she needed firewood, a section of fence had to be mended and the regular chores would have to be done. "I'm not sure that would be proper, Mr. Delaney," she managed to reply as she fidgeted with the napkin in her lap.

"Proper? I don't see anything improper about helping people when they need it. Besides, I think we would be adequately chaperoned." Logan grinned and placed his cup in the saucer.

"I don't see any harm in Mr. Delaney staying here for a few days," Maggie agreed. "Gustav could use his help, too."

"I don't know. There are no sleeping quarters, and well, I couldn't pay you very much." Johanna avoided looking directly him.

"Ma'am, you misunderstood. I don't expect to be paid. A gentleman doesn't charge for helping a lady in distress, and I like to think I haven't forgotten all my upbringing."

"I didn't mean to offend you, Mr. Delaney," Johanna said. "It's just that...that..."

"I understand, ma'am. As for sleeping arrangements, don't worry about that. I'm using to sleeping outdoors," Logan said.

"There is a cot in the harness room. I'm sure it would be more comfortable than sleeping on the ground."

Karl and Heidi raced into the room. "Mama, Uncle Gustav is awake."

"I'll clean up the kitchen while you take Gustav's soup," Maggie volunteered, rising from the table.

Johanna prepared the tray, and taking the lantern from its hook by the door, started for Gustav's room.

"Let me carry that," Logan offered, reaching for the lantern.

"Thank you. That would be a big help."

Soft yellow light spilled from the window of Gustav's room. He was trying to sit up when they entered. Johanna placed the tray on the trunk and piled the pillows behind his back. "I've brought you some potato soup and bread. There's jelly, too, and hot tea."

"I am such a bother," the old man fussed.

"You are not! I don't want to hear that again." Johanna arranged the tray and stepped back.

"I will be all right in the morning," Gustav said.

"No, Gustav, you can't get up tomorrow. You must stay in bed and give your back a chance to heal."

"*Liechben,* there is work to be done."

"Don't worry about that. Mr. Delaney has offered stay for a day or two and help out." She gently pushed Gustav back against the pillows.

"*Goot.* I am glad to hear that."

"Is there anything you need?"

"*Nein,* but maybe Mr. Delaney could stay a few minutes," he replied, glancing at Logan.

"You take the light," Logan said, handing her the lantern.

"Perhaps Mr. Delaney could rub some of that liniment on your back. I'll get it and the laudanum," Johanna replied as she hurried out the door.

After settling Gustav for the night, Johanna and Logan resumed their discussion. When Karl learned that Logan would be staying on, he asked to be excused and went to his room.

"Let me get you some bedding, Mr. Delaney." Johanna turned toward the bedroom.

"There's no need, ma'am. My bedroll will be just fine," he assured her. "And, ma'am, since I'm going to be around for few days, don't you think you could call me Logan?"

Johanna hesitated, then smiled, "Only if you call me Johanna."

"Yes, ma'am," Logan grinned, starting toward the door. "It's time I took care of *Él Campeon.* It looked like there were some empty stalls in the barn."

"Yes, use any one of them. And please take the lantern with you. It's very dark tonight."

Logan picked up the lantern. "Good night, Johanna."

Él Campeon nickered softly as Logan left his stall. A clean stall and fresh hay was a treat for the stallion after days on the trail with grass in short supply. Logan patted the horse's rump. "Just take it easy, old boy, while you have the chance. No telling how far we'll have to go, or how long it will take to pick up Greene's trail."

Él Campeon snorted in reply and began munching his late supper. Logan carried his gear to the harness room. Like everything else on the Bauer farm, it was neat and clean. Harness hung on pegs and the leather, though old, was well-oiled. He dropped his saddle on a bench in the corner and spread his bedroll out on the cot. Checking through his saddlebags for tobacco, he touched the wanted posters. He pulled them out and Joe Greene's likeness stared back at him. He shouldn't be staying here. He needed to get on with the search. A vision of Johanna smiling at him eliminated his twinge of conscience.

Stripping down to his drawers, Logan stretched out on the cot. His mind went over the day's events. Some unexplainable force drew him to Johanna Bauer. She was much prettier than he remembered. He knew she didn't trust him, might even be a little afraid him. And Karl was hostile. Now there were two obstacles that were challenge enough for any man. He was accustomed to planning his moves carefully and was known for keeping calm during the heat of battle, but this was a different kind of fight. One he was unfamiliar with and not even sure he wanted to be in, let alone win.

Turning on his side, Logan willed sleep to come, but instead he kept seeing Johanna in the green dress and how it accentuated her full breasts and slender waist. Visualizing her long, shapely legs, he felt the heat rising in his groin, and his body reacted accordingly. Taking a deep breath, he cursed softly. *Damn!*

While Logan was wooing sleep in the barn, Johanna and Maggie were preparing for bed in the house.

"How do you feel about Logan Delaney?" Maggie asked as she hung up her dress.

"I don't know," Johanna admitted. "He's very polite and certainly handsome, but there's something about him that bothers me."

"I think he's attracted to you," Maggie teased.

"Oh, no! Why would he be interested in me? An older woman with two children. He's more likely interested in you," Johanna protested as she pretended to concentrate on unfastening the tapes on her petticoat.

"Me? You met him before I came home, and he didn't know I was here when he stopped today. As for you being an older woman, that's ridiculous. No, he has an eye for you," Maggie insisted.

"I hardly know him. In fact, I don't know anything at all about him." Johanna picked up her hairbrush and began to smooth out the tangles.

"It's none of my business, and I certainly don't have the right to give advice. Logan Delaney is a good-looking man and has the manners of a gentleman, but I've seen too many of his kind not to recognize them. He's a hired gun. If you become involved with him, you could end up getting hurt. His kind doesn't settle down," Maggie warned.

"You don't have to worry about that. Remember, I have two children to think about. I don't intend to do anything that would bring disgrace on them."

As Johanna started breakfast the next morning, she glanced out the kitchen window. Logan was coming from the barn carrying his shaving things. She poured a small pan full of hot water and went to the back of the house. Her heart thudded and leaped into her throat when she saw him, shirtless, bending over the washbasin, the muscles in his back stretched tight under his smooth skin. Suddenly, he whirled around, his hand going to his hip. Johanna's face paled and fear flickered in her eyes. He flushed dark red, straightened and reached for his shirt hanging on a nearby peg.

"My apologies, ma'am."

Wordless, Johanna extended the pan of water. He reached for it, and as soon as his hand touched it, she turned and fled into the house.

*

"Karl, I will need wood for the baking," Johanna said as he sat down at the breakfast table.

"I'll be glad to take care of that, Mrs. Bauer," Logan said.

"Thank you, but that's one of Karl's chores." She avoided meeting Logan's eyes as she poured his coffee. During breakfast, she found it difficult to act normally. When Logan looked at her across the table his blue eyes darkened, and there was a grim set to his features. He will be gone in a day or two, she told herself, but the thought did not bring her a sense of relief.

"I need to harvest the last of the vegetables," Johanna told Maggie as she set the bread dough to rise.

"You go on, I'll tidy up inside." Maggie had taken on more than her share of the household tasks.

Johanna donned her bonnet and took a basket from the shelf. She could hear the rhythmic sound of the axe as Logan split the large logs for Karl to chop into smaller pieces. The woodpile was near the garden, and she bolstered her courage to work close by. Determined not let him affect her, her resolve wavered when she saw him swing the axe with a smooth calculated motion. Conjuring up a vision of his bare chest sprinkled with black hair, her throat went dry, and her hands tightened on the basket handles. Strange sensations stirred her body and coiled into a knot in her belly. *What is wrong with me? I've never had such feelings in my life.*

Logan watched as Johanna walked toward him. Before either could speak, they heard the sound of an approaching wagon. She put down her basket and went back to the house. Sam was driving the wagon, and Nick and Anne Marie sat on the seat beside him. Johanna hurried to greet them, calling out, "Maggie, we have company."

Maggie, in a brown calico dress, her golden hair covered with a bandanna, came out of the house with a feather duster in her hand. Nick jumped down from the wagon seat and swung Anne-Marie to the ground while Sam secured the horses. Maggie ran to meet them, arms outstretched.

"Nick, you're all grown up." Maggie's eyes filled with tears and they trickled down her cheeks.

"I could say the same thing about you," Nick said as they embraced. He drew Anne-Marie forward. "Maggie, this is my wife, Anne-Marie."

"I'm glad to meet you." Maggie clasped Anne-Marie's hands. "Johanna told you were pretty, but she didn't say how pretty."

Anne-Marie blushed and answered in a soft voice, "Thank you. It's amazing how much you favor one another."

"Yes, we take after Mama," Maggie answered.

Johanna watched the reunion between her sister and brothers with tears in her eyes. Now, if only Poppa would forget the past. Karl and Heidi raced up from the chicken house, and she put the thought from her mind. Seeing Logan standing at the corner of the house, Johanna felt a moment of panic. How was she going to explain his presence? Her thoughts raced and her palms grew sweaty. Since he was not wearing his gunbelt, he didn't look so formidable. Perhaps...

"Mary's not feelin' too good this mornin'," Sam said. Johanna wondered if that wasn't a convenient way for her to avoid seeing Maggie. Mary sided with Conrad, thinking Johanna should have refused take Maggie in.

Johanna turned and took a step toward Logan. "Mr. Delaney, I'd like you to meet my family." Johanna made the introductions. She explained that Gustav had been injured, and Logan had offered to help them out for a few days. The men shook hands, and Johanna felt the reserve behind the gesture.

Sam frowned. "You could have sent for Nick or me."

Johanna shook her head. "You two have enough to do right now." She watched Logan from the corner of her eye. His face was expressionless. Johanna bit her lip and searched for a way to ease the situation. "Mr. Delaney was passing through when Karl and Heidi brought Gustav home. If he hadn't stayed, Gustav would be up trying to work. You know how stubborn he can be." Johanna avoided Sam's stern gaze.

"Why don't we go inside, and I'll fix something to drink?" Johanna said.

"Mrs. Bauer, I know you want to visit with your family, so I'll get back to work." Without waiting for her response, Logan turned and walked away.

Heidi's blond head appeared in the harness room door. "Mama says you're to come to dinner now."

"Thank you, Heidi. I'll be right in."

The little girl nodded and scampered away. Logan put down the harness he had been mending and followed Heidi out of the barn.

The meal was a strained affair with Sam trying learn more about Logan's background. He answered Sam's questions without revealing much about himself. Johanna marveled at his self-control. In a land where a man's origins were not questioned, Sam's behavior was the next thing to being rude. His concern for her welfare touched her, yet she resented his interference.

In contrast to Sam's near hostility, Nick was open and friendly. He had noticed *Él Campeon* in the pasture and, being a lover of good horseflesh, was interested the stallion.

"Yes, he's a fine animal," Logan said. "He's part thoroughbred and part mustang. He's got speed and endurance."

"Where did you find such a combination?" Nick asked.

"He came from a ranch in west Texas where they breed horses for the army." Logan did not mention the ranch was his home.

To Johanna's relief, the meal ended and the menfolk went outside to smoke.

Anne-Marie turned to Johanna. "Mr. Delaney seems like a nice man. He's certainly handsome, and those blue eyes! I have a feeling you met him before today."

"Yes, he stopped here for water the day I received Maggie's letter telling me she wanted to come home." Johanna kept her eyes averted as she prepared a tray for Gustav.

"I don't see anything wrong with that. Don't let Sam upset you. He's a lot like Poppa Neicum, you know," Anne-Marie said.

"How is Poppa?" Maggie asked.

"He's fine. Don't fret, Maggie. We'll find some way to work things out."

"Mrs. Bauer," Logan called from the doorway. "If Karl will show me that section of fence that needs mending, I'll get started on it."

Nick stuck his head in the door. "Has Will DeVore been around lately?" Nick grinned, a devilish twinkle in his eye.

"No," Johanna replied. "Not since Maggie came."

Logan looked from Johanna to her brother, a puzzled look on his face.

Sam heard the conversation. "You'd do well to remember what I told you," he said.

Karl called from the barnyard. Logan nodded to the group and strode off to join Karl.

"It's time we started for home," Sam told Nick and Anne-Marie.

* * *

Milking time came and Logan had not returned. Karl picked up the buckets and started for the barn. He thought about Logan sleeping there and knew the man's gear was in the harness room. Setting the buckets inside the door, he ran toward the back of the barn.

Logan's saddle was on the bench and his gunbelt hung on a peg above it. The Peacemaker Colt .45 was in the holster. Karl had never handled such a weapon and had no intention of touching it. The saddlebags were another matter. They were lying on the cot, and he was drawn to them. Determined to learn more about Logan Delaney, Karl began his search. One side yielded meager supplies of coffee, sugar, salt, jerky hardtack and matches. The other contained a pair of drawers, a gray cambric shirt, blue denim trousers, a pair of socks, a red silk bandanna and a bunch of folded papers in the bottom. Curious about the papers, Karl unfolded them. A wanted poster with a man's likeness stared back at him. He read the description. Over six feet tall, long dark hair, dark eyes and a mustache. Karl's eyes widened in surprise. The description fit Logan Delaney. His hair wasn't long, but he could have cut it. He didn't have a mustache, but he could have shaved it off.

The poster said the man was dangerous, and Delaney sure gave that impression. There was a reward of one thousand dollars for his capture, dead or alive. Glancing around to make sure he was alone, Karl put one of the posters his pocket. He stuffed the rest of them and the remaining items back in the saddlebags. He had to show the poster to his mother. Was the man calling himself Logan Delaney really an outlaw named Joe Greene?

CHAPTER NINE

During supper, Johanna watched Karl sneaking glances at Logan. Something bothered the boy, but he would tell her in his own time. Maggie and Heidi washed the dishes while Johanna prepared Gustav's tray.

"Mama, may I go to see Uncle Gustav?" Karl asked, his voice strained.

"Of course." Perhaps Karl would confide in her.

"I need to check on *Él Campeon*." Logan reached for his hat hanging on a peg by the door. "He hasn't had much attention the last few days."

Karl did not speak as he and Johanna made their way to Gustav's room, and she made no effort to question him.

"How are you, Uncle Gustav?" the boy asked.

"*Besser.* I will be up tomorrow." The old man smiled, but there was pain his eyes.

"No, Gustav," Johanna insisted. "You have not healed yet." She set the tray beside the bed.

"Is Mr. Delaney still here? I thought heard him chopping wood this morning."

"Yes. He worked on the fence this afternoon," Johanna replied as she assisted him with his pillows.

"*Goot.* I am glad he is here."

Satisfied Gustav could manage, Johanna and Karl left the lean-to.

"Mama, I need to talk to you."

Johanna detected the quiver in his voice. "What is it, Karl?"

Karl dug in his pocket, brought out a crumpled piece of paper and handed it to her. She smoothed it out and, from the meager light coming through the window, read the bold black caption at the top: *Wanted,*

Dead or Alive. Joe Greene. One Thousand Dollars Reward. A man's likeness stared back her. She read the description beneath it.

"Where did you get this?" she asked, her voice thin and reedy.

Karl hesitated.

"Karl, where did you get this?" Johanna repeated, her tone sharp.

"From Mr. Delaney's saddlebags. He's got a whole lot of 'em."

"Karl, you know you're not supposed to go through other people's belongings!"

"I'm sorry, Mama, but I don't trust him. Do you think he's that man?" Karl pointed to the likeness on the wanted poster.

"I don't know. I guess he could be. But he's worked hard and helped with Gustav. He hasn't harmed us in any way." Her chest felt tight while the hollow feeling in the pit of her stomach made her legs weak. "Don't say anything to anyone about this."

"I won't, but what are you going to do?"

"I don't know. I need some time to think about it."

Mother and son returned to the house. By bedtime Johanna's nerves were strung tight, and the hollow feeling had turned to nausea.

"It's been an exciting day." Maggie broke into Johanna's thoughts. "It was wonderful to see Nick and Sam again. And you were right about Anne-Marie. She's a sweet girl."

"Yes, she is." Johanna forced her thoughts away from Logan Delaney, who might be an outlaw named Joe Greene.

"I don't think Sam and Logan hit it off very well." Maggie chuckled as she brushed her hair.

Johanna's heart a skipped beat. If Maggie only knew about the wanted poster. "No, but he's only trying protect us. Sam's like Poppa, you know, not very broadminded."

The women finished their preparations and climbed into bed. Maggie soon slept, but sleep eluded Johanna. Her thoughts kept going back to Logan and the possibility that he was an outlaw. After turning and tossing for what seemed like hours, Johanna slipped out of bed and reached for her robe and slippers. Taking the poster from its hiding place in the dresser, she picked her way carefully through the house. She took matches from the kitchen and lifted the lantern from its hook by the back door.

Once outside, Johanna lit the lantern and started toward the barn. Slipping inside, she walked to the harness room. She hesitated in front of the closed door. Swallowing hard, she took a deep breath and knocked. Before her courage could desert her, she opened the door and stepped inside.

Logan sat up, his eyes wide with shock. "Johanna! Is something wrong?" he asked, coming to his feet.

"I don't know." Her lips thinned and her features hardened.

He took a step toward her, and his eyes narrowed as he saw the paper in her hand. "Where did you get that?" he asked, his voice rough like sandpaper being rubbed over wood.

Johanna hesitated. She didn't want to admit her son had searched his saddlebags. "Does it matter?"

"Hell, yes, it matters! Karl went through my gear, didn't he?"

Johanna's face gave her away.

Logan's eyes flashed with anger. "Johanna, listen to me! I'm not an outlaw. I'm not Joe Greene. My name is really Logan Delaney. I admit I am looking for Greene. You saw the reward poster. Well, I aim to collect it." The sour taste of deceit filled his mouth as he spun the web of lies.

"You're a bounty hunter?" *That is almost as bad as being an outlaw.*

Logan flinched at the disdain in her voice. "Sometimes."

"And what about the rest of the time? What do you do then? Is your gun for hire to those who can afford the price?" Johanna asked, her voice thick with bitterness.

Logan did not answer. His eyes never leaving her face, he moved toward her. In her thin nightdress and robe, the meager light from the lantern outlined her silhouette. He came closer, she backed away. He followed her and grabbed her hands, pulling her toward him. She tried to pull away, but his hold was too tight.

"Let me go!"

"I can't," Logan answered, his voice tight with restraint. "You've been on my mind since the first time I saw you."

"I never gave you any reason to...to..." Johanna cried, her voice quivering.

"I know that."

Johanna shook her head. Her heart was pounding, and she knew he could feel it through her clothing. She twisted in his embrace, and Logan turned until his back was against the door. Her hazel eyes were wide with...what? Shock, fear, passion? Logan relaxed his hold and reached for the ribbon tied around her braid. He loosened it and touched her hair with something akin to awe. Thick and silky, its honey color glinted in the dim light. Long dark lashes tipped with gold framed her hazel eyes, and there were flecks of green in their depths.

Johanna's face flushed and her lips parted. He pulled her closer and brought her up hard against him. She knew she should push Logan away but, at the same time, she wanted to stay in his embrace. He smelled of tobacco, sweat and a musky odor she could not identify.

She raised her head and his lips claimed hers. They were soft and gentle. She was too shocked to move, and her brain refused to function.

Logan held her tighter, and her breasts flattened against his chest. A languid feeling enveloped her, and her body felt warm. She tried to move her arms, Logan shifted, and as though they had a will of their own, her hands crept up around his neck. Pressed against him, she felt the hard ridge of his arousal against her belly.

Reality broke through her consciousness, and she began to struggle. He loosened his hold but did not let her go. She stared at him, her gaze unfocused.

"Johanna," Logan groaned, his voice deep and raspy. He buried his face in her hair, his breathing ragged.

Johanna could not move. She could not speak. Watching him with bewildered eyes, she tried to understand the strange feelings that held her prisoner.

Guilt tickled Logan's conscience, but he couldn't seem to help himself. He kissed her again and pressed her body to his. Johanna tried to pull away. Her efforts succeeded in bringing her up against the cot. She lost her balance and tumbled onto the bed, taking Logan with her. They lay stunned for a moment.

Logan felt her softness beneath him and spoke between clenched teeth. "Oh, God, Johanna, I want you so bad I ache all over." He kissed the pulse beating her in throat, while his hands tangled in her hair. She squirmed under him, which only served to excite him even more. His lips returned to hers, and he ravaged her mouth. Her clothing had ridden up around her thighs and he caressed her smooth skin.

His hand moved down her leg and Johanna went rigid. He kissed her again, a long, drugging kiss, and her body relaxed.

She slipped her hands free and caressed his face.

Logan shuddered at her touch. His fingers went to the ribbons at the neckline of her robe.

"No, please, please don't," she pleaded, her voice barely above a whisper.

"I won't hurt you, Johanna,"

Johanna closed her eyes. Logan placed feathery kisses on her eyelids, her jawline and finally her mouth. His lips were warm and wet. "Johanna," he murmured, "don't be afraid."

Logan moved away, and Johanna eyes opened wide as he began to unbutton his shirt. Reality crashed through her passion-fogged senses. What was she doing? How could she permit such indecencies? What about her children? Overwhelming shame washed over her.

Logan glanced at Johanna. Her face was as pale as death, her eyes wide and staring. He knew he had to abandon his seduction of the woman lying before him. And seduction it would be. He could overcome her resistance with a few heated kisses, but he would not do that to her. With superhuman effort, he managed to tamp down his desire and straighten his clothing.

She was sitting up, her head down and her face turned toward the wall. Placing a finger under her chin, he turned her head and forced her to look at him. Tears clung to her lashes, and he knew she was overcome with embarrassment.

"Johanna, look me! There is nothing to be ashamed of. You didn't do anything wrong."

"I don't know what came over me," Johanna said, twisting her hands in her lap. She could not meet his eyes.

"I'm sorry, Johanna. Not for wanting you, but because I shamed you. The blame is mine."

Johanna rose to her feet, her legs barely able to support her and walked toward the door. As Logan stood watching she turned to face him. "I was wrong to come here."

"I think it would be best if I left in the morning," Logan said, his voice devoid of emotion.

Johanna nodded in agreement. Chin up, staring straight ahead, she left the room. As she fled into the darkness, guilt flooded every part of her being. Her behavior was beyond redemption. She could still feel Logan's hands on her body and his searing kisses. The fact that he found her desirable did not excuse her behavior. Although there was nobody to see, bright color flooded her face.

The image on the wanted poster flashed across her mind. Was Logan Delaney the bounty hunter or Joe Greene the outlaw? It didn't matter. She must put him out of her mind and forget the soul-shattering experience in the barn.

Logan watched Johanna run across the yard, his body still in a state of arousal. He knew if he had continued to seduce Johanna, the regret would have been worse afterward than the ache he was feeling now. She did not deserve the guilt and shame she felt now, to say nothing about what she would have suffered afterward. His feelings for her confused and puzzled him. Logan had always taken his pleasure when it was offered and thought little about it afterward. But this time was different. He wanted to protect Johanna, make things easier for her. Her life had been hard, and she knew little of pleasure and nothing of luxury. The only bright spot in her life was her children. Pa was right. He was caught between a rock and hard place.

* * *

Morning arrived too soon for Johanna, and she awoke feeling tired and irritable. How could she face Logan? Surely he would not leave without seeing her again. That would be the easy way, but Logan Delaney was not a man to avoid a confrontation. Deep inside Johanna knew he was not Joe Greene. She didn't know how or when she had come to that conclusion, but she could not risk her children's future trying to unravel the mystery.

* * *

Logan, too, spent a restless night, rose at dawn and did not bother to shave. After packing his gear, he saddled *Él Campeon* and led him out of the barn. Smoke was rising from the chimney as he walked to the house. Johanna answered the door. She looked at him, not quite meeting his eyes.

"I couldn't leave without seeing you," Logan told her, his voice strained.

Johanna wore a brown calico dress and spotless white apron that covered her from neckline to hemline. Her golden hair was wound around her head in a coronet of braids. Logan had never seen her wear it that way. She looked composed and somehow untouchable.

She stepped outside and closed the door behind her. "You shouldn't leave before you've had breakfast."

"I don't think that's a very good idea." Logan wore snug-fitting blue denim trousers and a gray shirt with a red bandanna knotted around his neck. His gunbelt with the tied down holster was in place. With a stubble of black beard, he looked more like the outlaw Joe Greene than a repentant suitor who had tried to seduce her the night before.

"Logan," Johanna said, "don't blame yourself for last night. I should have known better than to come to you the way I did." She raised her head and met his gaze head on.

Logan took a step forward and looked deep into her eyes. Her lashes fluttered, and she looked down at her feet. Gently clasping her hands, he felt the calluses on her palms. "What can I do to convince you it was my fault? Maybe if you weren't so beautiful, I wouldn't have been so tempted," Logan said with a rueful grin as he tried to make amends.

A faint blush stained her cheeks, and she tried to withdraw her hands.

Logan loosened his hold and stepped back. "I'll be leaving now. I have a job to do, but when I'm finished I'll be back," he promised, his eyes never leaving her face.

"Good bye, Logan. God be with you."

Logan mounted *Él Campeon* and reined him toward the lane. He touched the animal lightly with the spurs, and the horse broke into lope. He did not look back.

The sun had barely cleared the horizon when Logan rode into Meirsville. The hotel would be serving breakfast soon, and he could sure use a cup or two of hot coffee. The sheriff should be in his office by the time Logan finished eating. He wanted to make sure Koenig had the new reward posters.

The thought of the reward posters brought Johanna from the far recesses of his mind. Lord, how beautiful she had looked, her eyes dreamy and her lips swollen from his kisses. *Delaney, you fool! You have to get that woman out of your mind!*

As he drained his coffee cup, Logan focused on his plans to find Joe Greene. There were hundreds of miles where he could cross the border, but Logan had a hunch Greene had gone to Laredo. Dropping some coins on the table, Logan left the dining room. He crossed the street and entered the sheriff's office. Koenig came from a cell in the back and, seeing the Ranger, hurried forward.

"Howdy, Delaney. You're jist the man I wanted to see. There's a message here from Montgomery saying a fella matchin' Greene's description was spotted in Laredo." He rummaged through a desk drawer and retrieved a crumpled piece of paper.

The message was dated two days ago. "Looks like part of my problem is solved."

"Is there anything you want me to do?" Koenig asked.

"Think you could get a message to the captain and tell him I'm on my way Laredo?"

"Yeah, I'll put a letter in the mail."

"Much obliged," Logan replied.

"Good luck."

The two men shook hands, and Logan left the office. He purchased supplies and ammunition at the mercantile. After stowing everything in his saddlebags, he headed for Stein's saloon. He wanted a drink and a bottle to keep him company on the trail. He had a hunch his campfire was going to be mighty lonesome, to say nothing of what the memories of a golden-haired woman and a few minutes of thwarted passion would do to him.

Stein had customers when Logan laid his money on the bar. "Whiskey and a bottle to take along."

Emil poured the drink and set it in front of Logan. Reaching behind the bar, he picked a bottle off the shelf and held it up for inspection. Logan nodded. Stein wrapped it in brown paper and placed it in front of him. Picking up the shot glass, Logan downed half the liquor, savoring the smooth liquid as it slid down his throat.

"You been in here before?"

"Yeah, a spell back," Logan said, sipping the remainder of his drink. Glad the talkative Stein made no further effort toward conversation, he finished the whiskey. Nodding to the saloonkeeper, he strode out the door. Carrying the parcel containing the bottle of whiskey, he walked toward *Él Campeon* tied at the hitch rail in front of the hotel. A woman came out of the building, and before Logan could step aside, they collided. He put out his free hand to steady her, and wide green eyes stared into deep blue ones. Logan recognized her as the auburn-haired woman who had come into the hotel carrying a hatbox.

"Ohhhh!" Her face flushed a delicate pink.

Logan dropped his arm and she backed away.

"I'm sorry," she said, her voice soft and musical.

"No harm done, ma'am." Logan grinned, his teeth very white in his tanned face.

"Amanda!" Jane Reynolds appeared the doorway. "Is everything all right?"

"Yes. I wasn't paying attention to where I was going and ran into this gentleman," Amanda explained, her face still faintly pink.

Jane surveyed Logan with a critical eye. "Haven't you been our guest recently?"

"Yes, ma'am. About month ago," he replied, tipping his hat.

"I remember you, Mr. Delaney."

"I remember you too, Mrs. Reynolds. I'm not apt to forget a pretty lady."

"Thank you, sir." Jane smiled and turned toward Amanda. "This is my friend, Amanda Blair. Amanda has the dress shop next door."

Both women were fashionably dressed. A vision of Johanna in her calico dresses flashed through his mind. He'd wager she never owned a silk gown in her life, yet she was every inch a lady. "It seems a bit awkward to say 'pleased to make your acquaintance, ma'am.'"

"Yes, but I am pleased to meet you, Mr. Delaney," Amanda said.

"Will you be staying with us, sir?" Jane asked.

"Not this time, ma'am. I'm just passing through. I needed supplies and decided to stop at the mercantile."

"I hope you have a pleasant journey," Amanda said with a bright smile.

"Yes, and do come visit us again," Jane added.

"Thank you." Logan touched his hat brim and nodded. "Good day, ladies." As he approached *Él Campeon,* he wondered what the women would think if they knew the true reason he was in Meirsville. He slipped the parcel containing the whiskey into his saddlebags, mounted and rode to find Joe Greene.

CHAPTER TEN

Johanna's busy days gave her little to time to dwell on what had happened in the barn. The nights were another matter. She lay sleepless for hours, going over every incident that occurred since she had first met Logan Delaney. Although few in number, every meeting was burned into her memory. Her emotions ran from one extreme to the other: the strange feelings she had when he was near, the sense of excitement when he smiled at her, the sound of his voice when he said her name, and most of all the indescribable sensations she had experienced in the barn. She tried to deny the wanted poster, but all her old fears came back, and she was powerless to overcome them.

As they prepared for bed one evening, Maggie said, "Johanna, you seem worried or upset about something. Does it have anything to do with Logan Delaney?"

Johanna remained silent for a moment. She had difficulty admitting her innermost thoughts. "I'm afraid, Maggie. Logan said he was coming back."

"I don't think you need to be afraid of him, Johanna. I doubt he's the kind of man who would abuse a woman. Or isn't that what you're worried about?"

Bright red color stained Johanna's cheeks. She could never tell Maggie what happened in the barn. "No, I'm not worried that he will do me bodily harm," she said. "I don't know how I feel about him." Her nightdress clutched tightly in her hand, she blurted, "Maggie, he could be an outlaw!"

"Outlaw?"

Johanna shared the secret of the wanted poster. "He said he's a bounty hunter, but..." Her voice faded and her bottom lip trembled.

"Outlaw or bounty hunter? What do you think?"

"I don't know what to think. I can't believe he's an outlaw, although a bounty hunter isn't much better."

"Well, since you don't know when or even if he will come back, try not to think about it," Maggie advised.

Johanna began brushing her hair. Maggie's remark that Logan might not return brought Johanna a feeling of deep anguish. She turned away, not wanting Maggie to see her face. Her sister was too good at reading expressions.

The sisters settled down in the big brass bed.

"Maggie, have you given any more thought to seeing Poppa?"

"He's never going to come around."

"Yes, he will. You can't give up."

"But what can I do? He won't allow me on the place, and he won't come here."

"I've been thinking. You remember the Fourth of July picnics we used to have?"

"Picnics? Oh, yes!" Maggie's voice lost its defeated tone. "There was always a big celebration in town with a parade, and then everybody would go to the churchyard for the picnic. We used to have such fun." Nostalgia colored every word.

"We still have the celebration and the picnic. The Fourth is not far away. That might be a good place to try to make amends." Johanna searched Maggie's face in the dim light.

"I don't know, Johanna. It could be, well, awkward, you know. Besides Poppa there are the townspeople to consider. I don't want to embarrass you."

"You won't. Most of them don't care what happened ten years ago. I'm sure you've faced worse situations," Johanna said.

"Worse situations? Oh, yes." Maggie's laughter was devoid of mirth. "I've never told you about my life with Jack, but you know we moved around lot. Sometimes, depending on how the cards fell and the rules of the house, I served drinks. But that's all I did. Jack made that plain from the start. I was his wife, not his mistress. Oh, you can bet some of the situations were worse.

"Jack was killed by a man who accused him of cheating. He didn't cheat. He didn't have to. He was too good. But the man that killed him is the son of an influential man in Cripple Creek, so nothing was done about it. I was asked to leave town."

"Oh, Maggie, I'm so sorry." Johanna reached out and, putting her arms around her sister, cradled her close while Maggie wept bitter tears.

With the picnic less than two weeks away, Johanna searched through her wardrobe for something to wear. She felt dowdy and out of sorts.

"Why don't you wear one of these?" Maggie asked as she removed several gowns from her trunk.

"I couldn't do that," Johanna said, all the while admiring the fashionable garments.

"Please. You have done so much for me, let me do something for you." She held up a light blue dimity gown.

Johanna fingered the smooth fabric, and Maggie coaxed her to try it on. When she dressed in corset and crinolette, they discovered the dress was too short but had an ample hem.

"It's so pretty. Are you sure you want to alter it?" Johanna asked, twirling around to face Maggie.

"Yes. It would please me very much if you would wear it."

Johanna agreed, and Maggie hugged her sister.

"What are you going wear?" Johanna asked.

"How about this?" Maggie displayed a dark gray poplin gown trimmed with white pique.

"It's very pretty, and the color is suitable for mourning."

Karl had not mentioned Logan's name since the morning he left. Excited about the picnic, both children kept up a constant barrage of questions concerning the activities. Gustav, recovered from his skirmish with the hog house, was looking forward to the event.

Several days before the celebration, Johanna and Maggie were churning when Will DeVore rode into the yard. Maggie grinned as Johanna looked down at her cream-splattered apron. She shook her head, ran a hand over her hair and smoothed her skirt before going to the door.

"Howdy, Johanna." Will removed his brown Stetson.

"Hello, Will. Won't you come in?" she invited, stepping back across the threshold. "We're churning this morning." She turned to Maggie, who had taken over the chore.

"I'm sure you remember Margareth. We call her Maggie now."

Maggie nodded and smiled. "How are you, Will?"

"Howdy. I remember you as a little girl with long pigtails," he chuckled. "Looks like you're all grown up."

"We have a habit of doing that, don't we?" Looking at her sister's flushed face, Maggie continued, "It's awfully warm in here, Johanna. Why don't you and Will sit in the yard where it's cooler? I'll finish this."

Seated beneath the giant live oak trees, Johanna asked about Will's father.

"He's failin'. He never leaves the ranch these days. That's what I wanted to talk to you about. He's anxious to see you. You know he never objected to us seein' one another. It was your pa who didn't want you to have anything to do with me," Will reminded her, his eyes fixed on her face.

"I know, but that's all in the past. I'd be happy to visit your father."

"I'm mighty glad to hear that. Can I come and get you next Wednesday mornin'? You can take dinner with us. Mrs. Jenkins, our housekeeper, is a real good cook," Will coaxed.

"I'd like that."

"Good. I'll be here about mid-mornin' and have you back before supper." Will's plain features were transformed by the grin on his face.

The sound of voices intruded, and Karl and Heidi, followed by Gustav, came from behind the barn. Karl scowled and mumbled under his breath as he approached his mother and Will seated under the trees. Gustav and Will exchanged greetings.

Will turned to Johanna. "I need to be goin'. I'll see you Wednesday mornin'." He donned his Stetson.

"Yes. Good bye, Will."

"Wednesday morning? What did he mean, Mama?" Karl's brow furrowed as he watched Will ride away.

"Mr. DeVore's father is very ill, and I'm going to visit him."

Maggie joined them in the yard. "Is Will gone?"

"Yes." Johanna turned toward the house.

Gustav called to Karl and Heidi. "Come *kinder,* we need to grind feed for the chickens."

The little girl walked away with Gustav, but Karl gave his mother a long, searching look before following them.

As soon as they were out of sight, Johanna turned to Maggie. "Will asked me to visit his father next Wednesday. He's very ill and wants Will to marry before he passes on. Will's mother and brother died in an epidemic a few years ago," Johanna explained.

"I remember their ranch as being big and prosperous. I'm surprised Will never married."

"He said he never found anybody else." Johanna avoided Maggie's eyes.

"That sounds like you might get a proposal," Maggie teased.

"I don't want to marry again, but it's hard trying to raise the children alone. You know, Sam is all in favor of Will."

"He is?" Maggie stopped walking and turned to look at Johanna, her eyes wide in surprise. "Does Poppa know?"

"I don't think so, but if I were to choose Will, he wouldn't be able to do anything about it this time," Johanna vowed.

"Sam could be right. Maybe you should think about marrying Will. Logan Delaney may never come back, even if he wants to. Outlaw or bounty hunter, neither one lives very long. Sooner or later somebody comes along who is just a little faster or they get shot in the back." Maggie looked Johanna straight in the eye.

Johanna's heart skipped a beat. She had not thought about the possibility that Logan could be killed. He seemed invincible, too much in control. She knew that was unrealistic. Logan was mortal, all right. The scene in the barn had proved that. Johanna was shaken to her very soul. Her face paled and her hands trembled. She swallowed hard and hurried into the house without replying.

* * *

On Wednesday morning, Johanna prepared breakfast and straightened the children's room, all the while her mind occupied with the visit to Will's father.

"Maggie, what should I wear?"

Maggie rummaged through Johanna's meager wardrobe and took the gray calico from its hanger. "This is very pretty on you. An extra petticoat would help a lot. Maybe I can find some red ribbon in my trunk to weave through your hair."

Heidi ran into the bedroom and stopped short when she saw her mother all dressed up. "Mama, you look so pretty."

"Thank you, dear."

"Oh, I almost forgot. That man is here."

Johanna's heart a skipped beat. Had Logan returned? "What man?" Her voice sounded faint in her own ears.

"You know, Mr. DeVore," Heidi replied.

A wave of disappointment so intense it was like a physical pain washed over Johanna. She had not allowed herself to admit the depth of her feelings, but she now faced the realization that she was waiting for him to return. Giving herself a mental shake, she went to meet Will.

He was standing beside a shiny black buggy pulled by a handsome gray mare. Dressed in a black broadcloth suit, a fine white cotton shirt, his black boots polished to a high shine, he held a black Stetson in his hand.

Heidi followed her mother out of the house. Karl was nowhere in sight.

"Mornin', Johanna. You look mighty fetchin'," Will said, his eyes filled with admiration.

"Thank you," Johanna said with a smile. "You look very nice too."

Will settled himself beside Johanna and took up the lines. They turned into the main road, and Will glanced at Johanna from the corner of his eye. She sat erect and stiff, her hands folded primly in her lap.

"No need to be nervous, Johanna. I'm still the same Will I was ten years ago, but I hope I'm a little smarter than I was back then."

"It's just that...that..."

"I understand," he said and changed the subject. "Is Maggie going to stay here for good?"

"I don't know. We haven't talked about it. Poppa still hasn't come around, and that hurts Maggie. She lost her husband shortly before she came back."

"I didn't know that. Where did they live?"

"They moved around lot, but they were in Colorado when he died." Johanna saw no reason to go into detail.

"Well, she's young and pretty. She'll probably marry again," Will speculated as he guided the horse around the deep ruts in the road.

"I'm not sure about that. I can't get her to go to church or into town. She hasn't been off the farm since she arrived. I'm trying to convince her to go to the Fourth of July picnic."

"That sounds like a good idea. There's always a big crowd. Besides, all that happened a long time ago."

"Yes, but some people never forget." Johanna's voice carried a heavy trace of bitterness.

The buggy hit a rock and bounced high enough that Johanna grabbed for her bonnet. Will brought the mare under control, and they continued on in silence. The countryside showed the effects of the hot summer sun, and the rocky soil was cracked and dry.

"It's really dry," Johanna remarked. "Are you worried about water?"

"Not yet, but if we don't get rain soon, it could be a problem. That spring in the hills is still runnin', and that keeps the big hole filled." He turned his head and gave her a searching look. "You remember the big hole, don't you, Johanna?"

She kept her eyes focused on the horses. "Yes." The big hole had been the scene of their secret meetings. It was there she had told him she was going to marry Josef. To cover her embarrassment, Johanna said, "I'm not sure what to say to your father. Does he know the truth about his illness?"

"Yes, and he's doin' a good job of acceptin' it. He'll probably tell you he's anxious for me to get married. I hope that won't embarrass you. You don't need to promise him anything, Johanna."

"There's nothing I can promise him, Will."

The buggy rounded a bend the road, and the ranch house came into view. It was set in a grove of live oak trees with the bunkhouse, barn, corrals and other out buildings several hundred yards behind the main structure. Will turned into a short lane and drew the buggy to a halt in front of the house.

A long rectangular building constructed of rock, the house was low and close to the ground. There were chimneys at each end, and the roof extended over a porch that ran the entire length of the house. Will helped Johanna from the buggy, and they walked up the rock path to the house. A woman met them at the door, wiping her hands on a cup towel.

"This is Mrs. Jenkins, our housekeeper," Will introduced the woman. "Helen, I'd like you meet Johanna Bauer."

"How do you do, Mrs. Bauer." She was plump, her brown hair streaked with gray, and her brown eyes were bright behind wire-rimmed spectacles. "Would you like to take off your bonnet?"

"Thank you," Johanna replied as she untied the ribbons.

Mrs. Jenkins placed it on the hall table. "Your father is in the parlor, Will," she told him.

"Thanks. Would you care for some refreshment, Johanna?"

"No, thank you."

"If you'll excuse me, I need to get back to the kitchen." Mrs. Jenkins hurried away.

Will guided Johanna through a doorway to the left. A fireplace dominated one end of the large room. The furnishings, though dated, were in excellent condition. A patterned wool rug covered part of the polished wood floor, and lace curtains hung at the windows. A man was standing with his back to the fireplace. He came forward as they entered.

"Pa, I've brought Johanna."

"How are you, Mrs. Bauer? Seems strange to call you that," he added.

"Johanna will do fine," she answered and held out her hand. She remembered him as a big, robust man with light brown hair and a thick mustache. The disease slowly eating away at him had taken a severe toll. He was thin, his hair and mustache white. But his handshake was firm.

"Come, let's sit down." He indicated the sofa and chairs grouped around the room. Johanna sat on the horsehair sofa, and Mr. DeVore took a chair across from her.

"You two go ahead and visit," Will excused himself and started toward the door. "I'll be back as soon as I've tended the mare."

"I'm glad you came, Johanna. I've been wanting to talk to you. I guess Will has told you about my...illness?" Johanna nodded and he continued, "Then I'll get right to the point. I know you have your farm, but it's hard work, especially for a woman, and it will get harder. Think about your children. They need a father. You know how Will feels about you, and I know you cared for him at one time. You marry him, and he can take care of you. This is a prosperous ranch, and it will be Will's when I'm gone."

Johanna clasped her hands in her lap while she gathered her thoughts. "I don't know what to say. Although Will and I have known each other most of our lives, I'm not sure I want to marry again."

"Just say you will think about it. That's I all ask."

Will came into the room, and Johanna was spared giving him an answer. She didn't want to hurt Will's father, but neither did she want to give him false hope.

"Helen says dinner is ready," Will announced.

The dining room held a large oak table, chairs and sideboard. The table was set with a snowy white cloth and napkins. Johanna smiled when she saw the blue willow pattern dishes like the ones she had home. Mrs. Jenkins served a succulent meal of roast beef and gravy, browned potatoes and green beans seasoned with ham. For dessert they had luscious peach cobbler.

"I don't feel right not helping Mrs. Jenkins with the dishes," Johanna complained as they left the dining room.

"There's no need for that," Will answered.

"How old are your children, Johanna?" Mr. DeVore asked as they seated themselves in the parlor.

"Karl is nine and Heidi is seven."

"Jenny and me always wanted a girl, but it wasn't in the good Lord's plans." The old man's voice was tinged with sadness.

"Pa, I don't think Johanna would mind if you rest now," Will suggested.

"Oh, no. Please don't tire yourself out." Johanna saw the signs of exhaustion on Mr. DeVore's weathered countenance.

"Come and see me again, Johanna."

"I will, and thank you for inviting me. I've enjoyed my visit very much." As she retrieved her bonnet from the hall table, Johanna turned to Will. "I'd like to tell Mrs. Jenkins how much I enjoyed her delicious dinner."

"Helen, can you come out here for a minute?" Will called out.

The woman appeared, a puzzled look on her face.

"Mrs. Jenkins, I really enjoyed the meal. Will told me you were a good cook, and he certainly didn't exaggerate."

Mrs. Jenkins' face broke into big smile. "Why, thank you, dear. Your visit has done Mr. DeVore a world of good. He hasn't had such a good appetite in a long time."

"I'm glad to hear that. Good bye, Mrs. Jenkins."

Will guided the buggy onto the main trail. "I don't suppose you would consider going to the picnic with me?"

"I don't think it would be a good idea. If I went with you, I doubt Maggie would go. It's time for the family to put the past behind, and I think the picnic is the place to do it."

"I understand, but don't think I'm givin' up." Will grinned, his voice sounding determined.

The remainder of the trip was made in silence, each occupied with his or her thoughts. When they reached the lane leading to the farmhouse, Will spoke. "Maybe we'll have a chance to talk at the picnic."

"I'm sure we will. And I'll save you a piece of my chocolate cake."

"I'll hold you to that." Will brought the buggy to a stop and jumped down. He secured the lines and assisted Johanna from the conveyance.

"I'll keep your father in my prayers."

"We appreciate that. I'll see you again soon."

"Good bye, Will." Johanna watched until he was out of sight, her feelings more confused than ever.

CHAPTER ELEVEN

A million stars glittered in the vast Texas sky. Logan sat beside the dying campfire, his thoughts a jumble of bits and pieces. Johanna, Joe Greene, the Rangers, the Spanish Spur—all went around and around in his head. One day's ride from Laredo, he had to come to grips with his feelings for Johanna. The very thought of her set his pulse to racing.

In the pale light of dawn, Logan practiced his draw. If his timing was off one second, it could mean the difference between living and dying. Each time he drew was faster than the time before until the motion became a blur of movement. Satisfied with his performance, he holstered the weapon and went to fetch *Él Campeon*.

Logan rode into Laredo at suppertime, and the spicy odor of *frijoles* and *tamales* hung in the air. Looking forward to a hot meal and sleeping in a bed, he realized the trail didn't hold the appeal it once had. Like dozens of border towns, Laredo had a strong Mexican influence: adobe buildings, dusty streets and a surplus of men on the fringes of the law. The streets were crowded with cowboys, *vaqueros* and troopers from nearby Fort McIntosh. Unscrupulous lawmen often ruled both sides of the border, and Logan did not intend to reveal his true identity. Spotting a hotel up ahead, he reined *Él Campeon* toward the hitch rail. The building had a run-down appearance and was covered with layers of Texas dust. After signing the register "Hunter," he asked for a bath.

"Nah, don't provide 'em fur men customers since the barbershop's right next door," the clerk replied.

Logan climbed the stairs to the shabby room on the second floor. A faded Mexican blanket covered the bed that sagged in the middle. The cracked washbowl and pitcher sat on an oak washstand bearing signs of countless cigarette burns and watermarks. A wooden straight chair completed the furnishings. He wrinkled his nose at the stale odors, walked to the window and opened it wide. The room overlooked an alley littered with broken barrels, crates and other castoff items.

An hour later, shaved, bathed and dressed all in black except for a blue silk bandanna knotted around his neck, Logan went in search of his evening meal. Two doors from the hotel a sign advertised *EATS*. The clerk had told him he could get a decent steak there.

He found a table and sat with his back to the wall. "Steak, *frijoles* and coffee." He gave his order to a man wearing a soiled white apron.

"Got some dried apple pie baked fresh this mornin'," the man said.

"Sounds good."

"Comin' right up." The man hurried toward the kitchen.

In a short time, the food was placed before him, and the tantalizing odors whetted Logan's appetite. He found the food surprisingly good. The man refilled his coffee cup and Logan forked a mouthful of pie. The man had not exaggerated. The pie was fresh and seasoned just right with sugar and cinnamon.

Unbidden, the meals he had shared at Johanna's table flashed through his mind, followed quickly by the scene in the barn. Suddenly, the flaky crust tasted like cardboard. He washed it down with a swallow of hot coffee and cursed under his breath. He was tracking a dangerous outlaw. Joe Greene had strangled a woman, and he would not hesitate to kill again. If Logan did not put all thoughts of Johanna from his mind, he could wind up dead.

Numerous saloons had to be checked out. If Greene had seen the new reward poster, he would be a lot cagier. Whether or not he knew a Ranger was on his trail, Greene knew a showdown was bound to come. It was a known fact the Rangers dogged their man until they caught him.

Two days and five saloons later, Logan had no leads on Joe Greene. He had spent several hours in each one, playing a few hands of poker and nursing glasses of rotgut. If Greene was in the area, he would soon hear that Hunter was looking for him. Logan saw no alternative to the dangerous game he played. The sooner he apprehended Greene, the sooner he could go back to Johanna. Most of the time he managed to keep his head clear of her memory, but it crept in at odd moments. It was always there, locked away, like a treasure to be enjoyed.

Standing at the bar in The Frontier Palace, Logan debated if he should cross the border, something Rangers were forbidden to do. A young woman sidled up to him.

"Howdy, mister. You lookin' for a little excitement?" She was pretty, with blond hair piled high on her head, eyes heavily lined with kohl and vivid red lips. Her black satin dress hugged her slender figure.

"Evenin', ma'am. Can I buy you drink?"

"Sure. My name's Claire."

"Hunter."

"Oh, I've heard about you!"

"Let's get that table over there." Logan motioned to a secluded corner.

The Frontier Palace vehemently denied its name. There was the customary long bar down one side and the inevitable stairway to the second floor. Unlike Emil Stein's place, the glassware had lost its sparkle, and the brass rail and spittoons were tarnished. The sawdust on the floor was littered with tobacco wads and cigarette butts. Badly scarred tables and chairs crowded close together around a tiny dance floor.

Logan took a bottle and two glasses from the bartender and followed the woman to the table. He placed them on the table and pulled out a chair for her. With his back to the wall, he filled the glasses, pouring one only a third full. Claire smiled at him, winked and sipped from the glass. Logan grinned. He knew saloon girls usually drank watered-down whiskey or tea.

"What have you heard about me?"

"Nothin' much."

Logan took a swallow of whiskey. The girl began to fidget under his direct gaze.

"Well," she took another tiny sip, "there's talk you're lookin' for a fella named Joe Greene. Ever'body knows he's wanted, but so are half the men who come in here. You a friend of his?"

"You could say that. We got business. You know anything about him?"

The woman looked around the room, and then lowered her voice. "There's a fella been comin' here for the past couple weeks to see Bertie. He comes late and stays till daylight. I've only seen him once. Tall, dark hair, good lookin' guy. Bertie says he's real generous, but he must be kind a rough, 'cause she has bruises the next day."

Logan's heartbeat accelerated. "What's your reason for tellin' me this?"

"Guess I just like to gossip." She smiled, showing even white teeth.

"Yeah." Logan returned her grin before downing the rest of his drink.

"Will you be in town for awhile?" Claire asked as she rose from her chair.

"I'll be around."

She nodded and walked away. Logan headed for the hotel. If Greene came to see Bertie, and Claire would cooperate, he could finally nail him. What would entice the woman to help him? Money! The reward! He had told Johanna he was a bounty hunter. What better ruse to use with Claire? He could offer to share the reward with her and would see that she got all the money afterward.

Logan returned to The Frontier Palace the next evening, caught Claire's attention, and they sought out a table. A bright blue satin dress set off her blond hair, and he wondered what she looked like under the heavy face paint.

"Join me in a drink?" Logan gestured to an empty chair.

"Why not?" She sat down across the table from him and pushed the glass toward the bottle of whiskey. "Where are you stayin'?" she asked.

"The Traveler's Hotel."

"That's just down the street."

"Yeah."

Glancing around the room, Claire leaned toward him and spoke in a soft voice. "Bertie told me that guy didn't come around last night. How bad do you want to find him?"

"Why?"

"I might be able to help you. That is, if he comes back."

"Why would you do that?" Logan's eyes narrowed with suspicion.

"Maybe I like your looks." A mischievous smile curved her lips. She rose to her feet.

Logan stood and, before she could walk away, asked, "Can I take you to supper tomorrow night?"

Claire's blue eyes widened in surprise. "Sure, but I have to be at work at seven."

"That's all right. I don't know much about the eatin' places here. Where would you like to go?"

"There ain't many fancy places in Laredo, but the Casa Rio is right nice." Her expression held a mixture disbelief and hope.

"I'll call for you at five o'clock. That all right?"

"Yes, I'll be waitin'."

Promptly at five o'clock, Logan walked into The Frontier Palace and found Claire waiting for him wearing a light blue dress with a demure neckline. Her face paint had been applied with a light hand. A straw bonnet with blue satin streamers adorned her blond hair. "You look real pretty."

"Thanks. You ain't so bad yourself."

Logan grinned. He wore a white linen shirt and black string tie under his black leather vest. He offered Claire his arm.

"I'll be back at seven," she called to the bartender as they left the saloon.

During the meal, Logan learned Claire's family had been killed in an Indian raid. With no relatives in Texas, she was left to fend for herself. Drifting from town to town, she ended up in Laredo.

"I guess this is the end of the line." Despair colored her voice and showed plainly on her face.

Logan couldn't think of anything to say without sounding sanctimonious. Perhaps the reward would give her a new start.

"Where are you from?" she asked.

"West Texas, a long time ago." He paused for a moment. "Claire, you mentioned you might be able to help me find Joe Greene. You know, it could be dangerous."

"Yeah."

"I'll pay you to take the risk."

"How much?" Curiosity replaced the sadness in her eyes.

"I think I can trust you, so I'm gonna level with you. There's a thousand dollars reward for Greene, and I aim to collect it. If you help me, I'll give you two hundred and fifty dollars."

Claire's features froze in shock. "You're a bounty hunter," she exclaimed when she recovered her voice. "I don't know. If something goes wrong, I could end up gettin' killed."

"I won't let that happen. Just keep your ears open, and the next time Greene shows up, let me know. You said he comes late. I'm in Room 205. There's a back entrance, and you can slip in that way."

"Let me think about it."

"All right, but don't take too long."

Claire nodded. "I have to get back and change. I don't think the customers would appreciate this dress." Self-mockery colored her words.

"I do."

"That was the general idea." This time her smile was genuine.

Logan escorted Claire back to the saloon.

"I need some time to figure things out. Thanks for supper."

"My pleasure."

Logan watched Claire walk down the stairs. She came to his side.

"Evenin', Hunter." She smiled provocatively.

"Hello, Claire."

Claire's green silk dress bared her smooth white shoulders. A green plume trailed from the mass of curls piled on top of her head.

She's a pretty girl. It's a shame she had to end up this way. Logan walked toward a table in the far corner of the room while Claire picked up a bottle and glasses from the bar.

He poured the whiskey and handed a glass to Claire. Winking at her, he downed a swallow. They sat in silence for several minutes. Claire made no attempt to drink the liquor, but her hands toyed with the glass.

Finally, she spoke. "Hunter, I'll help you, but I'm takin' an awful risk. If somethin' goes wrong...Besides, how do I know I'll get the money if you catch this Greene fella?"

Logan realized her point was well taken. "All right, Claire. Just to prove I'm a man of my word, I'll give you fifty now and the rest when Greene is in custody."

Claire remained silent, her eyes downcast, while she chewed her lower lip. "It's a deal." She held out her hand. "Are you married?" she blurted out.

The question startled him for minute. "No," he said, releasing her hand.

"Is there somebody special?"

A vision of Johanna flashed through his memory. "Yes," he answered.

Claire, her smile wistful, replied, "I thought so."

"Does Bertie know when the guy is comin'?"

"No, he just shows up."

"Well, the only choice we have is to wait. When he comes, let me know. You know where to find me."

"Like I told you, he always comes late, after midnight."

"I'll give you the money now if you want." Logan reached in his pocket but Claire put a hand on his arm.

"No, somebody might see. Let's go to my room. That way you can see what the upstairs looks like, and I'll show you Bertie's room."

"Good thinkin'. Let's go."

Arm in arm they climbed the stairway. Logan grinned. The typical saloon architecture. A hallway ran the length of the upper floor. Three doors opened off each side, and a door at the end led to the outside. Logan had checked that out earlier.

Pointing to the second door on the right, Claire whispered, "That's Bertie's room."

They continued down the hallway, and Claire stopped in front of the last door on the left. Opening it, she stepped inside and Logan followed.

Logan's eyebrows raised in surprise. Most soiled doves did not worry about housekeeping, but Claire's room was neat and clean.

Claire shut the door and, lowering her voice, said, "These walls are kinda thin."

Logan nodded, reached into his pocket and brought out a small bag of coins. He counted six ten- dollar gold pieces and gave them to her.

"There's sixty dollars here!"

"Yeah," Logan grinned. "Your boss will expect his cut, won't he? The extra ten should cover it."

A faint blush stained Claire's cheeks, and Logan was filled with compassion. *She's little more than a girl.* "Claire, it's none of my business, but ain't there somewhere you could go, some relative or friend who would take you in?"

"That's why I decided to help you. I have an aunt in Illinois, and the money will get me there. I just hope it's not too late."

"It's not. You're a real pretty woman and a good one, too. The right man will know that."

"I hope you're right."

"I am. Now, we just have to wait till Greene makes his move."

Claire stood in front of him, her lips trembling and her eyes misty. Logan stepped forward and took her in his arms. He held her and stroked her back. She was frightened, and he offered comfort, as he would have to a child. Her body relaxed and she tilted her head to look up at him. "Don't worry, Claire. Everything will work out all right."

"I hope so, but I'm afraid."

"I won't let anything happen you, I promise." He brushed a soft kiss across her lips.

"She's a lucky woman, whoever she is," Claire whispered and stepped out of his embrace.

Logan grinned, winked and left the room.

Two days passed and Joe Greene did not put in an appearance. Once again Logan contemplated crossing the border to flush him out. He had spent the time in the saloons and, sick to death of rotgut whiskey and the smell of cheap perfume mingled with foul odors, had gone to his room. As soon as he delivered Greene to the sheriff at Llano, he would resign from the Rangers. It was time take a wife and settle down on the Spur. If luck was with him, that wife would be Johanna.

A soft knock sounded. Logan drew his revolver, stepped back and cracked open the door. Claire stood in the hallway; a dark shawl covered her head and shoulders. He holstered his weapon, motioned her inside and shut the door. She was breathless, and her face was pale beneath the paint.

"He's here. He's in Bertie's room right now." Her voice quivered with excitement.

Logan sat on the side of the bed and pulled on his boots. "I'm going to get my horse and gear from the livery. When you get back to the Palace, go on downstairs. That way, nobody can connect you and me."

"What about Bertie?"

"I'll have to tie her up and gag her. You can check on her later. Before we go, here's the rest of the money. We don't need to have any further contact. Get in touch with Captain Montgomery at Ranger Headquarters in Waco, and he'll see you get the reward." Logan started for the door.

"But you already gave me all the money you promised me."

"I'm a Ranger, Claire, not a bounty hunter. I can't accept the reward, but I want you to have it. The money will give you a new start."

Claire's eyes filled with tears. She tried to speak, but Logan touched his finger to her lips. Swallowing hard, she nodded. They slipped into the dimly lit hallway and made their way down the back stairs. Keeping to the shadows, they reached the back door of the Palace. A stand of mesquites loomed about thirty yards away.

"I'm gonna check those trees for his horse. It has to be somewhere close by."

"Be careful," Claire cautioned.

Logan returned, leading a piebald gelding. He tied the animal to a post, and they started up the stairs. Reaching Bertie's room, Logan motioned for Claire to continue on. She looked at him and mouthed the words, "Good luck."

He nodded as she turned and hurried away. Putting his ear to the door, Logan heard muted voices inside. He tensed, drew his revolver and kicked the door open. The man reclining on the bed raised up.

"What the hell!"

He was wearing only trousers, and his chest was covered with curly black hair. A gun belt with a pistol in the holster hung on the bedpost. The woman, a thin robe covering her fleshy body, cowered in the corner. Logan looked at the man and knew he had finally come face to face with Joe Greene.

It was easy to see why Johanna had mistaken him for the outlaw. Except for the color of their eyes, there was a slight resemblance. The killer's eyes darted to his gun.

"Don't try it!"

"Who the hell are you?" Greene snarled.

"Name's Hunter, and I know you're Joe Greene. In case you haven't heard, the price is a thousand dollars now."

Obscenities poured from Greene's mouth.

"Turn over on your belly," Logan ordered as he advanced toward the bed. He fanned back the hammer of the revolver. "Make a wrong move and I'll drill you. It'd be a lot easier to take you in dead, and it don't matter to me which way I do it."

Features twisted with hate, Greene rolled over on his stomach. Releasing the hammer, Logan brought the gun butt down on the outlaw's head. He grunted and his body went limp. Logan jerked the sheet from under Greene's prostrate form and threw it at Bertie. "Tear this up."

She had not said a word, and her hands trembled as she struggled with the sheet.

"Now sit down in that chair and keep quiet."

"Don't worry, mister. You done me a favor. That brute played rough even if he did pay good."

Logan quickly bound and gagged Greene, then did the same with Bertie. He opened the door and peered down the hall. It was empty. Hoisting Greene's limp form over his shoulder, he managed to push the door closed.

Logan was winded when he reached the bottom of the stairs. Draping Greene's unconscious body over the saddle, he used the man's rope to tie him securely. He led Greene's horse back into the copse of mesquites.

He grabbed the piebald's reins. Nudging the stallion forward, Logan left Laredo behind.

Greene regained consciousness, muttered strangled curses and struggled to free himself. Logan brought the horses to a halt and dismounted. He raised Greene's head and, in the faint moonlight, saw the hatred blazing from the outlaw's eyes.

"I'm going to untie you, but you make a wrong move, and I'll put a bullet in you." Logan freed Greene, and as soon the gag was removed, profanity poured from his mouth. Shoving his pistol against Greene's head, Logan pulled back the hammer. "If you want to see the sun come up, you better shut your filthy mouth."

The outlaw flinched, and then his body went rigid. Logan eased back the hammer and stepped away. Greene lunged and slammed into Logan, knocking the pistol from his hand. Grabbing Greene around the waist, Logan wrestled him to the ground. Kicking and clawing, they rolled and tumbled, both seeking and finding a target.

Greene landed a blow that connected with Logan's mouth, and Logan felt his lip split. Blood oozed from the wound. Retaliating with all the strength he could muster, he delivered a punch that snapped Greene's head back. Logan grabbed his gun and came to his feet. His finger quivered on the trigger as he looked down at the outlaw's dazed features.

"I should kill you for that." The deadly softness in Logan's voice belied the raging fury in his eyes. Greene lay on the ground, his eyes riveted to the gun in Logan's hand. He swallowed nervously but did not speak.

"That's the difference between us, Greene. You can strangle a defenseless woman because you're a cold-blooded killer. I won't kill you, but I'm going to make the trip to jail one you won't forget. You're going to spend the entire time on your belly tied over the back of your horse."

CHAPTER TWELVE

"It's going to be a fine day for the celebration," Johanna said. "Heidi, let me fasten your dress. We want to get started." She buttoned the red and white gingham frock and tied red ribbons around the little girl's pigtails.

"Karl, you may wear your new blue shirt, if you like." Since Johanna's visit to Will's father, Karl had been quiet and withdrawn. She knew he did not approve, but she would not discuss it with him.

Johanna felt Maggie's apprehension. How would the townspeople react when they saw her? And what would they say about her own changed appearance? Maggie had convinced her to use the creams and lotions, and Johanna had applied them diligently. Her complexion glowed, and even her rough callused hands were softer.

Maggie looked her over from head toe. "Johanna, you look wonderful!"

"Thanks to you."

"It's not much compared to what you are doing for me," Maggie said, a catch her voice.

"I don't want to hear any more of that. Let's get the food in the wagon. Karl and Gustav will help."

The parade and speeches over, the crowd gathered at the picnic grounds. Rows of tables were covered with a colorful collection of tablecloths, which added to the holiday spirit. Red, white and blue banners were in evidence everywhere. Townspeople mingled with ranchers and farmers. Today there were no social barriers. Johanna and Maggie placed the baskets of food on the center tables, before selecting a spot at the far edge of the picnic grounds.

Johanna wanted Maggie to have as much privacy as possible when Poppa arrived. The Neicum party came into view. Johanna saw Maggie clench her hands tightly together. "Don't worry, Maggie. Everything is going to be all right." Maggie's lips quivered, and Johanna saw the fear in her eyes.

During the parade, Johanna had seen people stare at Maggie. She had heard their whispers but ignored them. Sam pulled up the wagon and the family climbed down. He drove on to the area that had been roped off for conveyances. Karl and Heidi ran to join the other children at their games. Johanna watched as Conrad approached. She did not know if he recognized Maggie or whether he would acknowledge her if he did.

Suddenly Maggie was running toward him, and he opened his arms. Tears coursed down her cheeks as she ran into his embrace. "Poppa, oh, Poppa," Maggie sobbed.

Conrad hugged his daughter tightly. Johanna followed behind Maggie and could see his eyes were wet. He patted Maggie's shoulder awkwardly, all the while saying, "It's all right, *liechben*, it's all right."

Nick, walking behind his father, looked at Anne-Marie, his face wreathed in smiles. Mary's stern countenance revealed little emotion. Johanna knew the crowd had witnessed the reunion, but she did not care. Maggie and Poppa had been reunited, and that was all that mattered.

Pastor Mueller offered a short prayer, and the crowd descended upon the heavily laden tables. The women had prepared their specialties in abundance. Traditional German dishes vied with the hearty beef and beans the ranchers favored.

Amanda and her mother, George Taylor and the Reynoldses sat together several tables away. Amanda, angelic in white lawn, waved a delicate silk fan to stir the hot air. The men had removed their coats, and the party looked relaxed and comfortable.

Maggie and Conrad sat side by side, but they did not speak. That would come later. It was enough that the long estrangement was over. Johanna's heart was full. Her prayers had been answered.

After the meal, the menfolk joined a group of men pitching

horseshoes. The children resumed their games while the womenfolk cleared the tables.

"Hello, Johanna."

She turned to see Will standing behind her. Looking ill at ease, he held his hat his hand.

"Hello, Will. You know Maggie, and I think you've met my sisters-in-law." Johanna, flustered at his sudden appearance, motioned to Anne-Marie and Mary.

"Ladies." Will touched his hat brim.

The women acknowledged his presence with a nod and went on with their work.

"Could we go for a walk?" Will asked.

Johanna glanced at the crowd. They seemed busy enjoying themselves. Will motioned to the outer edge of the picnic grounds. They were soon out of sight of the crowd.

* * *

Logan made his way toward Maggie and two other women sitting at one of the picnic tables.

"Logan!"

"Hello, Maggie. How are you?" His eyes searched the crowd for Johanna.

"I'm fine."

"Johanna?"

"She's here, but..."

Logan waited.

"She went for a walk with Will DeVore."

Logan's face lost its pleasant expression. It had never occurred to him that Johanna might be interested in Will. He remembered Nick mentioning the man's name but hadn't given it further thought. Irritated at the feeling of jealousy that invaded his mind, he gave Maggie a brief nod. He wasn't going wait around until she returned. "Nice to see you again, Maggie." He turned to leave.

"Logan, wait. What should I tell Johanna?"

Logan shrugged and touched his hat brim. "Ladies."

He needed to notify Sheriff Koenig that he had Joe Greene in custody. When he had arrived at the jail, Deputy Perkins had told him the sheriff was at the picnic. Logan spotted the lawman among the men pitching horseshoes. He caught the sheriff's attention and Koenig hurried over to him.

"Delaney! I didn't know you were back. Any luck findin' Greene?"

Logan motioned toward the place where the conveyances were located. "Let's talk over there." When they were out of earshot, Logan explained, "Joe Greene is locked up nice and tight in your jail, Sheriff."

Koenig's rugged features revealed his surprise. "Congratulations."

"Thanks, but I still have to take him to Llano. I'll be heading out at first light."

"Do you think his gang is on your trail? I could send a deputy to Llano with you," Koenig offered.

"That's not necessary."

"Well, let me know if you change your mind. I'm going to assign a couple of extra men to the jail. Never pays to take chances."

"Much obliged, Sheriff. I'm a mite trailworn. Think I'll head back to the hotel and get some shut-eye."

The two men parted, and Koenig went in search of men to guard Joe Greene. Logan strode toward the place where *Él Campeon* was tethered. He passed a group of picnickers, and a feminine voice called out, "Mr. Delaney. How nice to see you again." He turned to see Jane Reynolds beckoning him toward the table. Amanda Blair and an older woman were seated beside her.

"Ladies." Logan tipped his hat.

"You've met Amanda, and this is her mother, Mrs. Blair. Please sit down, Mr. Delaney," Jane invited.

Logan sat down beside Amanda. Out of the corner of his eye, he appraised the young woman. *She's a beauty, all right.*

"Will you be needing a room, Mr. Delaney?" Jane asked.

"I've already registered for tonight, ma'am. I'll be leaving early in the morning." An awkward silence developed, and Logan decided it was time he went on his way.

Franklin Reynolds and another man approached. Franklin introduced George Taylor, and Logan scrutinized the banker while the man politely acknowledged the introduction. Taylor moved to Amanda's side.

So that's the way it is. Wonder if they're engaged? He thought about Johanna and Will DeVore. If she could forget him so fast, then he could find other interests, too. "Miss Blair, may I speak with you privately?" The question was out before Logan realized he had spoken his thoughts.

A shocked expression appeared on Amanda's face, and her skin colored faintly. "Why...why, yes." She rose and followed him several steps away.

"I apologize if I've embarrassed you, ma'am," Logan told her, a smile playing around his mouth. "I plan to return to Meirsville soon." He paused a moment before continuing. "May I call on you at that time?"

Amanda's green eyes flew open wide, and she stared him. After a moment, she found her voice. "I'm flattered Mr. Delaney, but we've barely been introduced. I don't think it would be proper for us to see each other socially."

Logan's smile was a bit sheepish. "I didn't mean to offend you, ma'am. And I appreciate your feelings. Perhaps we can get better acquainted when I return."

Well, at least she's not engaged. Whether she was impressed with his gentlemanly manners or wanted to know him better, Logan didn't care. He intended to seek her out the first opportunity he had.

"When you come to Meirsville again, I shall certainly be willing to discuss it." Amanda gave him an engaging smile. "Good day, sir."

"Good day, ma'am."

Logan reached the stallion just as a boy rushed up shouting at the top of his lungs.

"They took him! They took him! The outlaws took Karl."

Logan grabbed the boy's arm. "Calm down, son. Tell us what happened."

Gasping for breath, the boy related the story. "Me and Karl was on the way to my house and seen these men ride in behind the bank. We wondered what they was doin' so we hid and watched 'em. Two of 'em went in the sheriff's office. We peeked in the winda, and they tied up Perkins and brought some guy outta one of the cells. Then they shoved Perkins in it. I told Karl we should come and git the sheriff, but the men that was waitin' outside snuck up behind us and grabbed us. They told me to come and say they was takin' Karl with 'em and, if you follered 'em, they'd kill 'im." The boy swallowed hard, and his voice choked up.

A crowd began to form, and Koenig pushed his way through. "Easy, Henry. Easy." He put his arm around the boy's shoulder.

Logan saw Johanna and Maggie approaching. His breath lodged his in throat, and his heart thudded his chest.

Voices erupted and the crowd was yelling. "What man in the jail?" "What outlaws?" "What's goin' on?"

"Quiet! Quiet down!" Koenig looked at Logan, a question in his eyes. Logan gave a slight nod. "This man, Logan Delaney, apprehended the man and is taking him to Llano. Delaney stopped to rest a bit," the sheriff explained.

"What did the man do?" another voice asked.

Koenig hesitated. "He's suspected of murder and cattle rustlin'."

"Murder! That fella there had no right to put him in our jail. Now look what's happened!" The crowd grew restless.

Logan saw Johanna push her way to the front. Her face was ashen, her eyes wide with disbelief. She stared at Logan and her lips moved but no sound came.

"Quiet!" the sheriff shouted. "Delaney is a Texas Ranger."

"Ranger! He's a Ranger." The crowd quieted, but some of the men continued to grumble.

Logan held up his hand for silence. "It's time to stop talking and start doing." He turned to Henry. "How many men were there?"

"Five, countin' the man in the jail," the boy answered.

"We need to form a posse. Sheriff, can you get started? I'll be along in a few minutes." Logan walked toward Johanna.

The sheriff called for volunteers.

"I have horses for them that needs 'em," Angus McCray said.

A muffled explosion punctuated the liveryman's words. "They're robbin' the bank," came a roar from the crowd. George Taylor fought his way through and started toward the wagons.

Koenig grabbed his arm. "Hold up, George. They got the boy, remember? We don't want him to get hurt."

Angry cries ran through the crowd, and the men surged toward town. The sheriff ran for his horse.

Logan and Johanna stood facing one another. She stared at him, an expression of horror on her face.

"I'm sorry, Johanna. I didn't intend for anything like this to happen." Logan reached out to her, but she backed away.

"They've got my son. If you hadn't come back here with that outlaw, it wouldn't have happened. Why didn't you leave us alone?" Johanna sobbed, her control gone.

Logan's gut knotted up, her accusation slicing through him like a knife. "I'm sorry, Johanna. I'll bring Karl back. I promise."

Nick and Sam ran to join the posse while Maggie and Anne-Marie stood beside Johanna. Heidi clung to her mother's hand. Logan searched Johanna's face for some sign of understanding, but she was lost in grief.

When Logan reined the stallion to a halt in front of the sheriff's office, Koenig was coming out of the bank. Logan met him on the boardwalk.

"They blew the safe, all right," Koenig confirmed.

"I'll take a quick look around while you get the posse together." Logan stepped through the doorway. Taylor's office was intact, but the vault had suffered considerable damage. The door was hanging on its hinges, and debris littered the floor. Logan saw Taylor examining the contents of several metal boxes that had been blown off the shelves. Ledgers, records, and empty canvas moneybags lay in discarded heaps.

"Got any idea how much they took?" Logan asked the banker.

"We won't know for sure until we make a complete check. Probably close to fifteen thousand."

"No wonder Greene took the risk." Logan turned to leave.

"Greene? You don't mean that was Joe Greene in our jail," Taylor asked, his tone incredulous.

"Yeah. His gang must have been right behind me," Logan admitted, his voice bitter with self-blame.

"If you don't catch him and get the money back, this town will be ruined." Taylor's features were grim, his eyes hard.

"We'll get 'em," Logan promised as he left the building. He saw Nick and Sam talking with a tall man flanked by several cowpunchers. Logan stood beside the sheriff while he spoke to the crowd.

"I'm gonna pass out rifles to them that needs 'em." He turned to Max Hemmerlein. "You got any spare guns in your shop? And ca'triges? We'll need plenty of ammunition."

"I can open the mercantile," Adam Schmidt said.

"Delaney, you got anything you want to say?" Koenig asked.

"This is going to be a hard ride and maybe a long one. Those of you that need to look after your families and businesses better stay behind. It will be risky, no doubt about that. Greene is dangerous. He won't give up easy, but that's no reason to get trigger-happy. The boy's life is at stake, and I don't want anybody to forget that."

Angry muttering started and Sam confronted Logan. "You gonna wait all day?"

Logan's eyes narrowed, but his voice was level when he answered. "We'll ride out as soon as we're ready."

Koenig, who had disappeared from the crowd, returned. "They circled around the bank and headed north."

"You can bet they'll head west as soon as they clear town, then turn south. My guess is they intend to cross the border. Some of you gather supplies, and the rest get over to the livery."

The crowd dispersed, and Logan turned to Koenig. "Sheriff, I'm going to take a look at those tracks and see if I can pick up where they went back on the road. I'll meet you at the entrance to the picnic grounds."

Logan found the place the outlaws had tied their horses. The ground was scuffed and there were piles of fresh manure. He mounted and rode to the river to water the stallion and fill his canteen. Picking up a sign, he followed it to the edge of town. The tracks veered north. He rode slowly, his eyes on the ground, counting five sets of tracks. Greene's gang had probably stolen a horse somewhere rather than try to take the piebald from the livery stable.

The tracks continued through the brush for a quarter of a mile before turning westward. When Logan reached the place they joined the road, he was west of the picnic grounds. The bend in the road had prevented the picnickers from sighting the outlaws.

He rode back toward town. Reaching the spot where he was to meet the posse, he searched the grounds with his eyes. A few people remained, but he was too far away to see if Johanna was still there. His gut knotted and he fought the urge to look for her. He had to concentrate on getting her son back unharmed. Greene would not hesitate to kill the boy the minute he was no longer useful. Waiting for the posse in the shade of a live oak tree, Logan sorted through his mind for a plan. If it took the fifteen thousand to free the boy, then he would go after the outlaws once the boy was safe.

Ten men made up the posse that arrived at the meeting place, including Emil Stein, Max Hemmerlein, Angus McCray, and the Neicum brothers.

"Delaney, this is Will DeVore and his men." Nick introduced the strangers Logan had seen earlier. He nodded and sized the big man up. *So he's the man Johanna is interested in.* Mentally chastising himself that now was not the time, he forced his mind to concentrate on the task ahead.

"Did you pick up their trail?" the sheriff asked.

"Yeah. It came out on the road beyond that bend. They're headed for the border, all right."

The horses broke into a quick trot. The posse rounded the bend and Logan slowed *Él Campeon* to a walk, looking for a sign. Keeping an eye out for where they might have left the road, Logan studied the mingled tracks. Mostly flat, the distant terrain was broken by low rolling hills. It supported cacti, mesquite, and sagebrush but did not provide much cover. A dust cloud lingered on the horizon.

The setting sun streaked the sky with shades of orange and red that soon would turn to pink and lavender. Darkness would soon follow.

Continuing the search would be risky, because of the need to look for a sign and because of danger to the horses. There were gopher holes as well as ravines, and the animals were tiring.

Logan rode abreast of Koenig and pointed to a stand of mesquites. "Let's rest the horses a spell."

Koenig called a halt, and the men dismounted.

Nick asked the question uppermost their minds. "Delaney, what do you think of our chances of gettin' Karl back alive?"

"We'll get him back." Logan spoke with a conviction he was far from feeling.

"Maybe they already killed him," Sam broke in, his voice filled with accusation.

"I don't think so," Logan replied. "As long they keep him alive, they have some bargaining power. He's no good to them dead."

"Delaney's right," Koenig agreed. "Karl's safe for now."

"It's gonna be dark soon. We might lose them, especially if they decide to leave the trail and cut across country."

"Another thing," Logan added. "Their horses are about played out, and they're carrying those heavy money bags. They'll have to stop soon." He swung into the saddle. "We've got a little daylight left. Let's keep riding, and when we spot a good place to camp, we'll stop."

Less than hour later, they camped in a stand of live oaks. It was a dry camp without a fire. The outlaws might smell the smoke.

"It's a good thing we had lots to eat at the picnic," Emil Stein joked as he chewed a piece of jerky.

His meager meal finished, Logan covertly watched Will DeVore. He had learned DeVore was a local rancher of some prominence, but Logan could find nothing about the man to dislike. He wondered if DeVore knew about his interest in Johanna.

"We need to post a guard," Koenig interrupted Logan's thoughts. "Anybody want to take the first watch?"

"I'll take it," Nick said.

"I'll take the next one," DeVore volunteered.

Logan wanted the last watch, because he liked the quiet darkness before the dawn. It would provide time to organize his thoughts. Weary from the long days on the trail, he stretched out on his bedroll. Noise from the horses moving about and nocturnal creatures scurrying through the brush carried on the soft night air. Logan rolled over on his side, closed his eyes and slept.

The camp settled for the night. A sliver of moon hung in the midnight sky. Long shadows danced among the trees and bushes, creating strange shapes and images. The snores of the sleeping men punctuated the silence.

* * *

Silent and still, the woman seated in the rocker could have been a statue carved from marble. Her eyes, red and swollen, stared unseeing at her surroundings. The hysteria that had gripped her for a short time had given way to tight control, frightening in its intensity.

Maggie laid her hand on Johanna's shoulder. "It's very late. Why don't you try to get some rest?"

"I can't sleep knowing that Karl is out there somewhere with those outlaws." Johanna's voice was hoarse and ragged.

"I know, but at least get undressed and lie down. Logan will find Karl. I know he will."

"Yes, but will my son still be alive? If Logan hadn't brought that outlaw to Meirsville, this wouldn't have happened. I will never forgive him for it!"

CHAPTER THIRTEEN

"It's time, Delaney." Will touched Logan's shoulder. He came to his feet in an instant, revolver in hand.

DeVore sucked in his breath.

"Sorry," Logan apologized and holstered his weapon.

"I guess you're used to all this," Will said.

"You don't get used to it. You do what you have to do to stay alive."

Dawn streaked the sky as Koenig roused the sleeping men. After a quick breakfast of jerky and hardtack, they saddled their horses and rode out. Logan scouted ahead and picked up the outlaws' trail.

"These tracks were probably made about the time we camped," Logan said. "If they kept riding, they'll have a considerable lead by now." He saw the worried look on the faces of the posse and hastened to add, "But I don't think they did. Their horses were too played out."

The landscape flattened out and thick brush covered the area. In the distance, low hills ringed the plateau. Logan's instincts told him the outlaws would leave the trail soon. Less than a mile farther, the tracks veered off into the brush.

"They left the road here," Logan called out, bringing the stallion to a halt. He pointed toward the east and urged *Él Campeon* off the trail where he discovered the tracks turned south. The strong aroma from the creosote bushes and the smell of crushed sagebrush permeated the air. A half-hour later, the posse rode upon the remains of the outlaw camp.

Logan's careful scrutiny of the horse droppings, told him the lead-time was about the same. "Let's rest the horses a spell." Logan pointed to a stand of live oak trees. The posse gathered round, and Logan brought up the subject that had been on his mind for a while. "Sheriff, it might be a good idea if some of the men went back to town. This could turn into a standoff."

"Sam and me was just talkin' about that," Nick said. "His wife is ailin'. I'm a better shot than he is, anyway." Nick grinned as a scowl appeared on Sam's face.

* * *

Johanna scrubbed the already spotless floor. Since daylight she had been driving herself, keeping her grief locked inside. Images of Karl being tortured or worse kept filling her mind until she thought she would go insane. Heidi was quiet, and Gustav went about his chores, his pace slower than normal. It was if he had suddenly become the old man he really was.

Johanna wiped the perspiration from her face with the tail of her apron. She looked up to see Maggie's worried expression, her hazel eyes filled with concern.

"I'm going to make a pot of tea," Maggie said and hurried to fill the kettle. Johanna nodded but did not reply. The sound of hoof beats broke the silence. Her emotions, frozen into a hard knot, broke free. Throwing her scrub brush into the bucket of mop water, Johanna got to her feet and started toward the door. Hope flashed across her features, quickly followed by expressions of fear and dread. Running across the wet floor, she slipped, caught herself and flew out of the house.

"Karl, did you find Karl?" Her eyes searched the yard.

"Calm down, Johanna, calm down!" Sam grabbed her hands and pulled her into his arms, awkwardly trying to offer comfort. "No, we didn't catch up with them before I left, but I'm sure the posse has by now. Nick stayed, and Will is there too. They'll get Karl back."

Her control gone, Johanna sobbed, tears streaming down her face.

* * *

The posse was down to seven men. Koenig was an experienced lawman, and Hemmerlein certainly knew firearms. Nick was a good marksman, but hunting for game was not the same as shooting at a man. Logan surveyed their surroundings. The range of hills on the east and south were higher and covered with heavy growth. Thick green vegetation indicated water was close by. "How close is the river?"

"The Sabinal is less than a half-mile away," Koenig said.

"They probably crossed it last night," Logan speculated. "We may be closing in. Mount up."

Picking up the trail, the men moved ahead. Logan, eyes on the ground, reined *Él Campeon* to a halt and dismounted. "Take a look at these tracks, Sheriff. One of their horses has thrown a shoe."

"That should slow 'em down," Koenig responded.

The sun was climbing in the sky when they reached the river. The water ran low, swift and clear. The thirsty horses pranced nervously under tight reins. The animals were allowed to drink while the men walked upstream to quench their own thirst and fill the canteens. A quick swipe with a wet bandanna offered a welcome respite.

While the posse waited, Logan crossed the river, looking for the place where the outlaws left the water. East or west? West was the logical direction since they were heading for the border, but there was rougher country to the east. Greene was savvy, and if he headed east, he might think he could outsmart them. Again, Logan trusted his instincts. Staying close to the riverbank, he rode slowly, trying to pick up the trail. About a half-mile farther on, he spotted tracks leading out of the water heading in a southeasterly direction. His hunch had been right. Reining *Él Campeon* around, he rejoined the posse.

Koenig, his expression thoughtful, spoke. "There's some fairly rough country where he's headin'. River makes a bend and has washed out some big cut banks. Brush is thicker, too."

"Greene will be more desperate now with one horse less," Logan cautioned. "Keep your eyes open and your weapons ready. He won't hesitate to even the odds."

Single file, they followed the tracks through the tangled brush. Sunlight filtered through the leaves of the mesquite trees. Progress was slow, and the hot sun beat down from a bright blue sky. Shirts stuck to backs, and faces glistened with sweat. The horses' hides were lathered and dark. An hour later they reached the river.

"We're getting close. That manure," Logan pointed to a pile of horse droppings, "is only minutes old. Might be best if we went on foot from here. Keep some cover between you and the river."

The men dismounted and secured the horses. Fanning out, they crept forward. No movement was visible from the other side of the river. Logan's pulse speeded up and his breathing accelerated. He could almost taste the danger that lay ahead. A loud cry split the silence, and a head appeared above a stand of small hackberry trees.

"Help! Help! Somebody, please help me!"

The head abruptly disappeared from view.

"It's Karl!" Nick cried and started forward.

Logan stepped in front of him and grabbed his arm. "You trying get yourself killed? At least we know the boy is alive. They can't make a run for it, so they may try to bargain. We need to draw them out. Stay here and give me all the cover you can." Before the others could protest, Logan was threading his way through the brush toward the river. He stopped in a clump of stunted junipers.

"Greene," he called out, "we've got you pinned down. Turn the boy loose. It'll go easier on you."

No sound penetrated the silence.

"Greene," Logan repeated, "you might as well surrender. You can't ride out of here."

After what seemed an eternity, a voice called out, "We'll let the kid go if you back off and let us ride out. If you don't, we'll kill 'im."

Logan recognized Greene's voice, and his thoughts raced. They had to stall Greene to give them time to get Karl. Rushing the outlaws would be suicide. If they could come at them from above the drop off, their chances would better. He surveyed the top of the riverbank down to the water's edge and judged it to be about ten feet. The brush was thick enough to provide some cover. If the posse created a diversion, he could make his way to the top.

He laid out the plan, and Nick and Will immediately objected. "Karl's my nephew. It's my place to go," Nick argued.

"You know how I feel about Johanna, and it's her son they took,"

Will argued.

DeVore's statement raised questions Logan wanted answered, but now was not the time. Not a flicker of emotion showed on his face as he pushed the thought from his mind. "No. Greene was my prisoner, and I aim to get him back. Dead or alive. Besides, I get paid to take the risk." His grin took the sting from his words. "Koenig, give me ten minutes, then create a diversion and start moving in."

"It's too risky," Koenig insisted.

Logan did not answer. Picking up his rifle, he disappeared into the brush. The river had made a wide bend before Greene and his gang crossed the second time. Wading through the shallow water, Logan made his way to the other side. It was not a hard climb to the top of the bank except for a few places where the soil was loose. Logan threaded his way toward the outlaws' position and spotted the place where he thought the posse was concealed. He waved his arm over his head, hoping Koenig was watching. His answer came when he heard the sheriff yell out.

"Joe Greene, this is Martin Koenig, sheriff of Medina County. You release the boy, and we'll talk about the money."

Loud hoots erupted from several places in the brush. "You think we're crazy, Sheriff?" A rifle shot followed the outlaw's words.

"Careful where you aim," Koenig cautioned the men. "Delaney's on top now."

Before the posse could fire, more shots followed. None of them came close. Following Koenig's instructions, the posse fired far to the right and to the left of Logan's position. Max Hemmerlein, probably the best shot in the bunch, aimed high and peppered the area. Then, all was quiet as smoke from the rifle fire drifted skyward. Logan made his way toward the bottom and found about two feet of level ground between the bottom of the incline and the water's edge. Rocky soil and sparse vegetation provided little cover. The element of surprise was his only protection.

Another round of gunfire erupted, and Logan hoped the posse had closed the gap between their hiding place and the river. Heavy return fire from the outlaws followed. Logan chose that moment to move around the bend. The deep cuts the river had worn in the bank were choked with brush and debris. There was no sign of the outlaws or their horses. Watching for any sign of movement, Logan crept forward. He parted the brush and saw Karl, a gag in his mouth and his hands and feet bound. The boy's eyes were dull with shock, his cheeks tear-stained, and his lips bruised and bleeding. Logan's temper spiraled to the surface, but he tamped it down. Anger was man's worst enemy, and he needed all his faculties to capture Joe Greene. He untied the boy and, pointing in the direction from which he had come, motioned Karl away.

The boy hesitated, looked at Logan for moment, then turned and ran along the river's edge toward freedom. Logan heard the jingle of spurs and crouched down behind a clump of bushes. A man came into view, revolver dangling at his side. Stringy blond hair hung around his shoulders, and his face was covered with a sparse beard.

Peering into the hole where Karl had been, he let out a howl. "Joe, the kid got away." His whiny voice carried back to Logan. There was something vaguely familiar about him. Before Logan could place him, boot heels pounded down the riverbank. Logan's eyes widened in surprise. Greene had let his anger get the best of him.

"He cain't git fur and has to go back the way we come. Tell the others to keep 'em busy while I find the kid," Greene snarled.

Logan watched as the first man turned and ran back to the other outlaws.

Greene's eyes scoured his surroundings. Logan took a deep breath and walked into the open. "Greene!" His pistol left the holster before the word was out of his mouth. The outlaw whirled, pulling the trigger as he turned. The shot went wild. Logan fired, the bullet striking Greene in the chest. Shock registered on his face and his lips moved, but no sound came. He stood suspended in time, his body rigid, then pitched forward in the dirt. Logan looked down at Greene. Blood trickled from the corner of his mouth. He was dead.

Logan automatically punched out the spent shell and replaced it. The black feeling that always came over him when he took a human life manifested itself. His breath felt trapped in his throat and bile churned in his gut, turning it sour. The sound of movement in the brush brought him back to the present. This was no time for self-incrimination. Greene's gang would be on him in seconds.

Gunfire from both sides of the river was sporadic. Leaving Greene where he fell, Logan started his search for the rest of the gang. With their leader dead, maybe they would surrender. But fifteen thousand dollars gave a man all kinds of courage.

Beyond the place where Karl had been hidden, the vegetation grew thicker. Glancing up, Logan saw Nick and Will heading in his direction. He signaled his intention and moved along the riverbank. In the clearing ahead, he saw Greene's men, carrying the canvas money bags, making their way toward the top of the cut bank.

Stepping into the open, Logan called out, "Drop those bags and put your hands up!" They spun around, and in a split second Logan read their faces. They would not surrender. One of the men fired in his direction. The bullet whistled by his ear, and Logan went into a half crouch. The fleeting thought that Nick and Will were closing behind him surfaced, and he fired several shots in rapid succession. The two men close to the top dropped the moneybags and disappeared over the rim. A shot came from behind Logan, and one of the remaining men dropped the moneybag and clutched his shoulder. His partner, close behind him, got off a fast shot. Logan felt the impact as the slug hit him in the chest, high on the left side. There was no pain, just a burning sensation and a strange languid feeling. The brilliant sunlight faded to pale blue, then gray and finally black until the darkness closed around him.

* * *

Dark shadows gathered in the corners of the small room and crept across the floor. Johanna sat beside the bed where Logan lay unconscious, his thick black eyelashes resting against his pale cheeks. The healthy tan had turned a ghostly gray. Dr. Fischer had sent for her when Logan kept calling her name.

The past three days were like a bad dream. Johanna tried to sort out her feelings. Nick had come riding in with Karl, but her joy was short-lived when she learned Logan had been wounded. After a sleepless night, Martin Koenig arrived to deliver the doctor's message. Karl's hostility toward Logan had vanished. Johanna admitted the boy had been rescued due to Logan's daring and bravery.

As she prepared to leave, Karl came to the bedroom door. "Ma." The childish 'Mama' was gone. A part of Karl's childhood had vanished forever.

"Yes, Karl, what is it?"

"I never got a chance to thank Mr. Delaney for saving my life. Now he's gonna die, and I'll never be able to tell him how I feel." The boy's lips quivered as he tried to hold the tears at bay.

Johanna put her arms around him and hugged him to her breast. "Don't fret so, Karl. I'm sure Logan knows you're grateful."

"But...but I was ugly to him. And he's a Ranger, Ma. A Texas Ranger."

"Yes, that was a surprise."

Sitting at Logan's bedside, Johanna was filled with remorse. It would be evening soon, and he had not rallied except to utter unintelligible sounds that Dr. Fischer said reflected the pain he must be suffering. The doctor could not give her any encouragement.

She stood and stretched her cramped muscles. Placing her hand on his forehead, she felt the heat emanating from his body. Taking a cloth from the table beside the bed, she dipped it into the basin of cool water and bathed his face. It was covered with heavy black stubble, and she thought how sinister, yet how helpless, he looked. Again dipping the cloth in the water, she picked up his hand. It was fine-boned, the fingers long and slender. She felt only the slight impression of calluses.

Then she remembered. He made his living with a gun, and it looked as if he was going to die by the gun. Tears stung her eyelids, and she swallowed the sob in her throat. The flood of emotions that swept through her body stunned her. Johanna stared at his flat belly. A line of fine black hair ran down the middle and disappeared under the sheet that covered his lower body.

The memory of her nocturnal visit to the barn came flooding back. His burning kisses, his hands caressing her body, his rising passion, all replayed themselves in her mind. Her face flooded with color. How could she have such thoughts at a time like this? This man whom she barely knew had turned her placid world upside-down.

Logan stirred, and Johanna stepped back. His eyes opened, glassy and unfocused. He licked his cracked lips and whispered, "Water."

Supporting his head, Johanna held the glass to his mouth, and he drank greedily. He looked into her eyes, and she thought she saw a flicker of recognition, but it was gone as quickly as it came. He closed his eyes and slipped back into the black void.

The doctor entered the room and walked to the bedside. He was of average height, had a head of thick gray hair and a neatly trimmed mustache. "Any change?"

"He woke for just a minute and asked for water. I gave him a drink, but he slipped away again. Dr. Fischer, his fever is very high."

"You're right about that."

"Surely there is something we can do."

"I'm afraid we're doing all we can. Just keep bathing him with cool water." The doctor looked intently at Johanna. "Are you sure you want to stay here? Mrs. Perkins will be glad to come in."

"No, I'll stay, doctor. It's the least I can do after the man saved Karl's life."

The doctor nodded. "I'm going home for a bite to eat, but I'll return and bring you something. You need to eat."

Johanna resumed her vigil. Logan began thrashing about. Afraid his wound would start bleeding, she held his hands and tried to calm him. Speaking softly, she soothed him, as she would have one of her children. But Logan was no child, and even in his weakened state, she had difficulty restraining him.

Suddenly, he sat up and pushed her aside. His eyes opened wide and he stared straight ahead, but she knew was not aware of his surroundings.

"Johanna." His voice was a weak croak. "Johanna, I'll find Karl.

155

I'll bring him back, I promise."

Deep pain sliced through her entire being. Logan was reliving their confrontation after the kidnapping. How she regretted her hateful words! "Oh, Logan, I'm sorry I said those awful things to you. I didn't mean them. Karl is safe at home now, and I can never repay you for that."

He turned his head, and blue eyes locked with hazel ones, but she knew he did not see her or understand what she was saying. He was in the grip of a pain-filled delirium. Sinking back against the pillows, he closed his eyes, his breathing harsh and ragged.

She began wiping his face. His entire body was racked with fever, and putting modesty aside, she bathed his fevered flesh. The doctor returned and brought the food he had promised, but Johanna could not eat. She drank a cup of lukewarm tea and continued ministering to the man who had released emotions she didn't know existed.

Throughout the long night she bathed Logan's burning body and whispered words of comfort that she knew he did not hear. Logan's fever raged for two days, and Johanna fought with every ounce of her strength against the infection that threatened his life. The only respite she allowed herself was a quick trip to the doctor's house for food, which she barely managed to choke down, and a change of clothing.

When Johanna bathed his fevered body Logan quieted, but the fever soon rose again, Dr. Fischer and Mrs. Perkins came and went, but she was not aware of them. She could not recall what was said or her responses. The only thing she saw and heard was Logan's desperate struggle to win the battle he was fighting.

In the dark hour before dawn, his fever broke and the chills began. Locating blankets in the chest at the foot of the bed, Johanna covered him from head to toe and tucked the edges around his quivering body. How much longer could this strong man withstand the agony? The tears surfaced and ran unheeded down her face. Dropping to her knees beside the bed, Johanna beseeched her God to intervene.

Long after daylight, Dr. Fischer found Johanna asleep in the chair beside the bed. Her exhausted body had succumbed to the rest it desperately needed. He checked his patient and found his skin cool to the touch. The crisis had passed and Logan was sleeping peacefully.

"Johanna," the doctor whispered. "Johanna." He touched her shoulder.

She awoke with a start and looked at her surroundings. Reality flooded in. "Logan?" Coming to her feet, she leaned over to look at him. He was pale and still, his features relaxed.

"The worse seems to be over. I think he's going to make it," the doctor said.

"Thank God!"

CHAPTER FOURTEEN

Sunlight streamed through the open window. The branches of a nearby tree created shifting patterns on the wall beside Logan's bed. He opened his eyes, feeling drained and empty. The wound in his chest throbbed with every beat of his heart.

Nothing about his surroundings was familiar. Bits and pieces of what seemed like a bad dream: pain, thirst, heat and cold. Logan vaguely remembered the ride back to town after the showdown with Greene. At some point, Nick and Karl had left them. Logan's wound had bled and the pain had been excruciating, but he had managed to stay in the saddle until the posse reached Meirsville. He recalled the doctor saying the bullet had to come out. After a liberal shot of whiskey, the doctor began to probe. That was the last thing he remembered.

His eyes focused on a woman's figure at the other end of the room. "Johanna!" It had not been a dream, the hands that soothed him and the voice that whispered words of comfort. Logan did not realize he had spoken aloud until the woman turned toward him. The woman was not Johanna. She was of average height and plump, and her gray dress was covered with a voluminous white apron. Disappointment left a bitter taste in his mouth.

"Mr. Delaney, you're awake. I must let the doctor know." She hurried from the room.

The doctor smiled as he walked to the bedside. "You had a mighty close call, son." He waved a hand toward the woman. "This is Mrs. Perkins, my nurse."

"I guess I need to thank you, ma'am, for taking care of me." Logan smiled, a weak facsimile of his engaging grin.

"Oh, no, sir. Johanna Bauer has been looking after you. Doctor sent her home to rest."

Logan stared at the woman and then focused his attention on the doctor.

"There will be time for talking later. Right now you need nourishment and then to sleep some more." The doctor nodded to Mrs. Perkins and left the room.

With the nurse's help, Logan managed a few sips of broth. The effort exhausted him. *Christ*! He was as weak as a newborn colt. Mrs. Perkins insisted on administering a dose of laudanum. His eyelids grew heavy and he slept.

* * *

Johanna awoke to a room deep in shadows. From the moonlight shining through the window, she knew it must be late evening. She felt disoriented and confused. Dr. Fischer had insisted she accompany him home for a much-needed rest. Weary in mind and body, she had accepted his offer.

Memory came flooding back. Logan! She must find out about him. She threw back the covers and scrambled to her feet. Making quick work of her toilette, she opened the bedroom door and heard voices downstairs. The Fischers were in the parlor, a comfortable room filled with knick-knacks and family momentos.

The doctor rose to his feet when she entered the room. "Good evening, my dear. Did you rest well?"

Mathilde Fischer put aside her needlework and stood up. She was a buxom woman, her bearing regal, with thick braids that had once been dark brown. "You must be hungry. I did not wake you for supper because Gottlieb said you needed the rest. Let's go to the kitchen, and I'll fix you something."

"Thank you. I feel much better, but I hate to impose on you this way."

"Nonsense!" The Fischers spoke in unison.

Addressing the doctor, her voice not quite steady, Johanna asked,

"Logan? Is he going to be all right?"

"He's much better. In fact, he woke and was able take a little nourishment. I was just going to check on him. Would you like to accompany me?"

"Oh, yes! I'd like that very much."

Mathilde put together a hearty roast beef sandwich and made a pot of tea. Johanna discovered she was hungry. She finished the meal with a slice of apple pie. "The food was delicious, Mrs. Fischer."

"Thank you, dear." Turning to her husband, she added, "I'll wait up for you, Gottlieb." She handed him his medical bag.

The town was quiet and the streets were deserted. A short walk brought them to the doctor's office where they found a light burning. Logan was sound asleep.

"I've made arrangements with Deputy Perkins to look in on him." The doctor patted Johanna's hand. "He's young and healthy. It won't be long until he's back on his feet."

Johanna smiled, holding a prayer of thanksgiving deep inside. She would have been hard pressed to explain her feelings at that moment. "Would it all right if I stayed awhile?" Johanna asked, reluctant to leave Logan's bedside.

"Of course. Perkins will see you to the house when you're ready to leave."

Johanna settled in the chair beside Logan's bed. In contrast to the night before, his breathing was deep and even. She gazed at his face, relaxed in sleep. A vision of his clean-shaven face flashed before her mind's eye: broad forehead, arrow-straight nose, sharply chiseled cheekbones, firmly sculpted lips and remarkable sapphire eyes. She felt her face grow hot as she recalled the passion in those eyes and the feel of his lips on her skin.

As if aware of her presence, Logan stirred. Johanna bent over and stared into the blue eyes she had seen in her mind moments ago. Reaching for his hand, she clasped it to her breast.

"Johanna." His voice was little more than a whisper.

She squeezed his hand. "I was so afraid for you. Karl was worried, too."

Logan managed a faint grin. "I'm glad he wasn't harmed."

"Why did you let me think you were a criminal?" She gripped his hand and felt him wince.

"I'm sorry. I should have told you the truth."

"It doesn't matter now. I'm ashamed of the way I talked to you." She bowed her head.

"I understand. After all, you were right." He took a deep breath and closed his eyes for a moment.

Johanna placed her fingers over his lips. "You're tiring yourself out. We can talk later."

The doctor had left instructions to give Logan a dose of laudanum when he woke. Johanna prepared the medication, and after a feeble attempt to argue, Logan swallowed it down. He grew drowsy and succumbed to the drug's effect. Johanna looked down at his still form and felt a wild impulse to kiss him. She touched her lips to his and felt their dry, cracked surface in contrast to the hot, wet silk in the barn. Stepping away from the bed, she gazed at the sleeping man, turned and tiptoed from the room.

* * *

A week after the Fourth of July that Meirsville would remember for years to come, Johanna and Maggie were cleaning the kitchen after the midday meal. "Do you think we could work on those dresses I wanted to alter?" Maggie asked. Her wardrobe had not been designed with modesty in mind.

"I don't see why not. We can do the handwork outside where it's cooler." Johanna fit and pinned several frocks. Her thoughts strayed to Logan, and she did not hear the horse trotting up the lane.

"Johanna!" Maggie interrupted Johanna's reverie and pointed to the advancing rider. "I think it's Will DeVore."

Johanna felt a sense of apprehension. Will had ridden with Logan and the posse. Was Will aware of their friendship? Friendship! Johanna was honest enough to admit they shared more than friendship.

Will reined up and dismounted. "Afternoon, ladies." He doffed his hat.

"Hello, Will," Maggie said.

"Good afternoon, Will." Johanna put aside her sewing. "How is your father?"

"He's not good, Johanna," Will said as he toyed with his hat brim. "That's one of the reasons I'm here. He'd like to see you again. "

"I'm sorry to hear that. Of course, I'll be glad to go."

Will sat down and placed his hat on his knees. Johanna watched him from lowered lids. There was a grim set to his features, and his pale eyes held a worried look. Although not handsome in the conventional way, Will's features gave the impression of strength and determination. Unbidden, Logan's face flashed through her mind. She mentally chastised herself. Comparing the two men was unfair.

"How is Karl?" Will asked.

"I think he's going to be all right, but it was a terrible ordeal for a nine-year-old boy." Johanna shuddered, unable to shake the horror of Karl's close call.

"Yes, but he's a strong youngster. I could see that during the ride back to town."

Johanna smiled remembering Josef's quiet strength and how much Karl resembled his father. She shook off the bittersweet memory. "When would your father like me to visit?"

"Any time it's convenient."

"Would next Wednesday be all right?"

"Yes. I'll come for you like before," Will rose, hat in hand.

With a start, Johanna looked at Maggie, who had continued to work on her sewing. "Will you mind looking after the children while I'm gone?"

"You know I won't. I'm glad to do it. I enjoy spending time with them."

"They like being with you, too."

Heidi was in awe of Maggie's beauty regimen and fine wardrobe. Karl's reluctance to accept her had vanished when she pitched in to help Johanna with the housekeeping.

"I'll be here next Wednesday, Johanna." Will tipped his hat. "Ladies."

*

The heat of the day lingered on, and the family gathered in the yard after supper.

"Ma, will we be goin' to town Saturday?" Karl asked. He had been quiet and subdued since the kidnapping.

"I suppose so." Johanna's eyes lingered on her son's face as she tried to guess what was on his mind.

"Do you think it would be all right if I went to see Ranger Delaney?"

"Why, yes. Yes, I think Logan would like that."

Saturday arrived, and Johanna convinced Maggie to accompany them to town. They dressed in cool cotton frocks with a minimum of petticoats, although Maggie refused to give up her corset. An early start avoided the scorching heat that would build during the day.

"*Liebchen,* you wish to go to the mercantile first?" Gustav asked Johanna.

"Yes, I want to leave the list with Mrs. Schmidt." She turned toward the back of the wagon. "Karl, would you like to go and see Henry?" The boys had not seen one another since the kidnapping.

"Yes, ma'am, but I want see Ranger Delaney first."

As the women left the mercantile, Johanna spotted Martin Koenig standing outside his office and hastened toward him.

"Mornin', ladies." The sheriff tipped his hat.

"Good morning, Martin. Karl is anxious to see Logan. Could you tell us if he is still at Dr. Fischer's?" Johanna avoided looking directly at Koenig.

"No, he moved back to the hotel a few days ago. Says he's comin' along fine." The sheriff's face was devoid of expression, but his eyes glinted with amusement.

Karl assisted Gustav with the wagon and horses before joining the womenfolk on the boardwalk. Johanna and Karl entered the hotel lobby and climbed the stairs to the second floor. Gathering her courage, she knocked at the door. It swung open, and Logan stood before them. He was wearing Levis and a blue shirt that emphasized the color of his eyes. Pale and thinner by several pounds, he was still the most handsome man she had ever seen.

"Johanna!" His face broke into a smile.

"Hello, Logan. How are you?"

"I'm fine." He noticed Karl standing behind her. "Hello, Karl." He stepped back. "Please come in."

The room faced the street and ran the width of the building. A deep blue velvet settee and a pair of chairs divided the room into two areas. A floral rug in shades of blue and rose covered the polished wood floor. Johanna avoided looking at the other end of the room with its big four-poster bed.

"Please sit down." Logan motioned toward the sitting area.

Johanna hesitated before taking a seat on the settee. Karl followed and sat down beside her. Logan seated himself across from them. He and Johanna looked at each other, but neither of them spoke.

Karl seemed unaware of the tension as he gazed in awe at the room's opulence. Turning to Logan, he swallowed hard and said, "Ranger Delaney, I come to thank you for saving my life. And to tell you I'm sorry I acted so bad before."

Logan was silent for long moment before he spoke. "I was tracking Joe Greene, the outlaw who kidnapped you. It was better if you believed I was a bounty hunter."

Johanna watched the exchange between Logan and her son. "Karl, would you like to visit with Logan while Aunt Maggie, Heidi and I do some shopping?"

"Is that all right with you, sir?" Karl's eyes danced with anticipation.

"Of course, and why don't you call me Logan?"

Johanna rose, and Logan followed her to the door. "Come down to the lobby in a little while, Karl. You don't want to tire Logan out."

"I'm fine, Johanna," Logan assured her. "Doc says I can ride out to your place next week." Lowering his voice, he continued, "We need to talk." Blue eyes searched hazel ones.

Johanna wanted to touch him, assure herself he was recovering, but she knew she didn't dare. She clenched her hands tightly at her sides. "Take care of yourself, Logan."

She found Maggie and Heidi sitting in the lobby with Jane Reynolds. "Mrs. DuPree and I have been getting acquainted," Jane said.

"I've enjoyed visiting with you, Mrs. Reynolds." Maggie's hazel eyes sparkled with pleasure.

"Please call me Jane."

"And you must call Maggie."

"Mama, where is Karl?" Heidi looked toward the stairway.

"He's visiting with Logan."

"How is Logan?" Maggie asked.

Johanna frowned. "He says he's fine, but he has lost weight and he's too pale."

"I think that's to be expected, Johanna," Jane said. "He was gravely wounded."

"I know." Not wanting to discuss Logan any further, Johanna thought of the shopping she had mentioned. Amanda's shop was next door and Maggie loved fashion. What better way to spend the time?

"Maggie, would you like to see Amanda's shop while we're waiting for Karl?"

"Oh, yes, that would be a real treat."

"Johanna, may I borrow Heidi for a little while?" Jane asked. "We can have refreshments in the dining room."

"Mama, may I, please?" Heidi's eyes were shining, and she fidgeted from excitement. Johanna felt a stab of guilt. The little girl had few pleasures in her young life.

"It's kind of you to invite her, Jane."

"I must admit my reasons are selfish. She's a very special little girl. And please join us when you leave Amanda's shop." Jane smiled and held out her hand. Heidi accepted it without hesitation, and the two started toward the dining room.

Amanda's shop was small, but it was tastefully decorated. The color scheme of pale blue, rose and ivory lent an air of elegance to the atmosphere. As the sisters entered, the silver bell tinkled, and Amanda came from the back of the building. She was immaculately groomed, and her shining auburn hair and milk white skin were complemented by her green and white flowered dimity dress. Her eyes widened slightly, but she gave no other sign that Johanna's presence was anything more than an ordinary occurrence.

"Johanna, Mrs. DuPree, how nice to see you."

"I wanted Maggie to see your shop, Amanda. She wondered if you kept up with the fashions in this part of the country," Johanna teased.

"I know you do." Maggie smiled at Amanda. "You always wear the latest styles."

"Thank you. I feel I should live up to my advertising. Come, let me show you around."

For the next few minutes, Johanna and Maggie were treated to viewing the lovely items on display and Amanda's colorful description of the dressmaking business. Having shopped from St. Louis to San Francisco during her marriage, Maggie was impressed.

"The sewing room is in the rear. Would you like to see it?"

"Oh, yes. Johanna has been teaching me to sew, and I find I enjoy it."

A large portion of the building was devoted to the workroom. A cutting table, two sewing machines, a desk, several dainty chairs and small tables offered the clientele a place to rest and browse through the pattern books. Shelves on the walls held bolts of material and racks of ribbon, thread and other kinds of trim. Pink- and white-checked curtains draped a large window in the west wall. A pretty young Mexican woman was working at one of the sewing machines.

"Johanna, you know Rosa Perez," Amanda said. "Rosa, this is Johanna's sister, Mrs. DuPree. Rosa is my right hand. I don't know what I would do without her." Amanda's smile and voice revealed genuine affection for the young woman.

Rosa acknowledged the introduction with a shy smile and soft voice.

"The shop is small," Amanda admitted, "but I have a steady clientele. In fact, I have several ladies from San Antonio who come for fittings a twice a year. They usually make it a holiday and stay at the hotel for a few days."

"It's such a lovely place," Maggie enthused, fingering a bolt of rich green silk.

*

When the sisters returned to the hotel, Karl was sitting with Heidi and the Reynoldses in the dining room. The children were enjoying cookies and lemonade. Karl asked to be excused so that he might visit with Henry.

* * *

Logan lay propped up in bed, his mind focused on Johanna. Her visit had held a piquant quality. He had been happy to see her, but her presence had frustrated him to no end. God, how he had wanted to take her in his arms and kiss her. His whole body ached when he thought of touching her soft skin. He cursed and forced the thoughts from his mind.

Karl's wide eyes and animated expression flickered across Logan's consciousness. The boy had wanted to know all about Logan's experiences as a Ranger. He could see Karl was developing a case of hero worship and grinned thinking of his former hostility. Logan's amusement turned to bitter speculation. *When you come right down to it, there's not a lot of difference between a Ranger and a bounty hunter. Both hunt down their prey and often result to killing. One just carries a badge that makes it legal.*

* * *

The two men left Eagle Pass at first light, riding in a northeasterly direction. Back tracking would be risky but they needed money, and their chances of waylaying a lone traveler or attacking an isolated settler would be better. The older man's face was covered with a heavy stubble of salt and pepper beard, and his features beneath the brim his black hat were hard and lined.

His companion, a tall lanky young man with stringy yellow hair and a mustache, spurred his horse impatiently. "I still think we should try to find out if'n they kilt Joe," he whined.

"You said you thought that Ranger feller was the same one that yanked you out a that flash flood awhile back. If it was, don't you figger you owe 'im?" The older man reached in his shirt pocket for the makings.

The younger man's face colored, and he stared between his horse's ears. "I guess so. But that don't mean we cain't check on Joe."

"I seen him go down, Bud." Sims licked the edge of the paper before sticking the cigarette in the corner of his mouth. "'Course, they could a jist winged 'im, but I don't think so. Hawkins and Bennett was carryin' money bags, and if they wasn't kilt, they'll wind up in Huntsville." He struck a match against his pant leg and held it to the end of the crumpled white tube. "Anyways, we cain't ride into Meirsville to find out. It's too risky."

"Hell, Sims, we gotta do somethin'. Joe's our friend. Maybe we could sneak in there without anybody spottin' us."

"Kid, I been on the dark side of the law fur a long time." Sims inhaled a lungful of smoke and let it stream through his nostrils. "You don't have friends, jist fellers you ride with. When trouble comes, you're on your own. There ain't any way out fur me, but you could go to Californee and make a new start. If you go lookin' for Joe Greene or that Ranger, you'll jist buy yourself the end of a rope."

CHAPTER FIFTEEN

When Johanna visited Will's father, he urged her to marry Will as soon as possible. She tried to discourage him. Whether or not she had a future with Logan, he had awakened feelings she never knew existed. Perhaps those feelings would intensify or fade, but either way she could not marry Will. Mr. DeVore joined Johanna and Will for the noonday meal, but the effort cost him a great deal. It saddened her to think she would probably never see him alive again.

They were into the countryside and the road was deserted. Will pulled the buggy into a grove of trees. He turned to Johanna and reached for her hand. "Do you remember how it was between us, Johanna? Why did you let your father keep us apart?"

The anguish in his voice cut into Johanna's heart. She knew Will cared for her, but she had not realized the depth of his feelings. "I'm sorry, Will. Poppa would have disowned me if I had married you. Just like he did Maggie when she ran away. I couldn't face that."

Johanna reached out and touched his cheek, much as she would have Karl. But Karl was boy and Will was man. He pulled her against him, and his lips crushed hers in a bruising kiss. Johanna stiffened, but Will tightened his hold and continued to ravage her mouth. Behind closed eyelids, Johanna saw a pair of sapphire eyes and heard the words, *I want you so bad, Johanna.*

Will's hand was on her breast now. She struggled to free herself but he seemed oblivious to her resistance. She wrenched her mouth from his. "No, Will! Stop. Stop this instant!"

Will's body went rigid then his arms dropped away, and he slumped down in the seat. "Oh, God! Johanna, I'm sorry. I don't know what came over me. It's just that I've loved you for so long."

Will's kiss had been nothing like Logan's. Johanna felt only Will's wet mouth pressing against her lips. The kisses she shared with Logan were fire and ice. Her body was consumed in flames while her mind tried to freeze her emotions. His hands on her body made her feel warm and tingly. Outlaw, bounty hunter, Ranger, it made no difference. Logan Delaney had breached her defenses and laid claim to her heart.

"Johanna, say something," Will pleaded. "You don't know how bad I feel. I promise it won't happen again."

"I'm sure it won't," Johanna said, her voice cool and controlled.

With a pleading look, Will guided the buggy back onto the road. When they entered the lane to the farm, Heidi came running to meet them, her long braids bouncing and her eyes dancing with excitement. "Mama, Mama, Logan brought Karl a pony."

Johanna's heart fluttered as her eyes searched the barnyard. She glanced toward the house and saw Maggie standing near the door. Johanna took a deep breath and looked at Will from the corner of her eye. Did he suspect her feelings for the handsome Ranger?

Heidi, unable to contain her excitement, grabbed Johanna's hand. "Come on, Mama. Come and see Karl's pony."

"Logan is in the barn with Karl and Gustav," Maggie called.

"Let's see what this all about. Would you like to come along, Will?"

"Yeah. Haven't see Delaney since the shoot out. Guess he had a pretty close call."

Logan came out of the barn leading a piebald horse with Karl perched in the saddle. When the boy spotted his mother, his face broke into a big grin. Logan brought the horse to a halt, looked at Johanna and Will, and then urged the horse forward. Logan led the gelding to the fence and looped the reins around a post.

"Howdy, Delaney."

The two men shook hands.

"Looks like you're makin' a good recovery," Will said.

"Yeah," Logan answered.

Her eyes filled with concern, Johanna surveyed Logan from head to toe. He looked tired and the fine lines around his eyes were more pronounced. His black clothing emphasized his faded tan. The ever-present revolver in the tied down holster brought the memories flooding back, and Johanna shivered thinking about his near brush with death.

"Ma!" Karl yelled. "Logan wants to give me this horse. It belonged to Joe Greene. Is it all right for me to keep to him?"

"I don't know, Karl." Should she let Karl accept the gift? Could she deny him every farm boy's dream, a saddle horse of his own?

His voice curt, Logan responded, "The county was paying for his keep, Johanna, and they're glad to get rid of him." His eyes dark and piercing, Logan's features showed no emotion.

"Are you willing to take care of him? He will be your responsibility, you know."

"Yes, Ma, I'll take real good care of him," Karl promised.

"All right, you may keep him." The delight in her son's eyes brought a lump to Johanna's throat.

Maggie spoke for the first time. "I have supper on the stove. I'd better see to it. Heidi, will you help me?"

"Yes, ma'am." Turning to her mother, she added, "Mama, Logan is going to bring me a present the next time he comes." She followed Maggie into the house.

Johanna shifted her gaze to Logan and found his eyes pinned on her. Will was watching them, and she had to say something to ease the awkward situation. "Gentlemen, can you stay for supper?"

"It would be a pleasure," Will answered first.

Logan's features tightened, then relaxed. "You know I wouldn't turn down one of your delicious meals."

He smiled, and Johanna felt her heart drop into her stomach. "Good. I need to help Maggie. We'll call you when it's ready." She forced a smile and hurried into the house.

As they put the finishing touches on the meal, Maggie said, "Logan was upset when he found out you were with Will. He didn't say anything, but I spent too many years reading faces not to be able to tell."

"I don't know what do, Maggie. Logan said he wanted to talk with me, but..." Her voice trailed off.

MARY LOU HAGEN

"You two need to get things settled."

The atmosphere was strained during the meal. Johanna had little appetite and toyed with her food. Logan and Will exchanged polite conversation, but Karl and Heidi could hardly contain their excitement. Johanna threatened to withhold dessert before they quieted.

While Johanna and Maggie cleaned the kitchen, the men went into the yard to smoke. Logan and Will walked to the barnyard fence.

"How long have you been with the Rangers, Delaney?" Will leaned against the top rail.

"I rode with a Special Ranger Unit until the Rangers were officially reorganized the first of the year."

"Guess you move around a lot."

"Yeah, some."

"Be hard on a family man." Will's tone was casual.

Logan turned to DeVore, his eyes searching the other man's features. "Seems there's risk in about any work a man does."

Hoof beats sounded in the distance, and a horse and rider pounded down the lane. As the rider drew closer, Will hurried forward.

"Will, your pa done took a turn for the worse and Miz Jenkins sent me after you while Cummins went to fetch Doc Fischer."

"What is this about a present for Heidi?" Johanna questioned Logan after Will left.

Logan lowered his voice. "It's a doll. I couldn't give Karl the horse and not give Heidi a gift. I didn't bring it today because Miss Blair is sewing clothes for it."

The thought flitted through Johanna's mind that she could have sewn the clothing for the doll. She pushed it aside. "That's very thoughtful of you. But why did you choose that outlaw's horse for Karl? Besides, the children are not used to such luxuries."

"I would hardly call them luxuries, Johanna. A horse is a necessity, and little girls and dolls go together. As for why I wanted Karl to have Greene's horse, that's kind of hard to explain." Logan paused, then continued. "Sometimes a man needs to prove something to himself.

Karl had a rough time when Greene and his gang took him. Besides being afraid for his life, he feels guilty that he let the outlaws capture him. Offering him the horse that belonged to Greene gave him a chance to face his guilt and prove that he's not to blame for being abducted."

"*Yah.*" Gustav nodded in agreement. He stood up and knocked the ashes from his pipe. "It has been a long day, and I am going to bed. Logan, I am glad you are recovered. Will you come again before you go to Waco?"

"Yeah. Karl needs a few more lessons, and I want to bring Heidi's doll."

"*Goot.* I will say good night now." He disappeared into the darkness.

Karl and Heidi had whispered and giggled among themselves while the adults conversed. Now Heidi nudged her brother. "Go ahead, Karl. Ask Logan. Go ahead, ask him."

Karl scowled. "We don't know what that outlaw called the horse, but I been thinkin' 'bout a name for him. Is it all right if I call him Ranger?"

Logan grinned and ruffled the boy's hair. "I'd take that as a compliment, Karl."

"See? I told you he wouldn't mind," Karl told Heidi. "She wanted to name him Prince," he said, an expression of distaste on his face.

"Well, Prince is a nice name," Heidi defended her choice.

"Children," Johanna admonished, "I know it's been an exciting day, but it's time for bed now."

"I'll see to them," Maggie offered. "Come along, kids. Good night, Logan."

Logan assured the children he would return soon, and they followed Maggie into the house. The silence stretched out with neither Johanna nor Logan sure how to fill it.

"I need to get back to town."

"It's late. Why don't you stay the night?" As soon as the words were out of her mouth, Johanna knew she had said the wrong thing. Thank goodness it was dark and he couldn't see her face.

"I don't think that's a very good idea. I'll round up *Él Campeon* and be on my way." Logan moved toward the barnyard.

Moonlight filtered through the trees, and the light breeze cooled Johanna's flushed cheeks. She watched Logan blend into the darkness and thought about the dangers he faced in his work. A tremor ran down her spine. Someday there would somebody a little faster or Logan would get careless. How could a woman live with such danger? Her chest felt tight and her palms were sweaty. Every nerve in her body felt strained to the breaking point. Logan had made no further reference to the talk he mentioned earlier. Johanna had a feeling the reason had something to do with Will. It was not the ladylike thing to do, but she would bring it up herself.

Logan looped the stallion's reins over the fence. Before she could find the words, he made it easy for her. "Johanna, we should talk."

"Yes," she answered, her voice soft and low. She took a step closer, then another. His arms reached out and closed around her. As soft as the touch of a butterfly, he brushed his lips across her mouth. The thought of his near brush with death washed over her. He was lucky to be alive. She put her arms around him and rested her palms flat against his back.

Logan groaned deep in his throat, and his mouth plundered hers. Johanna returned the kiss and moved her hands down his back. She felt his muscles tighten under her hesitant exploration. He lifted his head, his breathing ragged. He did not release her, and she made no effort to free herself.

In the pale light from the moon, his eyes gleamed like obsidian. He relaxed his hold and, keeping one arm around her, touched her cheek with his other hand. He tipped her chin and kissed her again. Johanna knew she should stop him, but she was powerless to do so. Every thought of proper behavior fled. Her body felt boneless, and she clung to him for support.

He brought his hand to her breast and cupped the fullness in his palm. His body pressed against her, Johanna felt the hard ridge in his trousers. She felt warm and giddy and light-headed all at the same time.

Logan's mouth and tongue continued their assault. *Él Campeon* snorted and whinnied until the sounds penetrated Logan's passion-fogged senses. He released her. His hand went to the gun on his hip in a gesture so automatic that Johanna held her breath. His eyes scanned the darkness. "Get down," he whispered. "I'll take a look around."

Revolver drawn, Logan quickly disappeared in the darkness. *Él Campeon* snorted again and was answered with a loud whinny. The sound had come from behind the barn. Logan vaulted the fence as a gunshot exploded in the night air. Dropping into a crouch, he ran to the barn. Flattening himself against the building, he waited, his ears attuned for the slightest sound. "I know you're in there. Throw your gun out first and come out with your hands up."

There was no reply. Logan caught a slight movement from the corner of his eye and moved around the side of the barn. He called again. "All right, we'll do it the hard way." He fired a round of shots, hoping that all of the animals were in their stalls for the night.

A muffled cry came from behind the barn. Logan started forward but stumbled over an object laying his path. He caught his balance just as the sound of hoof beats reached his ears. The unknown assailant was getting away. Logan hesitated. He didn't have much chance of catching the fellow in the dark, and no doubt Johanna was frightened half out of her wits by now.

"Logan! Logan!"

He reached her in seconds and gathered her in his arms. "I'm all right. He got away, but I think I winged him."

"Oh, Logan." Johanna clung to him, her legs refusing to support her. "This is what I've been afraid of. Your work is too dangerous. You will always be hunting outlaws, and they will be looking for revenge."

"Johanna! Are you all right?" Maggie came running out of the house.

Logan released Johanna and stepped back. "She's fine. Everything is under control."

Gustav joined Maggie, and they hurried to Johanna's side. "What happened?" Maggie asked.

Logan related the event. It took more than a little effort to convince Maggie the danger was over before she and Gustav returned to their beds.

The excitement over, Logan broached the subject upper most in his mind. "What does Will DeVore mean to you, Johanna?"

"Will? I've known him all life. Why?"

"I've tried to see you twice, and you were with him both times. Is he courting you?"

"He has asked permission to call on me."

"What did you tell him?"

"I haven't given him an answer. His father is gravely ill. In fact he's dying, and I went to visit him."

"I see. Have you decided what your answer is going be?"

"Yes."

Logan waited. "Well?"

Johanna's temper rose. She resented Logan's questions. He had not declared himself. "I don't have to explain my decisions to you."

Logan took a step backward. "No, you don't, but I thought there was something between us. I guess I was wrong."

Johanna tried to see his face, but it was a blur in the darkness. She took a deep breath to calm her racing thoughts.

"What do you think is between us, Logan?"

"I've never felt this way about a woman before," he answered, his voice ragged. "But I think I'm in love with you." He moved toward her.

Johanna released her pent-up breath. Something inside gave way, and she went into his arms as he reached for her. She could feel his chest heave as he breathed deeply, then his lips came down hard on hers and all thought fled.

Logan was all leashed power and passion as he tightened the embrace and kissed her. "Johanna," he murmured against her lips. She returned the kiss with a intensity she didn't know she possessed. His hands roamed her body, lingering here and there, touched and explored. She felt his heart pounding and knew her own was beating just as hard.

"I want you so bad I ache all over, but not like this. You deserve more, much more. Will you marry me, Johanna?"

Johanna gasped. Had Logan just asked her to marry him? Her heart threatened to jump out of her chest, and she couldn't breathe enough air into her lungs. Her speech muscles froze. As the silence lengthened,

Logan's passion cooled and he released her.

"My first thought is to say yes, but there's much more to consider than my feelings. I need time to sort things out."

"We don't have a lot of time. I know you're concerned about the children, but Karl and I have mended our fences. Heidi is a sweet little girl, and I think she likes me."

"She does," Johanna replied as she clasped his hands. Her mind was torn between her feelings for him and what life would be like if she married him. The incident that had just occurred was fresh in her mind. He faced constant danger, and they would be separated for long periods of time. Could she live with the worry? Could their love survive such obstacles?

In a sudden move, Logan released her and stepped away. When he spoke, his voice was harsh. "Evidently you have a lot of doubts. Maybe DeVore is a better prospect."

Johanna's eyes rounded in disbelief. Did Logan think she could marry Will after the way she had responded to his advances? "You're being unfair, Logan. Do you realize I know very little about you? Where you come from, your family, nothing at all. You came along, hiding your true identity. You let me believe you were an outlaw, then rode off to God knows where and expected me to be waiting for you. The next time I saw you my son was kidnapped, and then you were wounded. You almost died! And look at what just happened. It's too much for me to deal with all at once."

Logan stood motionless for a moment. When he spoke, his voice held no emotion. "All right. I'll give you time, but I'm leaving for Waco in a few days." He strode to the stallion, mounted, urged the horse forward and was swallowed up by the night.

CHAPTER SIXTEEN

The silver bell tinkled as Logan entered Amanda's shop. She smiled when she recognized her customer. *Lord, she's a beauty.* He removed his hat, his eyes filed with admiration. "Good morning, Miss Blair."

"Good morning, Mr. Delaney. I just finished one of the dresses for Heidi's doll. The wardrobe will be completed in a day or two. Would you like to see what I've done?"

Logan's white teeth flashed in a grin. "I'm afraid I don't know much about ladies' fashions. I trust your judgment."

"That's very kind of you." She returned his grin with a bright smile.

"Why don't you call me Logan? I think we've been properly introduced. And the doll isn't the only reason I came here this morning." Logan's hands tightened on his hat brim. "Would you permit me to call on you, Miss Blair?"

A surprised look appeared on Amanda's face for instant. She recovered, smiled and answered, "I don't see why that would not be acceptable. And please call me Amanda."

She pointed to the back of the shop. "I'm afraid the only refreshment I can offer you is a cup of tea."

"Don't apologize. I've been known to imbibe the brew on occasion," Logan teased. "But I'll pass this time."

"Then I'd like to invite you to have supper with Mother and me tomorrow evening. Say, about six o'clock?"

Logan hid his surprise. "I would be honored, Amanda."

"We'll be looking forward to seeing you."

"I'm looking forward to it, too."

The Blairs lived a short distance off the main street. The house was built of stone and had a well-cared-for look. It was furnished with heavy pieces in fine woods Logan surmised must have come from their home in Boston. The overall result was one of quiet elegance.

Logan noted the snow-white linen, fine china, silver and crystal— rare treats for him these days. The roast chicken, buttered vegetables and fluffy yeast rolls, followed by a generous slice of pecan pie, took his memory back to the time he spent in Virginia before the war.

Amanda's mother was a gentle lady. She had reared her daughter in the same manner, although necessity had forced Amanda to become independent. Logan sensed the Blairs' curiosity through their polite conversation.

"Have you ever been to Boston, Mr. Delaney?" Mrs. Blair asked when they were seated in the parlor after supper.

"No, ma'am. But I went to school in Virginia before the war." Logan handled the demitasse with ease.

"But you are Texan, are you not?" Mrs. Blair asked.

"Yes, ma'am. My mother died when I was born, and my father had promised her he would see that I got an education. She had relatives in Virginia and I was sent there." He set his empty cup on the table beside him.

"Mrs. Blair, I would like to escort you and Amanda to church on Sunday. Perhaps you would take dinner with me at the hotel afterward?" He held out his hand for his hat, which Amanda had retrieved from the hall table.

"That's very kind of you, Mr. Delaney." The older woman looked her at daughter. Amanda nodded and smiled. "We'll be happy to accept your invitation," Mrs. Blair replied.

* * *

Her eyes wide with shock, Johanna's face paled as she watched Logan escort Amanda and her mother into the church. She stumbled, and Maggie grabbed her arm. She felt a deep pain in her chest, and her mind went blank.

"Johanna," Maggie whispered. Her grip tightened on Johanna's arm.

"Don't let them see how you feel. Didn't you say the banker is interested in Amanda?"

"Yes," Johanna answered. Numb with shock, she tried to clear the fog from her mind. "Her year of mourning was up some time ago, but she keeps him dangling."

Johanna could not remember a single detail of the service. As the congregation lingered in the churchyard, it was inevitable that Johanna and Logan would meet. She struggled with the emotions twisting her insides into knots. The group exchanged pleasantries. Not a flicker of emotion crossed his face. He was polite but distant. It was if they had never shared the intimate moments in the past.

"Logan, Logan," Karl and Heidi called out as they ran to his side. "When are you comin' to give me some more lessons?" Karl asked, his eyes dancing with excitement.

"Is my surprise ready yet?" Heidi piped up.

"Whoa, there. One at a time." Logan grinned at their youthful enthusiasm. "I'll be coming out to work with you soon, Karl. And Heidi, I'll bring your surprise. That is, if it's all right with your mother." His tone impersonal, he glanced at Johanna.

"Of course. You're welcome anytime," Johanna answered in the same tone.

The moment stretched into an awkward silence. Then, in a flurry of farewells, the group parted. Logan saw George Taylor approaching. The two men had met only once since the robbery, and Taylor had expressed his appreciation for the return of the bank's money. He tipped his hat to the ladies as he nodded in Logan's direction. "Delaney."

"Taylor," Logan matched the banker's brief greeting. Hell, he didn't blame the man for being curt. Taylor's interest in Amanda was common knowledge.

"Ladies." Taylor again tipped his hat and without another word strode off.

The buggy Logan rented from the livery, pulled by a gentle brown mare, responded well to his commands, and he found himself enjoying the leisurely pace. He glanced at Amanda from the corner of his eye. She was lovely in a pale green organdy gown. To his surprise, Logan had found her straightforward, with none of the coquette common in beautiful women. In spite of her beauty and charm, the spark that ignited when was he was near Johanna was missing. Perhaps if he knew her better...

"Amanda, is there an understanding between you and Taylor?"

"No, not really. My father was a minor partner in the bank, and George and I became friends. We have attended social functions together, and he usually escorts us to church. He has mentioned marriage, but I wanted to get established in the shop and prove that I could support Mother and myself. The business is doing well, and I'm enjoying my independence." Her smile was dazzling.

Logan nodded. "I can understand that. I guess I feel the same way about the Rangers. My father would like nothing better than for me to come back home and settle down."

Amanda's light laughter tinkled much like the silver bell above her shop door. "I guess it's natural for parents to want their children settled in a good marriage."

"I don't think you need to worry about that. A beautiful woman like you must have lots of offers."

Amanda turned her gaze full on Logan, and her green eyes lost some of their sparkle. "No. The war took so many fine young men."

Both were silent, thinking of the past.

"What about you, Logan? I thought perhaps you and Johanna Bauer...I'm sorry. You know how gossip circulates."

Logan hesitated. What could he say? He liked Amanda and did not want to deceive her. "I admit I have feelings for Johanna, but there are too many obstacles. You probably know Will DeVore has asked her to marry him."

Amanda laughed and shook her head. "Oh, that's an old story, Logan. Johanna could have married Will years ago. Perhaps she has no desire to remarry. She seems to be managing quite well."

Logan made no comment, and Amanda changed the subject. "Would you like to pick up the doll tomorrow?" Without waiting for a reply, she continued, "How do you plan to wrap it?"

A grin creased Logan's features. "You know, I haven't thought about that."

"I have an idea that might work." Amanda gave him a mischievous smile, and Logan saw another side of her very proper behavior. *It's a damn shame a man can't control who he falls in love with.*

The sun had made its way westward, and the light breeze, which had taken the edge off the heat, began to die. It would soon be suppertime.

"Would you like to walk a bit before we start back?"

"That would be nice."

Logan assisted Amanda from the buggy, and they walked to a huge tree with a wide trunk. Logan turned to face Amanda, leaning back against the rough bark. She removed a lacy white handkerchief from her reticule and lightly fanned her face. Logan watched her, his eyes turning a dark blue. She looked at him and smiled. He felt a stir of desire, straightened and reached for her hands. "Amanda, you are very beautiful."

She lowered her eyes but did not pull her hands from his. He took her in his arms, careful to be gentle. She didn't speak but continued to look at him, her green eyes wide in her pale face. Logan touched his lips to hers.

Amanda stiffened, then with a touch as light as a feather, she returned the kiss. Logan realized at once that Amanda had never known the heat of passion. Her kiss was as innocent as a child's. He wondered what would happen if he unlocked all those bottled-up emotions. Would there be fire under that auburn hair? Logan's desire escalated, but it was not the all-consuming passion he felt for Johanna. He broke the kiss and, still holding her in his arms, said, "You are truly a fine lady, Amanda."

Amanda remained still, her eyes searching his face. She stepped out of his embrace. "I think we should start back now. Mother will be worried."

Logan came out of the hotel just as Amanda was unlocking her shop.

He held the door for her and she stepped inside.

"Everything is in the back."

Logan followed Amanda to the workroom, amazed to see what was necessary for the operation of the small business. Amanda had brains as well as beauty.

"Could you lift that down for me, please?" Amanda pointed to a small trunk on the top shelf.

Logan reached for the trunk and set it on the cutting table.

"One of my suppliers sent it to me for display purposes, but I haven't used it for some time. The doll and its wardrobe should fit in the trunk beautifully."

"I'd be glad to pay you for it."

"Oh, no. There was no cost to me. I would like to give it to Heidi. I think she'll like it."

"I'm sure she will." Logan examined the trunk. It was crafted of dark wood, hand-carved and bound in brass. Amanda folded the doll's wardrobe and placed it in the trunk. Logan marveled at the tiny garments. There were dresses in several colors with bonnets to match and dainty lace-trimmed undergarments.

"I don't know much about such things, but it looks like you did a fine job. Heidi is really going to be excited."

"I enjoyed making the clothing. Heidi is a very sweet little girl. Let me get the doll."

When Amanda produced the doll, Logan wondered if Johanna would approve of his choice. It was an elegant creation with head and arms of French bisque, and a body constructed of fine leather with gussets at the hips and knees and a swivel neck. The doll's long blond hair was fashioned into ringlets framing a face with rosy cheeks and eyes of bright cobalt blue glass. Tiny gold earrings gleamed in the soft light.

Logan settled the bill just as Rosa entered the shop to begin her day. Amanda introduced her, and Logan was reminded of the two Mexican boys who had taken care of his horse and polished his boots. He wondered if Rosa might be their mother.

Logan realized there could be a problem transporting Heidi's gift. *Él Campeon* was inclined to be skittish and might object to having the trunk tied behind the saddle. An idea began to form. He could rent a buggy from the livery. Suddenly, he realized he and Johanna had never gone anywhere together. Maybe he could talk her into a buggy ride.

"Logan?"

Logan brought his gaze into focus to see Amanda watching him with a puzzled look on her face. "I'm sorry. I was trying to figure out how to transport Heidi's doll, but I think I've got it worked out." He picked up the trunk and walked toward the front of the shop.

Amanda followed. Before he reached the door, she spoke in a soft voice. "About yesterday. It wouldn't work, would it?"

Logan swallowed uneasily while he searched for an answer. What did you say to a beautiful woman who was everything a man could want but didn't set your heart to pounding or your body to aching?

Amanda smiled, and Logan saw a flash of regret in her eyes. "It's all right, Logan. I've been doing a lot of thinking about my future. I love the shop and being independent, but it doesn't take the place of a husband and children. George and I have much in common. He loves me, and I am quite fond of him."

"Then you plan to marry him?"

"Yes. I would appreciate it if you didn't mention it to anyone. We have a lot of details to work out before we can announce our engagement. And Logan, please don't give up on Johanna."

"I don't plan to. I wish you every happiness, Amanda. Taylor is a lucky man."

"Thank you." She held out her hand. "Good bye, Logan."

Logan placed a soft kiss on her palm. "Good bye, Amanda."

After leaving the trunk in his room, Logan started for the livery stable. Thoughts of confronting Johanna made him edgy. As he passed Stein's saloon, he admitted he could use a drink.

Two men were standing at the bar, and he recognized Will DeVore and one of his hands that had ridden with the posse. Logan sensed DeVore was agitated about something. Logan ordered whiskey. As he took a swallow, he watched the man's reflection in the mirror behind the bar. DeVore's expression was grim, and his skin was slightly flushed.

He's already had a few drinks. From under lowered lids, Logan examined DeVore for any sign of a gunshot wound. He saw nothing to indicate Will had been the would-be assassin. Of course, he had a sizable crew, but Logan did not believe any of them were hired guns.

"Thought you was leavin' town, Delaney. Guess you found a couple of reasons to stay on."

Logan's eyes narrowed. "You care to explain that, DeVore?"

Will laughed but there was no humor it. "Heard you was squirin' Amanda Blair around. I thought you was sweet on Johanna Bauer."

Logan placed his half-finished whiskey on the bar and turned to face DeVore. "I don't consider that any of your business."

The cowpuncher at Will's side spoke up. "Remember, Boss, he's a Ranger."

"That don't mean nothin' to me. He's makin' a fool outta Johanna." His hand crept to the butt of his revolver.

"Don't *you* be a fool, Will." Emile came from the other end of the bar and stood in front of DeVore. "You don't stand a chance against him. Besides, I don't want trouble here. Take your argument outside."

DeVore's hand dropped to his side. "I'm not afraid of you, Delaney, but I got sense enough not to draw against you. There's other ways of settlin' this."

"Yeah, like bushwhacking a man in the dark."

"I don't know what you're talkin' 'bout. Whenever I set out to even the score, I do it to a man's face. And I'm about to beat the hell outta you."

Without a word, Logan untied the leather thong that held the holster against his thigh. With nimble fingers, he unbuckled his gun belt and laid it on the bar. He turned and headed for the door. DeVore followed.

"Wait, Boss. Give me your gun," the cowhand coaxed.

Will shook his head as if to clear it from the effects of the liquor. He fumbled with his gun belt and handed it to the man.

Logan was already outside. DeVore plunged through the swinging doors, his eyes wild and his face scarlet. Logan stepped off the boardwalk into the street, and DeVore, close at his heels, lunged after him.

"Damn you, Delaney! Johanna shoulda been mine a long time ago. Now you come along and try to take her away from me."

"If you're determined to settle this, DeVore, let's have at it." Logan, his arms hanging loosely at his sides, stepped forward.

Will charged and caught Logan around the shoulders. Logan shrugged him off. As he regained his balance, DeVore brought his right fist up and punched Logan in the mouth. Blood spurted from his split lip. Logan swayed, the blow catching him off guard. He recovered and threw a hard right to Will's jaw. DeVore's head snapped back, and he teetered on his boot heels. Then he lunged forward and put his weight behind a jab to Logan's chest. Logan's wound was tender, and the blow sent shards of pain radiating through his body. He sucked in his breath. Then his anger exploded. With all the strength he could muster, he sunk his fist deep in DeVore's gut, and the man doubled over.

"What the hell's goin' on here?" Sheriff Koenig's voice roared above the murmurs of the small crowd that had gathered.

DeVore straightened up, and Logan backed away. Blood still trickled from the Ranger's lip. DeVore's jaw was swelling, and he would have a dandy bruise in a few hours.

"It's a personal matter, Sheriff," Logan told the lawman.

"Personal or not, I don't cotton to public brawls. This fight is over." Motioning to the crowd, he added, "Go about your business, folks. The excitement's over." He turned back to DeVore. "Will, it might be a good idea if you headed toward the Circle D."

A tension-filled silence followed. DeVore looked at the sheriff before turning his gaze on Logan. Without a word to either man, DeVore picked up his hat and crossed the street to the mercantile. The cowhand followed, carrying DeVore's gun belt.

"I left my gun at the bar," Logan told Koenig. He untied the bandanna from around his neck and dabbed at his bloody lip. His chest still hurt from the punch DeVore had landed. *Lord!* His knees were weak.

Koenig followed Logan into the saloon.

Logan's fingers trembled as he buckled the gun belt around his waist. He left the rawhide thong dangle down his leg.

"Whiskey," he told Stein. "Can I buy you a drink, Sheriff?"

Koenig grinned. "No, thanks. It's a little too early for me."

Logan grimaced as the raw whiskey burned his lip. He downed the drink and set the glass on the bar. "I'm going back to the hotel. That little fracas was a bit rough." He managed a grin as he left the saloon.

The next morning found Logan in the rented buggy setting a brisk pace toward Johanna's farm. The trunk rested beside him on the seat. It was time he told her the truth about himself and what he had to offer her. Whether not Johanna accepted his proposal, he was leaving the Rangers. The thrill of chasing outlaws and renegade Comanches was waning, and more important, his father needed him at home.

When Logan reached the farm, he saw Maggie sitting in the yard. There was no sign of Johanna. His mind conjured up a vision of Will DeVore. Was she with him? Would DeVore tell her about the fight? Somehow he doubted it.

"Logan! What a nice surprise."

"Hello, Maggie. I brought Heidi's doll." He gestured toward the buggy.

Maggie's eyes widened, and she pointed toward his bruised lip. "What happened?"

With a rueful smile, Logan answered, "I had a slight problem with Will DeVore."

"Will! You mean you two fought over Johanna?"

"Will was drinking and accused me of trying to take Johanna away from him. Koenig broke it up before any real damage was done." Logan looked around the yard. "Where is Johanna?"

"She and Heidi went see Lily Straum and her new baby." Maggie took a step toward him. "Logan, I'm probably sticking my nose where it doesn't belong, but I'm only trying to protect Johanna. She took me in after Jack was killed, and I had no place to go. I don't want to see her get hurt." Maggie's voice faltered.

"I would never hurt Johanna, Maggie. Surely you know that."

"Yes, but you're all wrong for her. The kind of work you do, the way you live. There's Karl and Heidi to consider, too. She needs security for them as well as for herself."

"Don't you think that's for Johanna to decide?"

A faint blush colored Maggie's cheeks. "Poppa forced her to marry Josef. He was an old man. She doesn't have the vaguest idea what love is all about. She has never met anyone like you. You showed an interest in her and she was overwhelmed. All of a sudden she had two men proposing to her."

A frown marred Maggie's face. "Then you showed up at the church with Amanda Blair. That was a hard blow. Now she's confused and unhappy. Don't take advantage of her."

"You've got it all figured out, haven't you?"

"I don't mean to offend you. It's just that I'm trying to protect my sister."

"I understand, Maggie, but you know things are not always the way they seem."

Maggie opened her mouth to reply, but the sound of an approaching wagon distracted her.

CHAPTER SEVENTEEN

Johanna, with Heidi beside her on the wagon seat, drew near the farmhouse. A strange buggy was tied to the hitching post.

She scanned the yard and saw Logan and Maggie standing beneath the trees. Her stomach did a flip-flop and her mouth went dry.

"Mama, it's Logan," Heidi said. "I hope he brought my present." As soon as Johanna brought the wagon to a halt, Heidi jumped down and ran to him.

Johanna continued on into the barnyard. The few minutes it took Gustav to take charge of the horses and wagon gave Johanna time to compose herself. " Hello, Logan." She glanced at him and saw his bruised lip.

Herman Straum, Lily's husband, had witnessed the fight between Logan and Will. Although Herman was reluctant to talk about the incident, Johanna managed to learn that Will had accused Logan of trying steal her away from him. She was at once worried that Logan might have been injured and angry with Will for provoking the fight. She added embarrassment to her teeming emotions when Lily said she thought it was romantic that the two men fought over her honor. Thank goodness Heidi and Karl were outdoors playing with the Straum children.

"Johanna." Logan touched his hat brim. "I've brought Heidi's doll." He strode to the buggy, removed the trunk and placed it on one of the benches. "Go ahead, Heidi. Open it," he urged.

The little girl fumbled with the clasp and lifted the lid. Her eyes opened wide and her mouth formed a large O. She stared at the doll but did not touch it.

"There are lots of clothes in the trunk. Miss Blair made them and wanted you to have the trunk to put them in." Logan leaned closer with Johanna right behind him.

"Heidi is overwhelmed," Johanna said as she viewed the contents of the trunk. "She has never seen such a beautiful doll. Nor have I. Come and look, Maggie."

"It's beautiful," Maggie agreed. Turning away, she murmured, "I have some stew on the stove, and I'd better check on it."

"You haven't thanked Logan, Heidi. And you must write Amanda a thank you note for the trunk. Perhaps Logan will deliver it for you when he returns to town."

Heidi threw her arms around Logan's waist and hugged him. He patted the top of the little girl's head. Heidi took the doll and lifted it from the trunk. She caressed its face and smoothed its golden hair. Handing the doll to her mother, she examined the tiny garments. As she displayed each one, her dainty features glowed with delight.

Johanna watched the scene unfold with conflicting emotions. She was happy for her daughter, but the memory of Logan escorting Amanda into the church was uppermost in her mind. Every nerve in her body screamed to lash out at him.

Karl and Gustav emerged from the barn. "Logan's here," Karl yelled and ran toward them.

Heidi grabbed Karl's hand and pulled him forward. "Karl, come see what Logan brought me. It's the most beautiful doll in the whole world. Miss Blair made lots of pretty clothes for it."

"Doll! Huh! Ranger's a lot better than any old doll."

"Karl!" Johanna reprimanded her son.

"I'm sorry," the boy said. He scowled, and then his face brightened. "Logan, can you stay and work with me and Ranger? I been takin' real good care of him."

"I'm sure you have, Karl. And yes, I have time to work with you."

"Heidi, you should take your doll to the house," Johanna said. Courtesy demanded she invite Logan to have supper with them. "Logan, can you stay for supper?"

Before Logan could answer, Heidi and Karl chorused, "Please stay, Logan. Please stay for supper."

"Yes, I'd like that. And thank you for the invitation."

"You're welcome. I need to help Maggie. We'll call when it's ready." Johanna picked up the trunk and motioned Heidi toward the house.

"Let's get started with Ranger," Logan said.

"Johanna, since I have the use of a buggy, would you care to go for a ride?" Logan asked as she and Maggie joined the men in the yard after supper.

Was he going to tell her that he was courting Amanda? How could she stand the pain that was sure to come? Her emotions were already strained to the breaking point.

"May I play with my new doll, Mama?" Heidi spoke from the doorway.

Grateful for the interruption, Johanna replied, "You must handle it carefully. It's very delicate."

"Oh, I will, I promise. And, Mama, I've been thinking about a name for her. I'd like to call her Amanda. Do you think Miss Blair would mind?"

Johanna swallowed hard and managed to answer, "No, I don't think she will mind."

"I think she would be very pleased, Heidi," Logan added.

The short respite had given Johanna time to consider Logan's invitation. He had betrayed her and she wanted to know why. "About that buggy ride, Logan. I think it's a lovely idea. I'll get my shawl."

"Where does this road lead to?" Logan asked, pointing to a narrow dirt track.

"It goes through some fields and winds down to the river, quite a distance from here." Johanna sat erect beside him, her hands folded in her lap. She had left as much space as possible between them.

"Then we should be able to find some privacy."

Johanna did not answer. Logan guided the buggy off the road and into the trees. He tied the reins to a tree limb before assisting her from the buggy. The silence stretched between them, neither seeming to know how to begin.

"Johanna," Logan began. "I know I've hurt you and I'm sorry. I thought you were playing me against Will DeVore, and that made me angry. Because you've known him all your life and he can offer you security, I thought you were going to accept his proposal. Are you, Johanna? Are you going to marry him?"

Johanna drew a deep breath and tried to calm her ragged emotions. She was not going to marry Will, but she did not intend to tell Logan that. Let him have a dose of his own medicine.

"What difference does it make if I marry Will? Evidently you have decided you prefer Amanda's company to mine."

"No, Johanna. That's not true. There's nothing between Amanda and me. She's going to marry the banker."

"But she permitted you to call on her."

"Yes, but we both knew it was a mistake. She hasn't told Taylor yet. She likes being independent. Taylor won't permit her to keep the shop after they are married, and she kept putting him off."

Johanna felt as if a weight had been lifted from her shoulders. Her heart fluttered, and her breath caught in her throat. Without conscience thought, she reached out to him. "Oh, Logan, I thought I had lost you."

Logan took a step forward, and she was in his arms. He brushed the outline of her lips with gentle kiss. Johanna responded and felt him wince. She had forgotten about his bruised lip. Before she could pull away, he pressed her body tight against his, ran his hands over her shoulders and down her back. Her senses whirled, and she was lost in the nearness of him.

Logan broke the kiss and loosened his hold. "Johanna, we've got to stop now, or I won't be able to." His voice was husky and his breathing ragged.

Johanna's face flooded with color, and she could not meet his eyes. Staring at her feet, she spoke in a soft voice, "Would that be so terrible, Logan?"

Logan drew in a sharp breath. "Not for me, but you would regret it later. I want you for my wife."

"I've tried to fight my feelings for you, but I can't deny them any longer." She looked into his deep blue eyes. "I know your work is dangerous, and you will have to be away most of the time, but even that will be better than the torment I've been going through."

Logan smiled and brushed her lips with a chaste kiss. "Johanna, I have a confession to make. I haven't been totally honest with you. I have a home." He stroked her cheek with his fingertips. "Do you remember I told you I was raised in west Texas? Well, my father is a rancher. It's a pretty big spread called the Spanish Spur."

Logan told her about Sean, the ranch and his plans to resign from the Rangers. "Can you leave your home and come live with me on the Spur? I think Karl and Heidi would be happy there, and I know my father would love to have them. We have a housekeeper. Her name's Consuelo, and she's been on the Spur since my father and mother were married. I know you two will get along just fine."

Johanna was overwhelmed. She had never considered leaving her home. Her fantasies had been limited to marrying Logan and having him make the farm his home.

"Johanna, say something. Will you marry me?"

Tears of happiness stung Johanna's eyelids, and the lump in her throat threatened to choke her. She swallowed and managed to whisper "Oh, yes, Logan, yes. I'll marry you."

Logan gave out a whoop and gathered her back into his arms. He placed a finger under her chin and looked deep into her eyes. "I love you, Johanna."

Johanna awoke with a start to discover the sun above the treetops. *Oh, I've never slept this late in my life.* She and Logan had talked late into the night, making plans for the future. Her face burned remembering their ardent embraces and passionate kisses.

Johanna made quick work of her morning toilette, and donning a brown calico dress trimmed with white rickrack, she hurried to the kitchen. She and Logan had decided to tell the family their plans after supper, and she wanted to prepare a special meal. Maggie was finishing the breakfast dishes. The children and Gustav had gone about their chores.

"Good morning. I'm sorry I overslept," Johanna's said, not meeting

Maggie's eyes.

"Everything is fine," Maggie said, a hint of laughter in her voice. "The children were a bit curious since you never sleep late, but I told them you'd been working very hard and needed to rest. How about some breakfast?"

"I'm too excited to eat. Maggie, Logan and I are going to be married."

"Are you sure, Johanna? Have you thought this through? What about the children? Do you realize..."

"Maggie, wait. It's not like you think." Johanna revealed the truth about Logan.

Maggie dried her hands on her apron, went to her sister and embraced her. "I'm so happy for you. Don't worry about me. It's time I was moving on. I've been here too long."

"Don't say that. I've loved having you with us. So have the children. You don't have to leave. I know we can work something out."

Johanna felt a stab of conscience. She had been so involved with her own happiness she had forgotten about Maggie's situation. She sat down at the table.

"Have you decided on a date?" Maggie poured two cups of coffee and carried them to the table.

"Yes. Three weeks from Saturday. Logan wants to be back on the ranch in time to help with the fall round-up. He also asked me to wear a pink dress, but I don't have anything suitable."

"Why a pink dress?"

Johanna dropped her eyes and looked at the steaming brew. "I guess because I was wearing pink the first two times we saw each other. Actually, the first time it was a faded rose calico. When I saw him again later that same day, I was wearing my pink gingham dress." She kept her eyes focused on the cup.

Maggie's smile turned to a frown, and she bit her lip in concentration. "That doesn't give you much time. You've taught me a lot, and I could help you sew a new gown."

Johanna placed her hand on Maggie's arm. "You do beautiful work, and it would please me very much to have you help."

"Will you buy the fabric for your dress from the mercantile or will you get it from Amanda? That is, if you're still speaking to her," Maggie teased.

"Oh, that." Johanna shrugged and shook her head. "It didn't mean anything. Amanda is going to marry George Taylor."

They heard sounds of the children and Gustav in the yard. Johanna cautioned, "Don't say anything to them. Logan is coming for supper, and we plan to tell them afterward."

The day seemed to fly and drag by turns. Johanna and Maggie spent the afternoon preparing the evening meal. Johanna baked a chocolate cake to celebrate the occasion. She caught Karl and Heidi watching her with curious expressions and realized she was not behaving normally. She was nervous, and her stomach felt like all the butterflies in Texas had found their way inside.

During the afternoon, Maggie brought up the question Johanna had pushed to the back of her mind. "What are you going to do about Will?"

"I was fond of Will when we were young, but I didn't really love him. Not the way I love Logan. If I had, I would have married him in spite of Poppa." Johanna felt the heat rise in her face. "Oh, Maggie, I never knew I could feel this way. When he touches me..." Johanna dropped her gaze to the floor.

"I know." Maggie's smile was tinged with sadness.

Johanna freshened up before Logan arrived. She repinned her hair and changed into the pink gingham dress. With a sigh, she covered it with an apron.

Johanna heard Logan's voice and hurried to the door. The sight of him, tall and handsome, did strange things to her entire body. He was wearing gray pinstripe trousers and a black leather vest over a white linen shirt with a black string tie. When her eyes took in the gunbelt and pistol, she felt a twinge of fear. *Oh, for the day when he will hang up his gun for good.*

When Logan reached her, she saw a mischievous grin appear and his eyes darkened. Johanna knew he recognized the pink dress in spite of the apron.

"Hello, pretty lady."

"Hello, Logan." Her voice sounded breathless even to her own ears.

Supper was almost over, but to Johanna the tasty food might as well have been paper. All her thoughts focused on the announcement she and Logan were going to make. Nothing but crumbs of the chocolate cake remained. Johanna rose from her chair and walked to Logan's side. He laid his fork on his plate, stood and placed his arm around her waist.

"Logan and I have something to tell you." Johanna glanced around the table. "We are going to be married."

There was complete silence for a moment. Gustav nodded and Karl and Heidi looked at each other, big smiles on their faces.

Karl let out a whoop and Heidi clapped.

"*Liebchen*, I am happy for you and Logan." Gustav rose and shook Logan's hand.

Maggie's eyes were misty. "Johanna knows she has my best wishes. Congratulations, Logan. I wish you many long years of happiness."

"Thank you. I'll do my best to make Johanna and the children happy." Logan's voice was husky.

Johanna's eyes were misty too, but the nagging thought buried deep in her mind surfaced. What would Poppa say? She forced the thought away. Nothing was going to destroy this glorious moment.

"Mama, Mama." Heidi tried to catch her mother's attention. "When is the wedding? Can I be in it?"

"We don't have everything planned, but you will certainly be in it."

Heidi's face broke into a big smile. Karl looked at Logan and shook his head. Logan grinned and nodded in agreement. When the discussion turned to gowns, wedding cakes and all the trappings associated with the ceremony, Logan and Gustav escaped to the yard. Karl followed on their heels.

Later the family discreetly retired, leaving Johanna and Logan alone. Drawing her to her feet, he pulled her into his arms and kissed her. "I've been wanting to do that since the minute I got here."

"So have I," Johanna admitted. "I can't seem to keep my wits about me when I'm near you."

Logan chuckled and held her tighter. His lips nuzzled her ear, traced a path down her neck and stopped at the pulse in her throat. He moved back to her mouth. Her lips parted and his tongue darted inside while he tasted, teased and seduced.

Johanna thrilled to Logan's caresses. He tasted faintly of chocolate and that special honey only lovers can know. The kiss went on and on until she felt her bones were melting. She tried to draw him closer, and he pressed himself more tightly against her.

"Lord, Johanna! What you do to me." Logan gasped for breath.

Johanna struggled to breathe. "I know."

Logan placed a soft kiss on her lips and set her away from him. "It's getting late. If I want to catch the stage in the morning, I'd better be getting back to town. I shouldn't be gone more than a week."

"Please be careful, Logan. I couldn't bear it if anything happened to you."

"Nothing's going to happen to me. I have plans to marry the most beautiful woman in Texas. Wait here while I fetch *Él Campeon.*" He started toward the barn.

Johanna resisted the urge to call out to him The memory of the attempt on his life filled her mind. *Oh God,* she prayed, *keep him safe from all harm.*

Within minutes, Logan returned leading the stallion. Johanna rushed to him and threw her arms around him. He dropped the reins and held her tight. She stood on tiptoes and pressed her mouth to his. He returned her kiss, his hands splayed against her back while her hands framed his face.

He tensed and broke the kiss. "It's a good thing I'm leaving for Waco in the morning," he told her. Moving away from her, he mounted *Él Campeon.* He looked down at her and, in the faint light of the moon, his eyes were as dark as the night sky. "Goodnight, my love."

CHAPTER EIGHTEEN

"Ma, do you think *Grossvater* will be mad 'cause we're gonna move away?" Karl asked.

Johanna and the children were on their way to tell her family the news. Her hands tightened on the lines. "I don't know."

Heidi patted her mother's arm. "He can come and visit us." She had solved the problem with childlike innocence.

Johanna guided the team into the familiar lane, and feelings of nostalgia surfaced. Her childhood had been happy until her mother's illness. She shook off the painful memories and pulled the wagon up to the house. The original farmhouse, built of rock, had been enlarged with a frame addition to accommodate Sam and Mary's growing family.

The atmosphere vibrated with excitement. Laura and Emily came running to meet them. "We got a new baby brother." Emily grabbed Heidi and danced her around and around.

"Be quiet, Emily," Laura cautioned. "You know Poppa said Mama needs to rest, 'member? We're supposed stay out here and not make a lot of noise."

Johanna instructed Heidi and Karl to behave and hurried into the house. Her father, Sam, Nick and Anne-Marie were in the sitting room. All of them showed signs of fatigue. "Is Mary all right?"

"Yes." Sam answered. "She's asleep now, but she's awful tired and weak."

"It was a difficult birth, Johanna," Anne-Marie said.

"Why didn't you send for me? You know I would have been glad to come." Johanna sat down beside her father.

"There was no need. Doc Fischer brought Mrs. Perkins with him," Sam told her.

Johanna nodded and looked around the room. She drew a deep breath and slowly exhaled. No use putting it off. "I've come to tell you I'm going to marry Logan Delaney."

Conrad jumped to his feet. "What is this foolishness you are telling us?"

"Please, Poppa," Johanna said. "I didn't come here to ask your permission or to argue about it. The wedding will be three weeks from Saturday. I hope you will all come."

Conrad glanced at his sons, and then settled his gaze on Johanna. His dark eyes bored into her. She held her head up, her eyes locked on his. He started to speak, then shook his head and walked out of the room.

Anne-Marie went to Johanna and hugged her. Stepping back, she gave Johanna a big smile. "I think it's wonderful news. I know you're going to be very happy." She watched Nick from the corner of her eye and added, "Mr. Delaney is certainly a handsome man."

"Is that so?" Nick teased. "And what is a married lady like you doing noticing a thing that?"

"I may be married, but I'm not blind," Anne-Marie shot back.

Nick laughed and embraced his sister. "We're glad for you, Johanna. Delaney seems like a good man."

"I hope you're not makin' a big mistake, Johanna. And what about Will DeVore?" Sam asked. Disapproval was plain on his face.

Johanna shook her head. "I never had any intention of marrying Will."

"I don't think he knows that," Sam insisted.

"I never made him any promises."

"Maybe not," Sam returned. "But he had hopes anyway."

Johanna turned to Nick and changed the subject. "Do you think you will be able to help Gustav and Karl with the corn?"

"Yes, we should finish here in a day or two."

Poppa had not returned to the house, and Johanna knew he would not appear as long as she was there. After a quick peek at Mary and the baby, both sleeping peacefully, she called the children and returned home.

*

Nick arrived alone early the next morning. The children, Maggie and Gustav went about their chores, but Nick lingered over a cup of coffee. "You mentioned you might rent the farm after you and Logan get married. Do you have anyone in mind?"

"No, but I'm sure I can find someone."

"We didn't intend to say anything just yet, but Anne-Marie is in the family way. I'm goin' to be a daddy." Nick grinned, his smile stretching from ear to ear.

"Oh, Nick, that's wonderful!"

"Yeah, we think so." Nick joyous expression turned to one of concern.

"Anne-Marie is all right, isn't she?"

"Yes." Nick shook his head in dismay. "It's just that she's upset it happened before we could get a place of our own." His face brightened. "Say, would you consider renting this place to us? You know we would take real good care of it. We could pay rent or a share of the crops, whatever works out best."

"What a wonderful idea! I don't know why I didn't think of it myself." Johanna looked a bit flustered. "I guess I was too caught up in my own plans." She hesitated for a moment, trying to collect her thoughts. "I could save the money for the children's education or whatever they might want to do with it when they're grown."

"That sure takes a load off my mind," he said. "And I know Anne-Marie will be tickled pink."

Johanna nibbled at her lower lip, a frown wrinkling her brow. "What about Maggie and Gustav? Logan asked them to come to the ranch with us, but they refused. Even though Maggie and Poppa have reconciled, you know she won't go back home."

"They can both stay right here. Anne-Marie is very fond of Maggie, and with the baby comin' and all...Besides, this has been Gustav's home since he came from the old country, and I can sure use some help around the place."

"That's very generous of you, but I don't think Maggie will accept your offer. She'll probably go to San Antonio." Johanna sighed. Maggie was determined not to go back to the saloons, and Johanna prayed that a solution to the problem could be found.

"I want to stop and see Pastor Mueller," Johanna told Maggie as she guided the team onto the road to Meirsville. Maggie lowered her voice so it would not carry to Heidi, who was riding in the back of the wagon. Karl had stayed home to help with the harvest.

"What do you think Pastor will say when you tell him you're going to marry Logan and move away?"

"I'm not sure, but I hope he won't refuse to perform the ceremony."

"What will you do if he does?"

Johanna straightened on the wagon seat, her voice firm and steady. "Then we'll go to San Antonio and be married there."

The parsonage came into view, and Johanna slowed the horses. She pulled into the yard and climbed down from the wagon. Her chest felt tight, and she fought down her rising anxiety.

"Heidi and I are going to take a walk through the cemetery," Maggie told her.

Johanna nodded and hurried up the stone pathway. Pastor Mueller answered her knock and ushered her inside. Johanna was relieved that Mrs. Mueller had gone to visit a sick parishioner.

"You can't be serious, Johanna! You hardly know the man."

The pastor's eyes bugged, and his voice ended on a high note.

"Logan would have come with me, but he's gone to Waco to resign from the Rangers. He told me all about himself, and he wouldn't lie to me. We want to be married in three weeks. I was hoping you would perform the ceremony."

"I'll have to give it some thought." Pastor Mueller hesitated, pursing his lips. "Do you know his faith?"

"Logan was baptized Catholic, but he hasn't attended church in years. There's a mission near Fort Concho, and a circuit rider stops at the ranch three or four times a year. I don't think it will be a problem." Johanna felt a twinge of guilt. She and Logan had not discussed religion in great detail.

"What about Karl and Heidi and their religious training? You're still a young woman, Johanna. You will probably have more children. I don't think you've really considered this as carefully as you should." A frown marred the minister's normally placid countenance.

Johanna swallowed a quick response. She was sick and tired of having to justify her actions. "I plan to teach Heidi and Karl their catechism and continue their schooling myself, at least for a while. I will not neglect their religious training or their education." Johanna's tone implied that argument was futile.

The pastor sighed in resignation. "I can see your mind is made up. I only hope you realize what you are doing. I'll perform the ceremony, but I would like to talk with Mr. Delaney as soon as he returns."

"Of course. And thank you, Pastor."

Maggie and Heidi were waiting in the wagon. "How did it go?" Maggie asked.

"He finally agreed." She looked from Maggie to Heidi and back again at Maggie. It was best to keep the details from the children. Maggie nodded.

They entered the mercantile, and Johanna rummaged through her reticule for her shopping list. She had cautioned Heidi not to say anything about the wedding. Johanna planned to make the announcement after Logan returned to Meirsville. If Mrs. Schmidt learned about it now, it would be all over town before noon.

Mrs. Schmidt greeted them with icy politeness. Johanna's heart ached for Maggie. *Will they never forget?* She walked to the display of yard goods and selected delicate lawn and other fine cotton for undergarments. As an excuse to keep Maggie occupied, Johanna asked her to choose the laces and ribbons.

"My, but you're getting fancy," Mrs. Schmidt commented as she measured and cut Johanna's order.

Johanna's lips curved in a faint smile. "Not really. I just decided it was time to indulge myself a little."

The woman looked at Maggie, her lips tightening in apparent disapproval. She wrapped the purchases without further comment while Johanna counted out the money.

"Thank you." Mrs. Schmidt gave a curt nod and hurried off to assist another customer.

"Are you going to Amanda's?" Maggie asked as they stood on the boardwalk.

"Yes, I'd rather do that than ask Mrs. Schmidt to see the special materials she keeps on the shelf."

The silver bell pealed out its welcome, and Amanda came from the back of the shop. Heidi saved Johanna from an awkward moment by running to Amanda. "Miss Blair, Miss Blair, thank you for making my dolly's clothes. They're beautiful. And thank you for the little trunk."

Amanda smiled and hugged the little girl. "I'm glad you like them. I enjoyed sewing the clothing."

Johanna took a deep breath and gathered her courage. "Amanda, I would like to purchase some fabric, and the mercantile doesn't have what I want." She cringed inwardly at the small white lie.

Amanda's eyes widened, then she turned a mischievous smile on Johanna. "Do I hear wedding bells?"

Johanna's face colored to the roots of her hair.

"I'm sorry. I shouldn't have said that," Amanda hastened to apologize.

"That's all right. Yes, Logan and I are going to be married. Maggie has offered to help me sew a new gown and suggested you might have the right fabric."

"Let's take a look. Do you have something special in mind?" Amanda asked.

"No, except I want something in pink. Maggie thought maybe silk. What do you think? I'd appreciate your suggestions."

"I'll be delighted to help. And I think Maggie's right. Silk would be lovely." Amanda stopped at the cutting table. "Have you decided on a style?"

"No. Maybe we could look at the pattern book."

"Of course." Amanda selected the latest *Godey's Ladies Book* and laid it on the cutting table. She took three bolts of fabric from the shelf and laid them beside the pattern book.

The brocade and taffeta were delicate shades of pink, while the corded silk was deep rose.

An elegant gown with an overskirt and asymmetrical draping caught Maggie's eye. It had a high round collar, and the bodice, opening to the waist, formed a deep vee in the front. The underskirt was trimmed with poufs and shirring and had knife pleating at the hemline.

"That's a lovely gown," Amanda agreed. "I haven't used the pattern myself. There's quite a bit of handwork involved, but I'm sure you'd have no trouble with it."

She unfolded the bolts of brocade and taffeta, suggesting the brocade for the overskirt, and the taffeta for the underskirt, ivory lace trim for the collar and long straight sleeves. Ivory crochet-covered buttons would complete the bodice.

Johanna, abandoning her conservative nature, agreed it was perfect. She accepted Amanda's suggestions and added the items necessary to finish the dress.

While Rosa cut the fabrics and packaged them, the women returned to the front of the shop. Heidi was enthralled with the merchandise on display in the glass-fronted cases.

"Amanda..." Johanna hesitated.

"Is there something else?"

"May I offer my best wishes on your engagement to Mr. Taylor." Seeing the surprised look on Amanda's face, she hastened to add, "I hope you're not offended that Logan told me."

Amanda shook her head. "No, we just don't want to announce it until George and I work out the details. I need to do something about the shop. I have a good business built up and would like to sell it if I can find a buyer."

"I promise I won't mention it to anyone," Johanna assured her.

"Thank you. And let me offer you my best wishes. I know you and Logan will be very happy."

Several days later Johanna and Maggie were working on Johanna's trousseau. "I've been thinking, and I have something I want to talk to you about," Johanna said.

"What is it?" Maggie asked, concentrating on the tiny stitches as she sewed lace on a petticoat.

"Promise you'll think about it before you answer."

Maggie stopped sewing and looked up. "Whatever is on your mind?"

"I know you like to sew, but would you want to do it for a living?"

"What do you mean?"

"You know Amanda wants to sell her shop. If you want to buy it, I will loan you the money." Johanna held her breath, waiting for Maggie's reaction.

"I can't let you do that," Maggie answered. "What if I don't make it? You know how the people here feel about me."

"You won't fail. As for the people, I wouldn't worry about them. Amanda has several clients from San Antonio, and I'm sure they would come back. Please think about it, Maggie," Johanna begged.

"All right. I'll think about it."

"Good. That's all I ask."

When Nick returned the next day, he brought Anne-Marie with him. "I came to help with your trousseau," she told Johanna.

"I'm glad you came. I've wanted to tell you how happy we are about the baby. And we can certainly use the help." Johanna gathered up an armful of undergarments.

"I'm excited you're going to let us have the farm. You don't know what it means that we will have a place of our own. And I wanted to ask about the furniture. Are you taking all of it with you?" Anne-Marie's pretty face glowed.

"No, only my sewing machine, the cherry cabinet and china dishes. If you would like to use what's here, it's fine with me."

"That would be wonderful." Anne-Marie blushed and dropped her head. "We don't have much money and with the baby coming and all..."

Johanna laid aside her sewing and embraced her sister-in-law. "I understand, and I'm glad I can help."

The women prepared a hearty noon meal. Harvesting the corn was hard work. A shucking peg was used to remove the husks, and the ears were tossed into the wagon for the trip to the corncrib. Part of the crop would be sold and the rest left to feed to the livestock.

As Johanna and Maggie bustled around the kitchen after supper, Maggie said, "I've decided to accept the loan. I can't stay on the farm, although I appreciate Nick's offer. And I don't want to go to San Antonio. I'll repay you as soon as I can. But there's still a problem with where I'm going to live. I can't afford to stay at the hotel."

Johanna smiled and breathed an inward sigh of relief. "I'm glad you decided to do it. We should go into town tomorrow and make the arrangements. I'm sure Mr. Taylor can take care everything."

Johanna's eyes narrowed in concentration. "You know, Maggie, since Amanda's not getting married right away, maybe she'll agree to help you get started. You know, get the hang of things. It won't hurt to ask her. As for a place to live, there's Marta Albrecht's boarding house."

"Oh, no. She would never let me stay at her place, and I wouldn't give her the satisfaction of turning me away."

"Well, don't worry about it now. I'm sure we'll be able to figure out something."

Early the next morning they started for town. Karl asked to go along to visit Henry. "I won't get to see him after we move to the ranch."

Johanna felt a moment of panic. Was she making a mistake taking the children away from all that was familiar? She forced the thought from her mind.

Amanda was delighted to learn that Maggie wanted to buy the shop. The women started for the bank to complete the transaction. As they waited for a passing freight wagon, Johanna approached Amanda about helping Maggie learn the business.

"That's a good idea. I'm hoping to have a Christmas wedding so there will be lots of time for me to help out."

When they entered the bank, Taylor came to meet them, his eyes focused on Amanda.

"George, I have the most wonderful news. Maggie wants to take over the shop."

"That is good news," he replied, a smile lightening his stern features.

"Mr. Taylor," Johanna stepped forward, "can you handle the arrangements?"

"Of course. Please step into my office."

When the ladies were seated and Heidi had been given a picture book to keep her occupied, Taylor sat down behind his desk. He picked up a pencil and leaned forward. "How should I draw up the papers?"

"I want to make Maggie a loan. There should be enough in my account to take care of it."

Taylor nodded and replied, "I'm sure there are more than adequate funds in your account." He opened a desk drawer and pulled out a pad of paper. "I'll need some information. Will you be a partner in the venture?"

"Oh, yes, Johanna. We should be partners," Maggie said.

"No, I don't want to be a partner. That would be impractical with my being so far away." She turned to the banker. "I'm sure Amanda has told you Logan Delaney and I are going to be married."

"Yes, and I would like to offer my best wishes."

Johanna smiled, thinking he was probably relieved he no longer had a rival for Amanda's affections. The details were settled, and Taylor promised the papers would be ready to sign by noon. He insisted on celebrating the occasion by treating them to lunch at the hotel.

When they gathered after the papers were signed, the Reynoldses joined them. Jane offered to help Maggie with the shop, and Johanna felt her burden lighten. Perhaps in time the townspeople would accept Maggie.

Maggie volunteered to do the delicate handwork on Johanna's trousseau. This freed Johanna to use her beloved sewing machine, and the work progressed quickly. Maggie was sitting in the yard with her lap full of sewing when Will DeVore rode up.

"Is Johanna here?" he asked without preamble.

"She's inside. I'll tell her you're here." Maggie gathered up her work and hurried into the house.

Will was watering his horse when Johanna walked into the yard. Maggie remained indoors. Johanna watched, her apprehension building.

Had Will heard about the wedding? "Hello, Will."

"Is it true? Are you going to marry Delaney?"

"Yes." She stood facing him, her calm manner belying the hollow feeling in the pit of her stomach.

Will's face paled beneath his tan. He moved closer. "Why, Johanna? Why? You hardly know him. He's nothing but a legal killer. He can't offer you anything. And what about your children? He won't be around to be a father to them." His voice was ragged with emotion.

Johanna's face flushed with color. "I'm sorry you had to hear about Logan and me before I could tell you myself. But you have no right to come here and talk this way. You know nothing about Logan. Although it's none of your business, he's resigning from the Rangers. His father owns a large ranch near Fort Concho, and we're going there to live. As for Karl and Heidi, they are very fond Logan and he of them."

"You're going to leave your farm?" Will asked, his expression incredulous.

"Yes. Nick and Anne-Marie are going take over the place."

"I see you have everything all worked out," Will said, his voice filled with bitterness. "But I still think you're makin' a big mistake. When is the weddin'?"

"In two weeks."

"Two weeks!" Will's eyes raked her from head to toe. "I hear Delaney left town."

The color left Johanna's face and anger such as she had never felt surged through her body. "Just what are you implying, Will?"

"I'm not implyin' anything. But if you find yourself needin' a husband and Delaney don't come back, I won't be waitin' around."

Johanna's face blanched, and her body stiffened. Her vision blurred while she stared at him. When she spoke, her voice was coated with ice. "Perhaps you *were* the one that started that ugly gossip when Karl and Heidi were born."

"You don't really think I would say those things about you?"

Johanna did not reply but continued to look at him.

He dropped his eyes and stared at his boots. "I'm sorry I hurt you. I've loved you for a long time, and you've turned me down for the second time. It's hard to accept."

Will's voice was filled with pain, but his cutting remarks still rang in Johanna's ears. "We have nothing more to talk about, Will."

CHAPTER NINETEEN

"I can't believe I forgot about the Harvest Dance," Johanna said as she and Maggie finished the breakfast dishes.

Maggie laughed. "Well, you have had a few other things on your mind."

"I hope Logan returns in time for us to go. Do you realize that we have not really courted?"

"It might stop a lot of wagging tongues to see you together," Maggie said, drying her hands on the dishtowel.

"I suppose so. What about you? If Logan gets back in time, will you go with us?"

"I don't think so. It could be embarrassing, and I don't want to cause any more problems."

"That's nonsense. I'm sure Nick and Anne-Marie will go, and Poppa usually does. The Reynoldses, Amanda and her mother will be there. Practically everybody for miles around comes. As for the *old biddies*, don't worry about them." Johanna injected as much force as she could muster into her reply.

Later that day, Maggie suggested they look through her trunk for gowns to wear to the dance. The upper floor of Stein's saloon, the social gathering place for the community, would be decorated to resemble a ballroom, and Maggie was eager to dress for the occasion.

"There isn't much time for alteration," Maggie said as she searched through the trunk. She held up a dragon green corded silk dress with black passementerie. "This should do nicely for me." The style was modest with a high neckline and elbow-length sleeves. "I have some jet beads and earrings that go very well with it.

"Is there anything here you like?" Maggie asked as she continued taking gowns from the trunk. She discarded most of them as unsuitable. "How about this one? I know the color is a bit unusual. *Godey's* calls it red mahogany, and it's perfectly respectable."

Johanna's hand flew to her mouth. In spite of, or maybe because of, its simplicity, it was the most unusual dress she had ever seen. The bodice formed a deep vee in the front and buttoned down the back. The slightly scooped neckline and elbow-length sleeves would reveal more skin than Johanna had ever displayed in public. The full skirt, requiring a crinolette and at least three petticoats, was caught in the back in a bustle effect.

Her eyes wide with wonder, Johanna said, "It's the most beautiful dress I've ever seen. But I couldn't wear it."

"And why not?" Maggie asked, her hands on her hips. "After all, you are engaged. Besides, let people talk. They will anyway."

Two days after Johanna had chosen the red dress, she was leaving the spring house and glanced up to see a rider coming down the lane. Maggie, taking clothes from the line, broke into laughter as she watched Johanna hike her skirts up and run to meet him.

"Johanna!" Logan was off *Él Campeon* in an instant and caught her in a tight embrace. Oblivious to anyone who might be watching, he kissed her passionately, and she returned it in full measure.

"You did come back," Johanna said as he released her mouth.

Logan's body stiffened. "You didn't think I left for good?"

Johanna's face colored bright red, and she dropped her eyes. "Oh, no, it's just that..." she stammered, Will's callus remarks fresh in her mind.

"Not a chance, lady. You promised to marry me, and the devil himself couldn't keep me away." He kissed her again.

Logan picked up *Él Campeon's* dangling reins and looped them over the hitch rail. "Were you able to make the arrangements?" he asked, putting his arm around her waist.

"Yes, but Pastor Mueller wants to talk with you before the ceremony. It's set for eight thirty Saturday morning. I hope that's all right."

Logan looked into her eyes and said in a voice filled with meaning,

"The sooner the better. And everything on my end is taken care of, too. I even managed to write my father. Captain Montgomery would have liked for me to stay in the Rangers, but he understands. In fact, he's sending two of his men to make the trip to the Spur with us."

Johanna looked at him, the shadow of fear in her eyes. "Do you think there will be any danger?"

"No, it's just the captain's way of showing his appreciation for my service with The Rangers."

Maggie drew abreast of them, carrying the basket of clothes. "Hello, Logan. Welcome back."

"Hello, Maggie. Let me carry that." He reached for the basket. "Johanna, I'd like to meet your father and have a word with him before the wedding," he said.

Although it pleased Johanna that Logan wanted to make the first move, she felt a stab of anxiety. "We could go tomorrow, if you like." Without waiting for Logan's response, she hurried on. "Come, let's go in the house, and I'll make some coffee."

While the coffee heated, Johanna cut thick slices of strudel, and Maggie set the table. As she served the refreshments, Johanna brought Logan up to date concerning the wedding plans. She also told him about Nick and Anne-Marie and the arrangements they had made for the farm.

"You certainly get things done when you set your mind to it," Logan said when he learned Maggie was taking over Amanda's shop.

"Thank you, sir." Johanna smiled, and then her expression grew serious. "Karl is quite upset with me. He wants to visit his friends since he won't see them when school takes up. Do you think I should allow him to ride Ranger around the countryside?"

"I think he's capable of handling the horse. The animal is not mean-tempered in spite of its previous owner. Let me check him out again before you give Karl permission."

The remainder of the day passed swiftly. The children and Gustav returned from visiting a neighbor, and Heidi and Karl welcomed Logan with enthusiasm. He had brought them small gifts: for Karl an intricately carved horse that the boy said looked just like Ranger, and colorful hair ribbons for Heidi.

After a delicious meal that included lots of discussion, Johanna went with Logan to fetch *Él Campeon*. It was a warm night, and the sky was ablaze with stars.

"What time should I be here tomorrow?" Logan asked.

"If you'd like to come for dinner, we can leave right afterward. There are some things I want to talk with Nick about, but I was waiting until you returned."

"I'll help any way I can. You know that." Logan dug into his saddlebags and removed a small object. "I have a gift for you, too, but I wanted to give it to you when we were alone." He placed a small velvet box in her hand.

Johanna's fingers fumbled with the lid. She managed to open the box, and a heart-shaped locket gleamed in the faint light from the moon. She gasped, her throat going dry while her eyes grew misty. "Oh, Logan, it's beautiful!"

"I'm glad you like it. Be sure to look on the back when you get inside." Logan took her in his arms and brushed a soft kiss across her lips. "I want to give you so much." He kissed her again, and she responded with so much feeling he felt the blood begin to pound in his veins. "I'd best be going," he said, his voice hoarse with restrained passion. "I'll here about mid-morning and work with Karl for awhile." He looked into her face, which the moonlight had turned to tawny gold. "Good night, love."

Johanna watched as Logan disappeared in the darkness. How was she ever going to learn to control her emotions when she was near him? She needed a moment to compose herself and sat down on a bench. The breeze cooled her heated skin. She caressed the velvet box, anxious to see what was on the back of the locket.

When she returned to the house, Gustav was leaving for his room. Maggie was sewing, and Heidi and Karl were engrossed in a game of checkers.

"Children, Logan and I are going to visit your grandfather tomorrow. Would you like to come along?"

"Yes," they chorused.

"Then you'd better be off to bed."

The children were tucked in, and Maggie retired. Johanna sat at the kitchen table and opened the velvet box. She turned the locket toward the light. The inscription read: *L.D. - J.B., 1873*. Johanna swallowed, took a deep breath and clasped the locket to her breast.

* * *

Logan arrived and worked with Karl and Ranger until Johanna called them for dinner. "Karl is going to make a fine horseman," Logan said. "I don't think you have a thing to worry about."

Karl grinned from ear to ear.

"I'm glad to hear that. Now, I need to freshen up before we leave."

"You look fine to me," Logan said, a knowing look in his eyes.

A telltale blush spread across Johanna's cheeks, and she hurried into the bedroom. Looking into the mirror, she tucked a few wispy curls into place, removed her apron and inspected her dress. The gray calico looked neat and proper, and the red trim helped bolster her courage.

"I told Johanna I wanted to meet you. I think we have a few things to talk about." Logan held out his hand.

Conrad ignored Logan's gesture of friendship. "What is there to talk about? You have filled Johanna's head with foolish ideas. She is leaving her home and her family to go where she has never been. How do we know what you say is true? That you have a fine ranch and can provide for her and my grandchildren?"

"Poppa," Johanna pleaded.

"It's all right, Johanna. I understand your father might have doubts about me." Logan looked the older man in the eye. "I love Johanna and would never lie to her. You can check me out with Ranger Captain Montgomery in Waco. I promise you I will take good care of Johanna and the children."

Anne-Marie came out of the house wiping her hands on her apron. Her usually smiling countenance was pale and drawn.

Johanna suspected Anne-Marie was suffering from morning sickness.

"Won't you come in? I've made coffee and I baked cookies yesterday. I don't think the children have eaten them all." Anne-Marie smiled and gestured toward the house.

Johanna looked up to see Nick and Sam coming from the barn and felt the urge to grab Logan's hand and run to the wagon. She knew Sam was bound to voice his objections.

Johanna had difficulty keeping a straight face when Mary was introduced to Logan. The woman's face mirrored total surprise. She acknowledged the introduction but contrary to her usual tactless manner, did not offer any further comments. With some misgivings, Johanna left Logan with Nick and Sam while she helped Anne-Marie with the refreshments.

"Nick," Johanna addressed her brother when they had been served. "I think we need to discuss the terms of our agreement. I won't be taking the farm implements and livestock. Do you want to buy them now or wait until your crops come in next year?"

"We could probably pay for the livestock and implements now."

"All right. Should I rent the farm or accept a share of the crops? What do you think, Logan?"

"It's your property, Johanna. Do whatever you feel is best. It doesn't matter to me. I just want you to be happy."

"A woman's property usually belongs to her husband when she marries," Sam interrupted, his tone harsh.

"Not in this case," Logan answered. "Johanna wants to keep the farm for Karl and Heidi. Besides, I'm not a farmer. The Spur covers over a hundred and fifty thousand acres. That's enough for me to take care of."

"No matter," Conrad spoke up. "Johanna, you are being too hasty making these decisions. I see no need for all the rush. Why not wait awhile? You may change your mind."

"No, Poppa, I won't change my mind."

"Pa, this is a chance for Anne-Marie and me to get started. We need a place of our own, and Johanna deserves to be happy," Nick said, his expression anxious.

"Thank you, Nick."

Nick suggested the agreement be put in writing, and Johanna asked for Logan's help in preparing the documents. After a great deal of deliberation, she agreed to leave the Percherons behind.

"They aren't suitable for ranch work," Logan told her. "They would be of more benefit to Nick."

"I thought we would need them to pull the wagon." Johanna used her last argument.

"I'll pick up a team at the livery stable. They can always be traded or sold to the army later. My father sells a lot of horses to the army," Logan added by way of explanation.

"I guess it's settled then," Johanna sighed. "It's just that I'm so fond of them."

"I know you are. Maybe you'll find a horse to your liking at the ranch and we can do some riding."

"I don't know how to ride."

Logan chuckled. "It will be fun to teach you."

When the conversation turned to the Harvest Dance and the gowns the ladies would be wearing, the men escaped outside.

"I'm not sewing anything new this year." Anne-Marie's fair skin turned a delicate pink.

"Since I won't be going, I'm not concerned about it." Mary's lips puckered in disapproval.

"Maggie has offered me one of her gowns." *If Mary could see that red dress, she really would have an attack of the vapors.*

"I've been thinking, Johanna," Anne-Marie said. "Since you will be going to San Antonio right after the wedding, there won't be time for a party."

"No, the stage comes through about noon. That doesn't leave much time after the ceremony."

"Well, what about having a wedding breakfast at the hotel? I'm sure Jane Reynolds would be glad to arrange it. If you think that would be all right with Mr. Delaney?"

"I'm sure it will, but I'll ask him and let you know."

"Good. If you'll give me a list people you want to invite, I'll be glad to see that they get an invitation."

"That's very sweet of you." She was going to miss this sister-in-law.

As they prepared to leave, Conrad walked up to the wagon and stopped in front of Logan. "I can see that everything is all settled, Mr. Delaney. I just ask that you take good care of my daughter and grandchildren. Maybe you will bring them to see me sometime." Conrad held out his hand.

"I give you my word, Mr. Neicum," Logan promised as he shook the old man's hand. He looked around at the others. "You are all welcome at the Spur anytime."

* * *

"Is he gonna make it, Doc?" The speaker looked down at the young man who lay unmoving on the table. His long blond hair was damp with sweat, and his skin was pale and waxen.

"I don't know. I've done all I can. That bullet should have come out several days ago." The doctor wiped his hands on a bloodstained towel. "It's infected, and the poison has spread through his system."

"He wouldn't let me take it out, Doc. Wanted you to do it. It took two days ridin' to git here."

The doctor shook his head but made no reply. He washed his hands and asked Simms to help him move Bud to the cot. When they had transferred the boy and made him as comfortable as possible, the doctor told Sims he had to make a house call.

"You can sit with him while I'm gone, but he'll be out for quite a while yet. I had to give him a sizable whiff of chloroform. If he does come to, don't give him any water. It won't stay down."

"I'll look after 'im, Doc." Sims pulled up a chair and seated himself close to the cot. His mind replayed the conversation with Anderson before he ended up getting shot. *Damn!* If only the kid had listened to him, but he was determined to learn what had happened to Joe Greene.

Bud had ridden into Meirsville under the cover of darkness and stopped at the saloon. It was there he had learned the Ranger, Delaney, had killed Greene. The two outlaws who had been captured by the posse had been tried and convicted. It had proved to be Anderson's lucky night when he discovered the Ranger was still in town. It seemed he was courting a widow woman in the area. After that it wasn't difficult to keep an eye peeled for him and follow him when he left town. His youth and inexperience had earned Bud a bullet in the leg when he attempted to shoot the Ranger from ambush.

Although Sims disapproved of Anderson's actions, he had stayed in the camp and waited for Bud. After all, he had nowhere else to go. Sims had ridden with Greene for two years and now he was alone. When Bud had shown up, barely able to stay in the saddle, Sims hadn't known whether to treat his wound or ride off and leave him. He had ended up doing what he could to stop the bleeding, all the while telling the kid he needed a doctor. The kid had insisted on riding back to Llano where Doc Moore could tend him.

Sims ran his hand over the stubble on his face. He could use a shave and bath, but he wasn't likely get either one soon. Bud hadn't moved, and his breathing was shallow. His pale face had grayed even more. Sims had seen many men cash in their chips during his infamous career and had little hope for the boy.

Anderson's eyelids fluttered, but he did not open his eyes. Moaning, he cried out, "Mama, it hurts. Where are you, Mama?" He began to toss about, and Sims tried to restrain him. The doctor arrived and decided a dose of laudanum was in order. They managed get it down the suffering boy, but he was still calling for his mother when he drifted off to sleep.

Taking a bottle and two glasses from one of the cupboards, the doctor sighed. "I could use a snort of this. How about you?"

"Sure thing, Doc. Much obliged."

"It's a damn shame. Addie was a good, decent woman."

As Sims' eyebrows raised, the doctor continued, "His mother. She did my laundry and cleaning for years. That worthless bastard she married deserted her and the boy when he was just a tyke. She did the best she could for him. She died about year ago, and Bud's been flirting with the law ever since. You want to tell me how he got that bullet in his thigh?"

Simms hesitated. Could he trust the doctor? Well, no matter. He owed the man that much. "We was involved in a little fracas at Meirsville, but the posse caught up with us. Me and Bud managed to git away, but the Boss was shot. We didn't know if'n he was killed or not, but Bud wouldn't let it be. 'Cause Joe got him out a little scrape here in Llano awhile back, he wanted to know for sure. Told 'im it was too risky, but he wouldn't listen. When he tried to git the Ranger that killed Joe, he bought a bullet in the leg."

The doctor listened without interruption as the tale unfolded. Slowly shaking his head, he remarked, "It's just as well Addie is dead and gone. This would break her heart." He paused. "Care for another?" He held up the bottle.

"That's mighty fine whiskey, Doc. Don't git to sample that kind very often."

The doctor refilled Sims' glass but did not add to his own. As soon as darkness fell, the doctor sent Sims out for sandwiches and coffee. The two men kept their vigil over the wounded man. In his delirium he continued to call for his mother. A few times he muttered Greene's name.

The doctor kept Bud sponged off and administered another dose of laudanum. Just as the dark hour before dawn arrived, Anderson opened his eyes. Motioning Sims to join him at the bedside, the doctor strained to hear the young man's last words.

"I'm sorry, Doc. Do you think Ma will forgive me?"

"It's not your mother's forgiveness you need now, Bud. It's the Almighty's. Make your peace, son. I've done all I can for you. You can thank your friend here for that."

The dying man looked at Sims standing beside the doctor. His eyes wet, Sims was thankful for the dim light.

"Sims, I'm beholdin' to you fur bringin' me home."

"Wisht I coulda done more, Bud."

"Doc, will there be place for me beside Ma?"

"Yes, Bud, I promise there will be."

The young man's eyes opened wide, and he seemed to stare at something in the distance. His breathing faltered, and with a small sigh he slipped away.

CHAPTER TWENTY

The sky was sprinkled with stars when Logan came to take Johanna to the Harvest Dance. Bartell, who had arrived with Helderman the day before, accompanied him. When Logan had asked Bartell if he would escort Maggie to the dance, he grinned. "Why would I object when I get to take a pretty lady to a dance, and she didn't have a chance to turn me down?"

Maggie answered the door, swung it wide and stepped back. "Come in. Johanna will be out in a moment."

"Maggie, this Ranger Dan Bartell. He's going to be my best man, and he'd like to escort you to the dance."

"How do you do?" Maggie held out her hand. She was stunning in the dragon green gown.

Bartell's Adam's apple bobbed up and down several times down before he found his voice and answered, "My pleasure, ma'am."

Johanna stepped into the sitting area. Logan's breath caught in his throat. He had thought her beautiful before, but the woman in the dark red gown was a stranger. Her honey-gold hair was swept atop her head in a mass of curls, and tiny gold earrings glinted in her lobes. The exposed skin of her neck, shoulders and arms resembled polished ivory. He smiled when he saw the locket around her throat. Oblivious of the others in the room, Logan moved forward and caught her hands, looking deep into her eyes. "You are beautiful," he told her, and brushed her lips with a soft kiss. He released her. "Dan, I'd like you to meet my fiancée, Johanna Bauer. Johanna, Dan Bartell."

"Ranger Bartell, I'm happy to meet you." Johanna smiled and offered her hand.

"I'm might proud to make your acquaintance, ma'am." He turned to Logan, his eyes filled with admiration. "You're one lucky galoot, Delaney!"

"I'm well aware of that," Logan replied.

"I'll get our wraps from the bedroom," Maggie said. She returned with a black silk shawl over her shoulders and a silk paisley one which she handed to Johanna.

"Shall we go?" Logan asked.

The second floor of Stein's saloon was decorated with colorful paper lanterns and streamers. Johanna's eyes focused on the snowy white tablecloths covering the refreshment table that was laden with pies, cakes and other delectable sweets. She recognized Mrs. Blair's crystal punch bowl and cups. Several different patterns of china and cutlery occupied one end of the tables.

On the opposite side of the room, a row of chairs had been arranged to provide a place to rest between dances or to sit and visit. The musicians tuned their instruments on a raised platform at the front of the room. Meirsville boasted its own German band, which provided music for any occasion. The far end of the room was partitioned off for the ladies and sleeping children.

Johanna felt the eyes upon her as she and Maggie crossed the floor to deposit their contributions on the refreshment table. Everybody must know about the wedding by now. Maggie and Bartell were drawing their share of attention. The ones who remembered the scandal were quick to recognize her and tell the ones who did not.

The Blairs, George Taylor and the Reynoldses entered together. Amanda's blue-green taffeta gown contrasted with Jane's elegant purple silk. A white lace collar relieved Mrs. Blair's customary black dress.

Logan spotted Helderman in the crowd and motioned him to join them. Logan made the introductions, and he could see the admiration in the young Ranger's eyes.

"I'm glad you will be with us on the trip to the Spur," Johanna told him.

He grinned and replied, "So am I, ma'am. It will be a real treat to eat somebody else's cookin' for a change."

"She's a fine cook," Logan assured him.

Emil Stein stepped up to the platform and called for attention. "On behalf of the town council, I want to welcome you to our annual Harvest Dance. It's good to see such a big crowd. The harvest has been good this year, and we have much to be thankful for. There are plenty of refreshments, thanks to the ladies. The musicians are ready, so let's begin the festivities."

The music began and couples paired off. Logan and Johanna joined the dancers on the floor. He held her in his arms and whispered in her ear, "You're the most beautiful woman in the room." She smiled at him, and her eyes held the promise of delights to come.

Maggie and Bartell danced, ignoring the stares and whispers caused by their presence. Johanna saw her father, Nick and Anne-Marie enter the room and urged Logan in their direction.

"The invitations to the wedding breakfast have been taken care of," Anne-Marie told Johanna.

"I really appreciate your help," Johanna said.

The dancing continued, and Johanna found herself partnered with her father.

"I hope you will be happy, daughter, but you know we are going miss you." He did not try to conceal the sadness in his eyes.

"I will miss all of you, Poppa. But we'll come back for visits," Johanna said, her eyes damp.

The children, sleepy and beginning to fuss, were carried to the sleeping area. The musicians called for an intermission, and the thirsty dancers headed for the refreshment tables. Logan and Johanna, followed by Maggie and Bartell, left the dance floor. The dancers surrounded them, but a woman's voice could be heard above the chatter.

"Save face! Ha! That's rich. There's no way she can hide what she's done. She was probably run out of some town and had nowhere to go. Conrad would never let her come back home. Of course, Johanna has lost all sense of decency, too, so it don't matter to her."

A sudden silence enveloped the room. Johanna recognized Mrs. Schmidt's nasal tone. She was stunned by the hurtful words, and her breath caught in her throat. She looked at Maggie, whose pale face matched her own. Johanna gripped Logan's arm. She felt his body stiffen.

Pastor Mueller stepped onto the platform. "May I have your attention, please?"

Through the fog that numbed her senses, Johanna saw the Blairs and George Taylor standing beside the minister.

"On behalf of Mrs. Josiah Blair, I wish to announce the engagement of her daughter, Amanda, to George Taylor. Now, you all know the happy couple, and I'm sure you'll want to congratulate him and wish them every happiness."

The pastor's announcement eliminated the possibility of a confrontation between the sisters and Mrs. Schmidt. Amanda and George became the center of attention. The musicians returned to their instruments and struck up a lively folk tune.

"I'm not sure I know the steps to this one," Logan said, "but let's give it a try." He urged Johanna toward the crowded floor.

Johanna searched for Maggie and found her with Bartell sitting by themselves at one end of the room. Her heart ached for her sister, and as much as she would have liked to strike back at the tactless woman, she controlled her anger. Nothing would be gained by creating a public display.

The tune ended, and Johanna and Logan joined Maggie and Bartell. "Let's sit the next one out. I'm out of breath," Johanna confessed, sitting down next to Maggie.

Max Hemmerlein approached and stopped in front of Maggie. "I know we haven't been properly introduced, Mrs. DuPree, but I'm Max Hemmerlein. I own the gunshop here in town. I would be honored if you would allow me the next dance. That is, if Ranger Bartell don't object."

"I guess I have to be accommodatin', but only one dance, mind you." Bartell frowned in jest.

Maggie smiled and answered Hemmerlein, "I would be delighted, sir."

Martin Koegnig tapped Logan's shoulder. "Do I have your permission to dance with your intended?" he asked.

Logan grinned, his eyes twinkling, and replied, "I don't guess I could refuse since you're the only law around here now."

"You're lookin' mighty pretty tonight, Johanna," the sheriff told her.

"Thank you, Martin. I hope you can come to the wedding breakfast."

"Can't say I was surprised the weddin' is real soon. I know Delaney's anxious to get back to that ranch of his. You know I wish you much happiness, and I wouldn't miss the breakfast."

Johanna and Koenig came abreast of Maggie and Hemmerlein. Maggie's face was chalk white. She took a step away from the gunsmith. "Mr. Hemmerlein, I haven't given you any reason to make a remark like that."

"Ah, come now, Mrs. DuPree. It is Mrs., ain't it? A *lady* with your reputation shouldn't object to a sociable drink and a stroll in the moonlight."

Before she could respond, Dan was at her side. "Is something wrong, Maggie?" he asked. His eyes, narrowed and penetrating were focused on Hemmerlein.

Maggie laid her hand on Dan's arm. "Please, Dan, it's all right. Mr. Hemmerlein just forgot his manners for a moment."

"Mistakes like that can be mighty costly, Hemmerlein," Dan said. "You owe the lady an apology."

His face flushed, Max responded, "Yeah, sure, I'm sorry, ma'am. It won't happen again." He turned and hurried away.

Johanna knew the incident would circulate faster than a brush fire. "Maggie, would you like to go to the ladies' room?"

Maggie nodded.

"We won't be long," Johanna said as she followed Maggie toward the other end of the room.

Two young women leaving the ladies' room stifled giggles as they passed Johanna and Maggie. An older woman was rocking a child, and Johanna recognized her. "Good evening, Mrs. Frederick."

The woman rose, nodded and answered, "Evenin', Johanna." She ignored Maggie and carried the sleeping child to a pallet.

Two fainting couches, a dressing table and two rockers made up the furnishings in the room. The chamber pots were concealed behind a folding screen in the corner.

"Would you like to lie down?" Johanna felt overwhelming sympathy for Maggie.

"No, I'll be all right in a minute." Maggie's eyes were misty. "If this were any other place, I could handle it without any trouble at all, but anything I say will only make the situation worse." She dabbed at her eyes with a handkerchief.

Johanna nodded. "I know, and what really bothers me is that I'll be leaving soon. I won't be here to help you. Not that I've been much help. The gossips have had their fun with me, too. But I'm not sure how much more I can stand without giving them a piece of my mind."

Maggie smiled through her tears. "I'll bet they'd sit up and take notice if you did."

After a quick toilette, Johanna and Maggie returned to Logan and Dan. Nodding toward Amanda and George, Johanna said, "I think we should go talk with the happy couple."

When congratulations and best wishes were offered, Taylor smiled and Amanda blushed. Afterward, they all moved onto the dance floor. When the music ended, Logan suggested they get a breath of fresh air, and Johanna agreed. She fetched their shawls, and the two couples descended to the first floor. The saloon was closed to the public, but Emil was dispensing free beer to the men who wanted something stronger than the punch served upstairs.

Stepping into the moonlight, Logan put his arm around Johanna's waist. "Do you think we would start a scandal if we walked down to the river?"

"Probably," Johanna laughed, "but let's do it anyway."

"We're getting away from this viper's nest for awhile, Dan. Why don't you two come along?" Logan asked.

"Would you like to walk with them?" Dan asked.

"Yes," Maggie answered, taking his arm.

They walked without speaking until they reached the water's edge. Maggie and Dan moved away in the darkness. Logan drew Johanna into his arms. His hands spanning her waist, he teased her with feathery kisses along her jawline. Impatient, she drew his head down and captured his mouth. The kiss went on and on until Johanna thought she would explode from sheer lack of air.

"You're dangerous, lady," Logan said.

Johanna laughed softly and tightened her arms around him. " It's just that when you touch me..."

"I know, love." He kissed her again, and then set her aside. "It's time we were getting back to the dance."

When they reached Stein's, Johanna admitted her reluctance to go back inside. "It's such a beautiful night, let's sit in front of the hotel for awhile."

"I almost forgot this." Logan withdrew a crumpled paper from his pocket. "The marshal in San Antonio sent a messenger with it." He smoothed the wrinkles from the yellow sheet and handed it to her. The light filtering from the hotel was barely adequate for Johanna to read the message.

Logan Delaney - Meirsville, Texas
Glad to get your letter. Stop. Not too surprised. Stop. Looking forward to meeting my new daughter and grandchildren. Stop.
Your father, Sean Delaney

"It's from your father! You know, I confess to wondering how he would feel about your marrying a woman with two children."

"You don't need to worry about that." Logan squeezed her hand. "Pa is pleased that I'm coming home for good. We talked a little when I was there last. He joshed about not having to wait for grandchildren."

Johanna's thoughts flew to her conversation with Maggie. Now was the perfect time to find out if Logan wanted children of his own. "Logan." This was going to be harder than she thought.

"What is it? Is something wrong?"

"No, not really. It's just that we never discussed having a family."

Logan took her hands in his and looked deep into her eyes. "I love you, Johanna, and whether we have children or not doesn't really matter. We have Karl and Heidi, and they would make any man proud."

Dropping his head, he placed a soft kiss on her palm.

"I had a fairly easy time with Karl and Heidi. It would make me very happy to have your child."

Logan placed his arm around her, drew her close and whispered in her ear. "Then, why don't we just let nature take its course?"

He kissed her, and she felt the passion all the way to her toes.

"Don't you think it's about time we went back to the dance?" Maggie called as she and Bartell joined them.

"I suppose," Johanna replied, "but it doesn't matter. They're probably all thinking the worst anyway."

The musicians were playing a lively tune, and the dancers whirled around the floor.

"Why don't you stay here with Logan and Dan while I take our wraps to the ladies' room?" Johanna offered. She heard the whispers as she passed the women sitting in the chairs, but she ignored them. The ladies' room was empty except for the sleeping children. She was spared an embarrassing encounter and hung the shawls on a hook.

Joining the others at the refreshment table, she murmured softly, "Hold your head high, Maggie, and look them straight in the eye. They won't be expecting that, and you can bet they'll not look you in the face."

Amanda and George joined them. "I've been wanting to ask you, Maggie. Do you plan to keep the same hours at the shop?"

Maggie's brow furrowed in concentration. "I haven't really thought about it, but I see no reason to change them."

The dancers drifted toward the refreshment table, and Amanda turned to face them. "I'm sure the news has gotten around, but in case you haven't heard, Mrs. DuPree will be taking over my shop soon."

The room grew still for a second or two, and then the whispers started. Bits and pieces of conversation carried back to Johanna and Maggie. The words *flaunt herself, disgraceful* and *shameless hussy* reached their ears.

Oblivious to the reaction of her announcement, Amanda continued, "Of course, I plan to stay and help out until my wedding. The date isn't set, but it will be some time during the holidays." She focused a brilliant smile on the gathering.

Turning back to Maggie, Amanda asked, "Have you made a decision concerning where you will live when you move into town?"

Before Maggie could formulate an answer, a voice rang out. "She don't need to think I would let her stay at my place. After all, I run a *respectable* boarding house," Mrs. Albrecht proclaimed for all to hear. Everybody knew she ran the *only* boarding house in town.

The room became deadly quiet. The men began to shuffle their feet, and the women avoided looking at one another. Maggie's face was pink with embarrassment, her body rigid. Knowing she was close to breaking down, Johanna reached for her hand. She drew a deep breath, her anger rising to the surface. They had endured insults all evening.

Amanda took up the challenge. Her green eyes flashed with anger, but her voice was soft when she said, "Why, Mrs. Albrecht, there is no need for Maggie to stay at your establishment." Her smile guileless, she continued, "You know we discussed this, Maggie, and Mother and I won't take 'no' for an answer. We have plenty of room and will be delighted to have you stay with us. And, after my wedding, you will be company for Mother. There now, it's all settled."

* * *

The two boys were slopping the hogs. Karl, excited about having a horse of his own, had been regaling Michael all afternoon about becoming a cowboy on Logan's ranch. Michael had listened to Karl with little response.

Now, Michael blurted out, "I'm sick and tired of hearin' 'bout that ol' horse of your'n. He can't be very good 'cause he belonged to an outlaw. An' I'm sick of hearin' 'bout that Ranger. Pa says he's really a gunman. You're bein' taken in by him and Aunt Johanna's makin' a fool a herself."

"That's not true, Mike Neicum! Logan would never gun a man down less'n he had it comin'."

Michael set his bucket down and turned to face Karl.

"He really pulled the wool over your eyes, didn't he? Ma says Aunt

Johanna always acted like a perfect lady, but she had ever'body fooled, too," Mike smirked.

Karl, his face a bright scarlet, balled his fists and demanded, "You'd better be careful how you talk about my mother."

"Yeah? What you gonna do about it?"

"Take back what you said or you'll be sorry." Karl's heart was pounding since Michael always came out the winner in their disputes.

"Ha! You know you can't whip me. I already proved that lotsa times. Ma says birds of a feather flock together, and ever'body knows Aunt Maggie is a whore."

Karl had a vague idea what the term meant, and he knew it didn't apply to his mother or his Aunt Maggie. A rage like none he had ever known enveloped him. It spread over him like a heavy blanket, smothering him in its intensity. Throwing caution to the winds, he charged Michael, and they went sprawling in the dirt. Righteous anger lent Karl strength, and he pummeled his opponent. So great was Michael's surprise at the vicious attack that he failed to respond. By the time he gathered his wits, his nose was bleeding. He grunted and swung at Karl. The blow landed just below Karl's left eye.

Sam came out of the barn in time to see his son and nephew rolling about on the ground. Setting down the bucket of milk, he hurried to the boys and managed to pull them apart. "What the devil is goin' on here?"

The boys stood glaring at one another, neither willing to offer an explanation.

"Well, I'm waitin'."

"Ah...ah..." Michael stuttered.

"Karl," Sam turned to his nephew. Karl, too, was reluctant to reveal what the fight was about. "It...it was my fault, *onkle*," the boy confessed. "I was braggin' 'bout Ranger and Logan's ranch and all, and Mike got tired a hearin' it. That's all."

Michael stared at Karl in disbelief.

Sam looked from one to the other. "Mike, Karl will be movin' away soon, and you may not see him for a long time. As for his horse and livin' on a big ranch, well, you'd be excited about that too, wouldn't you?"

"Yeah, I guess."

Karl stuck out his hand. "I'm sorry, Mike. I shouldn't have done so much braggin'."

Michael hesitated, then shook Karl's hand.

CHAPTER TWENTY-ONE

"It's going to be a beautiful day!" Johanna reached out as if to embrace the sunshine streaming through the window. She turned to see Maggie waiting to help her dress. Logan had suggested the wedding party stay at the hotel and avoid the early-morning drive to town. Gustav and the children were waiting in the lobby.

As she fastened the tapes of her petticoats, Johanna felt the panic take hold. Was she making a mistake? She and Logan hardly knew one another. And what about the children? He was used to his freedom. What about the physical attraction between them? She was untutored in the ways of love, and Logan was a virile young man.

Maggie came to her side, smiled and squeezed her hands. "Don't worry, Johanna. Everything is going to be fine. Logan loves you and you love him. That's all that really matters."

Johanna managed a weak smile. "I know." She reached for the elegant pink creation spread out on the bed.

"You look beautiful, Maggie." Johanna tried to focus on the present rather than what would take place later.

Maggie, gowned in pale gray silk trimmed with matching lace, shook her head. "There's only one beautiful woman here today."

In spite of the remarkable resemblance, there was no mistaking the one to be married. Johanna had that special glow reserved only for brides. Maggie fastened the delicate buttons of the bodice.

Johanna took a deep breath. "Maggie, I'm really nervous." Her face flushed a bright scarlet.

Maggie grinned, her hazel eyes bright with knowledge. "What are you nervous about?"

Johanna dropped her head. "Josef was an old man and Logan is young and...I...I..."

"Well, he's no stranger to a woman's bedroom. But Logan loves you and you will be his wife. What happens between you will be natural and right."

"But...but there's something else." Johanna could hardly get the words out. "Logan said it didn't matter if we had children and I want to give him a child, but..."

Maggie smiled, then seeing the stricken look on Johanna's face, grew serious. "Just because a man and woman...well...she doesn't have to have a baby every year."

Johanna stared, her mouth agape.

"I didn't mean to shock you, but I learned a great deal about preventing pregnancy working in the saloons. Not that I'm an expert myself. I had a miscarriage and was told I wouldn't be able to have any more children. It must be true, because I never conceived again."

Johanna's surprised expression turned to shock, then softened with sympathy.

Maggie shook her head. "It was a long time ago."

By the time Johanna was arrayed in her wedding finery, Maggie had added to her education considerably. It was difficult for Johanna to imagine putting the knowledge into practice, and her face colored every time she thought about it.

Conrad had given her in marriage to Josef, but Johanna and Logan wanted to walk down the aisle together. Maggie, matron of honor, and Heidi, bridesmaid, and Bartell, best man, with Karl beside him, would precede the bride and groom to the altar.

Johanna stepped into the narthex and Logan smiled, his eyes filled with love and admiration. She was a vision in her pink gown, her golden hair encircled by a wreath of pink silk flowers. She carried a matching bouquet. Both had been fashioned by Amanda as her gift to the bride.

As she walked down the aisle at Logan's side, Johanna struggled to draw a deep breath. Maggie had laced her corset too tight. From the corner of her eye she watched Logan. How handsome he looked in his black broadcloth suit and white linen shirt.

Mrs. Mueller played the ending notes of the German wedding hymn, "Lord Who at Cana's Wedding Feast?" just as the bridal couple reached the altar. Johanna and Logan repeated their vows, and he slipped the heavy gold band on her finger. She thought she saw a hint of moisture in his eyes. As they knelt for prayer, Mrs. Mueller sang, "Oh, Perfect Love."

"You may kiss the bride," Pastor Mueller said.

Logan brushed a soft kiss across Johanna's lips, and they faced their guests. The faces of her family and friends were a blur. They started down the aisle to the strains of "O Blessed Home Where Man and Wife" flowed from Mrs. Mueller's talented fingers.

The wedding breakfast was a merry affair, but Johanna remembered little of it. She and Maggie finally escaped to their room where Johanna changed into her traveling costume. Maggie had altered a navy blue suit, which Johanna wore with a white silk waist and a navy hat with velvet bows.

* * *

San Antonio

The stagecoach pulled up across the street from The Menger Hotel. Reputed to offer the finest accommodations between New Orleans and San Francisco, it was located next to the Alamo and faced the plaza. A glazed iron canopy across the main floor supported by iron columns formed a balcony for the second floor. Thin iron columns enhanced the cantilevered tile-roofed porch over the second floor. Shutters provided shade from the strong west sun. The Menger boasted several spacious suites as well as single rooms, a dining room, saloon and indoor plumbing.

During the few trips she had made to San Antonio, Johanna had seen the building but never been inside. She tried hard not to stare at the opulence surrounding her. Three stories high, the lobby was oval in design and dominated by several Corinthian cast iron columns. Wrought-iron scrollwork comprised the balustrade that encircled the second floor. Oriental rugs placed on the decorative tile floor defined the conversation areas. An enormous crystal chandelier hung suspended from the ceiling. A curving stairway lead to the upper floors. Elegant damask sofas, velvet chairs and heavy rosewood and walnut furniture promised comfort for weary travelers.

Logan seated Johanna in a chair near the door. "Rest here while I check with the desk clerk. There shouldn't be any problem. I made reservations."

Johanna gave him a strained smile. It had been a long day, and she was tired. She tried to take a deep breath, but her corset protested.

Logan returned with the key. "We're on the second floor. Someone will bring our baggage up."

Johanna rose and smoothed her skirts. Her legs felt weak, and there was a hollow feeling in her stomach. Placing her hand on Logan's arm, he guided her toward the stairway.

"Everything is going to be fine, I promise." Logan whispered in her ear. Stopping in front of Room 214, he unlocked the door and swung it wide.

Johanna walked into the room and found herself overwhelmed. Logan had reserved a suite. An Oriental rug covered the center of the polished wood floor. The windows were draped in deep red damask over fine lace curtains. The furniture, similar to that in the lobby, consisted of a settee covered in the same deep red damask, two chairs in deep blue velvet, a large dark red leather chair and ottoman. Small tables and lamps with ornate glass chimneys were artfully arranged. Between the two windows overlooking the plaza, a small round table and two chairs provided a cozy spot for dining.

"It's been a long day, and I know you're tired. Would you like to have supper sent up?"

"Could we do that?" Johanna did not want to face a room full of strangers.

"Just tell me what you'd like, and I'll go downstairs and order it."

"I really don't know. Why don't you decide?" Johanna knew he had much more experience in such matters.

"All right. If you'd like to freshen up, the bedroom is through that door and the bathroom is down the hall."

A knock sounded at the door. A man was standing in the hall with their luggage beside him. Logan motioned the man inside. He picked up the bags and took them to the bedroom. When he returned, Logan handed him a coin.

The man nodded. "Obliged."

Johanna moved toward the bedroom to find even more opulence. A large four-poster bed dominated one corner. The bedcover was deep blue with red braid trim. The same red draperies hung at the windows. An ornate screen occupied another corner, and huge armoire and dresser with marble top took up the other wall. Two armchairs in deep blue tufted velvet with a rosewood table between them provided comfortable seating.

"Logan, it's lovely!" Johanna's frugal nature surfaced. "But it must cost a lot of money."

Logan took her in his arms and kissed her gently on the lips. "Let me worry about that. I want this to be wonderful for you, Johanna. Something we can remember for the rest of our lives."

Johanna looked deep into his eyes and saw only love and desire in their sapphire depths. The effects of the long, exhausting day disappeared like magic. Smiling, she stood on tiptoe and touched her lips to his. He groaned and tightened the embrace. She pressed against him and he deepened the kiss. Just when Johanna thought her lungs would burst, Logan ended the kiss, leaving them both gasping for breath.

"Lord, woman," he moaned, "do you know how close I am to ripping your clothes off and taking you right here?"

Johanna looked at him for full minute then, with the newly discovered weapons of the seductress, she smiled and replied, "Do you need any help?"

Logan blinked, and seeing the expression on his face, Johanna dropped her head. Had she been too wanton? She kept her eyes focused on the white linen stretched across his chest.

Logan grinned, titled her chin up, and teased, "I can see you and I are going to spend a lot of time taking off our clothes."

Johanna heard the laughter in his voice, sighed gently, and relaxed against him. She had much to learn about this man she loved with all her heart.

"Why don't you rest while I order something to eat? I won't be long." Logan kissed her again. "I'm going to lock the door. This is a respectable place, but it doesn't pay to take chances."

After removing her jacket, Johanna investigated the other side of the screen. She found a washstand equipped with a fine china pitcher and bowl as well as the necessary chamber pot. Afraid Logan would return before she was presentable, she did not change out of her skirt and waist.

Logan found her standing in front of the window watching the street below. People were moving about in all directions.

"Quite a sight, isn't it?" Coming up behind her, he drew her to his side and put his arm around her waist.

"Yes, it is."

For several minutes they watched the scene below. Then Logan turned Johanna in his embrace until she faced him. "I love you, Johanna."

His lips claimed hers in a gentle caress. She opened her mouth to him and tasted the liquor she had smelled on his breath. Perhaps Logan's control had felt the need of liquid reinforcement. A loud knock sounded at the door, and Logan released her mouth. Johanna thought she heard him mutter, "Damn!"

"It's our supper," Logan called over his shoulder.

The waiters set the trays on the table between the windows, took off the covers and began arranging the dishes. Tantalizing aromas wafted upward, and Johanna realized she was hungry.

"There wasn't much of a selection," Logan apologized. "I hope you like roast beef. There's apple pie for dessert."

"It smells delicious." Johanna's eyes widened in surprise when one of the waiters placed a bottle of wine on the table. Logan handed them each a coin. They thanked him, grinned and left the room.

After seating Johanna, Logan opened the wine. He poured the glasses half-full, picked up one and handed it to her. "To my lovely bride," he toasted.

Johanna was familiar with the homemade wines of her friends and neighbors, but this deep red liquid was nothing like them. It had a puckery taste that was strange yet not unpleasant.

"It's Burgundy, imported from France," Logan explained. "I'm sorry there wasn't any chilled champagne."

Johanna took another sip. "I like it."

"I'm glad." His eyes clung to hers as she sipped the wine. As the meal progressed, the contents of the wine bottle diminished. They gathered up the soiled dishes, and Logan placed the trays outside the door.

When Johanna was comfortable on the settee, Logan relaxed in the big leather chair. "There's a traveling theater group playing at the opera house tomorrow night. Would you like go?"

"If you want to." Johanna's mood was mellow.

"I sure do. I want to show off my beautiful bride."

His remark brought a warm flush to Johanna's face. "Did you enjoy that big bathtub?" he teased.

Her cheeks turned bright red. "I didn't use it." She avoided meeting his eyes.

"Well, there's plenty of time."

"Perhaps tomorrow."

He rose and walked to her side. His arms encircled her, and she could feel his heart beating through the linen shirt. "Don't be embarrassed, love. I'll wait out here while you get ready for bed."

Logan entered the bedroom and found Johanna, clad in a pale pink nightdress, sitting before the mirror. She laid down her brush and began to braid her hair.

"Please leave it down." Logan stood behind her and ran his hand over the top of her head, his fingers tangling in the half-formed braid.

Johanna shook the long tresses free, and they spread over her shoulders like a golden cape. She watched Logan's reflection in the mirror. His eyes were twin flames of blue fire. She held out her hand.

He led her to the bed and sat down on the edge. She stood between his outstretched thighs, reached for his hands and brought them to her lips. Logan groaned deep in his throat and fell back on the bed, bringing her with him. They turned to face one another, bodies barely touching. He kissed her temple, moved to her eyelids, then the pulse in her throat.

She placed her palm on his chest, and his breathing grew ragged. With a gentle push, he rolled her over on her back. The kisses they had shared seemed innocent compared to the assault Logan mounted now. Breaking the kiss, Logan stood up and placed his fingers on the top button of his shirt, a question in his eyes. Johanna's face colored as she rose to her feet, but she looked him squarely in the eye as he made quick work of shrugging off his shirt. He tugged off his boots and pulled her down on the bed beside him. He fumbled with the ribbons of her nightdress while his long drugging kisses swept all rational thought from her mind.

"I want to love you," he whispered, his voice ragged with desire.

Passion too long denied could not be stayed! Logan collapsed against her, his head resting upon her breasts. She could feel his heart pounding and hear his heavy breathing. Their union had been quick, leaving Johanna feeling strange and incomplete.

"I'm sorry, love, it will be better next time. I promise."

His words penetrated Johanna's dazed senses. Her eyes flew open and she gasped, "You mean you...you...?"

Logan chuckled. "Oh, yes. I've waited a long time for you." He stood and began removing his trousers.

Johanna tried to keep her eyes averted, but the temptation was too great. She had seen his body when he was wounded, but the man standing before her was vitally alive. Evenly proportioned, he was all lean muscle and corded sinew. The puckered scar from the bullet wound that had nearly cost him his life was now a dull pink. Johanna shuddered, thinking how empty her life would be without him. Her face grew hot when she found Logan grinning her.

"Might as well get used to this ol' carcass, Mrs. Delaney. You're going to be seeing a lot of it."

"Oh, Logan, don't tease me. I know it's brazen of me, but I like looking you."

"Not half as much as I enjoy looking at you. Now, let's get you out of this thing." Before Johanna could protest, he pulled her nightdress over her head and tossed it on the floor.

This time their lovemaking was slow and tender with Logan the tutor and Johanna the willing pupil. As they lay entwined afterward, she told him, "I...I...never knew anything could be so...so..."

"I suspected as much that night in the barn."

Johanna fell asleep in Logan's arms only to awaken as dawn streaked the sky. Logan was laying on his side looking at her. Memory came flooding back, and she sucked in her breath. She glanced at him out of the corner of her eye.

Logan rolled to his back and Johanna's eyes grew misty as she traced the puckered scar on his chest. He whispered, "I love you," and kissed her softly on the mouth.

With a quick twist, Logan reversed their positions. He kissed her again. "Look at me, Johanna. I want to watch your face when I love you."

Her thoughts scattered like leaves in the wind. She kissed him back, her body straining against him as their lips clung.

Logan sucked in his breath. "If we don't slow down, it's going to be over before we get started."

Comprehension dawned, and Johanna turned her head away.

"Don't." He turned her face toward him. "Please love, look at me."

Johanna surrendered to Logan's caresses. As she climbed higher and higher toward the peak she had discovered only a short time before, a million bright colors burst before her eyes, and she was sure she had touched heaven itself. Logan was trembling from head to toe.

"I know I'm too heavy for you, but I can't move."

"No, you're not. You feel good. It's like...like..."

Logan rolled over on his back. "I know, love. I've never experienced anything like it, either."

"You mean you...but surely you..."

Logan chuckled. "You don't want me to answer that." He reached for her and looked deep into her eyes. "I have never loved anyone the way I love you."

"And I love you so very much."

Logan grinned. "If they are real lucky, like you and me, that's the way it is between a man and his wife."

Johanna was silent for a long moment.

"What are you thinking about?" Logan asked.

"You."

"What about me?"

"I was wondering how..." Johanna turned her head.

He ran his fingers along her jaw line. "Come on now, let's hear it. There should be no embarrassment between us."

"Well...I wondered how you could, well...you know...so often?"

Logan laughed. "Easy. I get worked up just looking at you."

Johanna's smile hinted at thoughts she was not ready to share. It looked as if she just might have need of Maggie's secrets.